#MOONSTRUCK

OTHER TITLES BY SARIAH WILSON

The #Lovestruck Novels

#Starstruck

#Moonstruck

The Royals of Monterra

Royal Date

Royal Chase

Royal Games

Royal Design

Stand-Alone Novels

The Ugly Stepsister Strikes Back

Once Upon a Time Travel

#MOONSTRUCK

SARIAH WILSON

Montlake
Romance

Published by Montlake Romance, Seattle

www.apub.com

Amazon, the Amazon logo, and Montlake Romance are trademarks of Amazon.com, Inc., or its affiliates.

ISBN-13: 9781503902831
ISBN-10: 1503902838

Cover design by Eileen Carey

Printed in the United States of America

For my dad, who at seventy-one years old still plays bass in a rock band.

CHAPTER ONE

If you'd asked me two hours ago what I thought about pop star Ryan De Luna, I would have told you that he was an overproduced, talentless, washed-out has-been.

But as I stood here in the crowd of screaming, giddy, exuberant (mostly female) fans, I could admit that I might have been just a little bit wrong.

Especially since the last time I'd seen him in concert had been seven years ago, when I was fourteen. He'd been seventeen at the time, with shaggy bangs, wearing an oversize basketball jersey, and he had lip-synched the entire thing.

The boy I'd swooned over couldn't begin to compare to the well-groomed man I watched now. He sang live. No more mouthing the words, no Auto-Tune. He wore modified suits and stylish clothes he could move in. He danced less than he had before, mostly because dancing full-out and singing at the same time was pretty much impossible.

And I should know, being the lead singer of my band. I do not dance while I sing.

Even though I had been to approximately a million live concerts, thanks to my love of music, I could honestly say I'd never seen any performer who was so magnetic or so charismatic. Ryan De Luna had the entire crowd mesmerized. Totally in his thrall. He could have ordered them to go out and invade a small country, and I was pretty sure the sobbing, screaming, fainting women around me would have done it.

Heck, at this point I probably would have even joined in.

I was not exaggerating the fainting part, either. It seemed to be worse the closer they stood to the stage. One smile, one hip shake, one high note from Ryan De Luna and they dropped like flies. So far they'd taken thirteen women over to the ambulances to be checked out.

It probably didn't help matters that he was ridiculously gorgeous. I knew his mom had been Latina, and I'd read something about his dad being Irish. Ryan melded both heritages together perfectly—he had lightly bronzed skin, dark-brown hair, and bright-hazel eyes.

Hazel eyes that appeared to have winked at me. Even though logically I knew that wasn't possible, my traitorous heart still fluttered and raced in response.

I tried to put that image of him at seventeen back in my head to erase what I was currently witnessing, but my brain refused. I even had to admit that my musical tastes changing from pop to rock music had tainted and altered my memories of him and his songs.

Because there was still one song of his that I really loved. The one I had listened to on repeat over and over again: "One More Night." I liked it so much that recently I had done an acoustic cover of it on my band's YouTube channel.

Not that I would ever admit how much I still loved that song. My second-oldest brother, Parker, would probably die laughing if I told him. Or he would after he got rabidly outraged about the general lack of music and soul in today's Top 40.

The backup dancers kicked it into high gear behind Ryan as his band and the DJ coordinated to play a live club mix of the song. Every woman in the audience broke into absolute hysterics as the first strains filled the arena. Strobe lights flashed around him and the dancers as they moved together. I knew so many guys who had the rhythm of a sea slug. But Ryan De Luna could dance, and it was hypnotically sexy.

Have I mentioned yet that he was super good-looking, too?

Controlled fire burst from the corners of the stage as the massive screen behind him showed the original video for the song. I couldn't imagine my band, consisting of me and my brothers, Fitz, Parker, and Cole, ever having a show like this. We could barely manage to book gigs at local clubs. Ryan De Luna was one of the few artists in the world who could sell out entire stadiums.

"Maisy! Maisy! Let's head backstage now!" My best friend, Angie, had to yell this in my right ear, and even then I could barely make it out.

Embarrassingly enough, part of me wanted to stay and watch him sing this song. Another part of me wanted to tell Angie no, to suggest that we head for her car and get out of there before the parking lot and roads got too congested. But I knew I couldn't. It meant too much to her to meet Ryan De Luna, and I really owed her.

I was probably the only woman in the whole stadium who didn't care about the All-Access pass Angie had given me. In fact, I was pretty sure I could have staged my own Hunger Games by tossing it into the group closest to the stage.

But not wanting to be personally responsible for starting a riot, I refrained.

Instead, I nodded, and we shuffled through the sweaty, tearful mass of hormones that screamed out all the things they wanted to do to Ryan. Which involved marriage proposals and various other unspeakable acts.

When we cleared the crowd, Angie yelled, "This way!" and then pointed at the same time in case I didn't hear her.

I snuck one final glance at a grinning, disgustingly hot Ryan. So freaking pretty. I allowed myself that look because it would be the last time I'd see him in person, no matter what Angie hoped.

A burly, scowling security guard with a headset stared us down as we approached him, but one flash of our badges and we were in. Girls without passes would probably have to flash other things to get past.

"Down the hall. Take the first left," he directed us, and we proceeded inside.

I'd been backstage at concerts multiple times. Once even at a Rolling Stones concert, thanks to the A&R rep my oldest brother, Fitz, was dating at the time. I had tried to prepare Angie for the reality of what was about to happen. Ryan De Luna wasn't doing any meet and greets, which essentially involved fans paying a small fortune, waiting in line for hours to stand next to him and have their pictures taken, and then being ushered out the door to make way for the next person. Pathetic as it was, at least then Angie would have stood a chance of saying hi.

Instead, given past experience, I knew we would be shoved into a room with crappy food and radio-contest winners and various music-industry professionals—like label execs with their tween daughters, bloggers, and journalists. Maybe the opening act would show up, maybe a PR person or his manager, but there was zero chance of Ryan De Luna stopping by.

No matter how I tried to warn her, Angie wouldn't listen. She just kept telling me to trust her.

Before the concert I'd wondered aloud if her goal was to hook up with Ryan or something. After a twinge of sadness in her eyes that made me feel extremely guilty for joking that way, she said, "I'm old enough that I don't think Ryan De Luna wants to get with me and my mom body. And even if he did because he was either drunk or off his medication, my answer would be no."

We definitely had that in common. If propositioned by any musician, my answer would also be an emphatic no, but for very different reasons. Although Angie's definition of "mom body" was probably off, given that she looked amazing and was only twenty-six years old.

"You, on the other hand," she continued, "are free to say, 'Ooh yes, baby, one . . . more . . . night!'"

I shot her a side-eye to let her know what I thought as she laughed at her own quip. Did she seriously not remember my rules?

We walked down a massive concrete hallway lit with buzzing, fluorescent bulbs, and I felt the temperature drop. We were underneath the stadium bleachers, but despite all the potential interference (including my currently partial deafness from all the loudness), I could hear Ryan winding down his show. He thanked his band, the dancers, and the crew and then told the women of Los Angeles how much he loved them.

Considering he'd dated roughly half of them, it was probably an accurate statement.

Manwhore, thy name is Ryan De Luna.

The audience chanted Ryan's name repeatedly, trying to get him to do an encore while we took a left at the end of the hallway. Just as I'd predicted, there was a roped-off area marked "VIP." It had a catering table set up and a bunch of people milling around, including a hysterically sobbing teenage girl whose face had gone purple. Like she'd cried and screamed so hard she'd burst blood vessels.

"I told you!" Such a waste of time.

"And I told you. That's not where we're going."

Just then I heard yelling and turned to see a bunch of security guards wearing the same black polo that the guard out front had worn, telling everybody to get out of the way. Angie and I pressed up against the wall. Behind the guards, a bunch of guys were carrying guitars and then . . . Ryan De Luna.

A very sweaty Ryan De Luna. Which I should have been grossed out by but instead had some strange, lurid thoughts about.

If I'd thought he was attractive onstage, it was about a thousand times more potent up close.

Kind of like the difference between running your fingers though a candle's open flame versus hopping on a rocket ship, going into outer space, and then being shoved onto the sun's surface.

5

No wonder the media had nicknamed him El Caliente.

He used a white towel to mop up the (still not gross) sweat from his forehead and then flung his hair back. And I swear, it happened in slow motion.

A drop of his sweat landed on my hand.

I was overcome with the desire to never wash my right hand ever, ever again.

I looked up, and the impossible happened. Ryan locked eyes with me. He smiled. "Hey."

How was I supposed to respond to a smile and "Hey"? Was there a response? It seemed like there should be a response. An easy one, even.

Before I could figure it out, he was gone, caught up in the current of the security guards pushing him along.

What had just happened to me? I was nobody's fangirl.

Unlike the purple-faced teen in the VIP area who was currently being revived by a concerned-looking adult.

Disgusted with myself, I rubbed off what was left of his sweat.

"Tell me again about how Ryan De Luna doesn't affect you at all?" Angie said in a singsong voice.

"The only part of me he affects is my gag reflex."

Her dancing eyes let me know she did not believe me.

I couldn't blame her. I didn't believe me, either.

She grabbed my wrist. "That's where we're going." It took me a second to realize she was following Ryan. She trailed behind the group like a determined little caboose. Some detached part of my brain wondered how this would end up. Which brother would be the least angry when I called and asked them to bail me out of jail? Because obviously we would be prison-bound for trespassing and physical assault after Angie, despite her protests to the contrary, cornered Ryan and flung herself at him. I didn't know what her plan was. Would some sort of favors have to be performed to even get us close to him in the first place? If that were the case, Angie was on her own. That was not me.

Not that it was Angie, either, but she'd been a little "moonstruck" lately. Since I had been a fan for about five minutes before I got over it, I knew that Ryan's last name meant *moon* in Spanish, and his fans would talk online about their obsessive love and how Ryan made them "moonstruck." As a group they called themselves his "Luna-chicks." One particularly stalkery branch of fans called themselves the "Luna-tics," and they failed to see the irony of the name at all. And now I was worried my friend had gone full-on Luna-tic.

As Angie tugged at me, I kept trying to make her stop so I could look at stuff—there were some gorgeous, expensive Mesa Boogie amps sitting in the hallway—but she refused to slow down.

We rounded a corner, and I saw yet another black polo-ed security guard. He stood in front of a door marked LOCKER ROOM. This guard had shaved his hair down to a buzz cut and had wicked burn scars on the right side of his face near what was left of his earlobe. His biceps bulged so much that he had a hard time keeping his arms crossed.

This was not a man you'd want to physically restrain you while waiting for the police to arrive.

Imagine my shock when he broke out in a huge smile that softened his entire appearance. "Heya, Angie."

Even more surprising, Angie launched herself at him, and he engulfed her in a hug, the top of her head just reaching his shoulder. "I'm so excited to see you again, Fox!"

He let her go, and she stepped back. "Thanks so much for everything—for the passes and the tickets. I can't tell you what it means to me."

"Anything for you. You know I'm only a phone call away."

"And a flight away, considering you're on tour with the biggest pop star on the planet."

Was I imagining things, or was that a flirtatious tone in her voice? I'd never seen her do that before, and we'd been out together tons of times. Well, we went out whenever she could wrangle up a babysitter for her two-year-old. But even then, she spent all her time shooting guys down. She did not encourage them.

What I didn't imagine was the interest in Fox's eyes. He was definitely attracted to Angie, which he obviously should have been because she was beyond amazing.

But it didn't seem like she knew he liked her.

Hmm.

"Have a good time," he said as he opened the swinging door for us and gestured inside. "And don't do anything that will force me to haul you guys out."

He was teasing, but I was still worried about what Angie might do.

Because there was no greenroom or dressing room in a stadium, somebody had hung up a bunch of thick blue-gray curtains to cordon off certain areas. One of the curtains swung open, and I had a brief glimpse of brown-leather couches and a massive big-screen TV. Angie marched us straight ahead, and despite the fact that she was half my height, I had a hard time keeping up with her.

"How did you manage this?" I asked. I knew Angie was resourceful, but what she had pulled off was seriously impressive.

"Fox was in Hector's . . ." Her voice caught, and I knew from experience she didn't want me to comfort her. Her husband, Hector, had died in combat a little over a year ago. IED. Angie still couldn't say his name without getting emotional. She wanted to be able to talk about him without that happening. "He was in Hector's unit."

That explained the burn marks on Fox's face and why he was doing this for Angie. After Hector died, the other soldiers in his unit and their wives had basically adopted her. She became their family, and they would do anything for her.

Including unfettered access to Ryan De Luna.

Although Fox hadn't been looking at Angie in a particularly familial way.

"Fox called me to say he'd be in town and wanted to check in on me. When he told me he'd started working as a bodyguard for Ryan, well, one thing led to another, and here we are."

Here we were.

She pushed the curtain aside, and I quickly glanced around the room, noting the two guys playing a video game on the big screen and a bunch of groupies talking to each other and twirling the ends of their hair. The other women sized us up and immediately dismissed us as possible competition.

I could see why. We were not from the groupie/pop-star girlfriend mold. Like, my clothing covered my body and stuff.

Them: Outfits that, if they sat down or bent over, revealed the parts that made them female.

Me: Black, ratty jeans and a worn (but soft) black Beatles T-shirt that had once belonged to my mother. (I worried sometimes that I was too much of a clichéd "lead singer in a rock band" with my choices but then decided if I was actually cool, I wouldn't care what anybody else thought about my clothes. I was still working on that part.)

Them: Mostly various shades of blonde, with perfect waves and hair extensions for days.

Me: Unwashed, naturally long brown hair with scarlet streaks that I'd recently added.

Them: Enough makeup to properly audition for clown college.

Me: Okay, I liked to look quasi-nice and wore some makeup, especially when I performed, as the lights tended to wash me out. But I was not giving the scary thing from Stephen King's *It* a run for his money.

Basically, we were total opposites in every way possible.

But then my brain stopped working entirely.

Ryan De Luna had entered the room.

He'd been in the middle of putting on a new shirt while walking around the curtain farthest from us to join everybody. He pulled the white jersey material down over some lightly tanned abs. Despite my telling Angie not two days ago that they must have been airbrushed on for photos, I could now see that those hard bumps and ridges were very real.

No airbrushes of any kind were harmed in the forming of that deliciousness.

Then Ryan De Luna winked at me with a little smile, letting me know he understood exactly what I'd just been looking at. I forced myself to turn away from him. I would not worship him with excessive adulation.

I wouldn't.

Even if every part of me wanted to. Which was kind of a problem, given that I planned on staying abstinent until marriage. I couldn't let myself think these kinds of things.

The air-conditioning must have been on high, as the room was extremely cold. At least that's what I told myself to explain my shivers.

"I'm going to say hi," Angie announced, apparently unaware of my inability to form coherent thoughts. "Are you sure you don't want to come with me?"

"So sure," I finally managed. Even if my bad opinion of Ryan had slightly bettered after seeing him perform, he still represented everything I hated about the industry. Mass-produced, soulless, tuneless, synthesized dreck.

Ab ogling aside, I really wasn't interested.

Really.

"Suit yourself." She shrugged and went over to introduce herself to Ryan. He'd better be nice to her, or else.

When she left, I wasn't sure what to do. The surgically enhanced women wearing Band-Aid–size "clothes" flocked around him, cooing at him like presenting peacocks. They literally draped themselves all over him like overgrown leeches. Plastic peacock leeches. Pleeches.

Ryan grabbed what looked suspiciously like the Martin custom acoustic guitar made of Honduran rosewood that I'd been lusting over last month online. I could never afford it, and he had one just lying around. He took the beautiful instrument to a couch and sat down. He held it . . . weirdly. Something felt off.

Through some kind of mental code, his flock of pleeches established a pecking order about who got to sit where. They gathered around him—one on each side, a few sitting on the back of the couch behind him, and the others around his feet. Like he was the Lord Master of Music and would dispense all his worldly knowledge to them.

Poor Angie circled around the group, unable to find a way in.

If she didn't find one soon, I was going to help by shooing them away. Or pulling some hair. Whatever worked.

I rolled my eyes so hard over his groupies that I saw the inside of my skull. I sat down next to a guy who strummed what looked like another custom Martin guitar. Were they breeding them or something?

"Not a fan?" he asked, surprising me. Because normally I hung out with my brothers, and they wanted to cut off the air supply of any male who looked twice at me.

"What? Oh. Not really."

"Of me?"

"I don't know who you are." I'd probably just seriously insulted the guy. While I could tell you the name and preferred instrument of almost every rock guitarist on the planet, I was not up on the pop scene.

I'd abandoned that when I was fifteen.

Right after my father left us.

"I don't know who you are, either," the guitar player shot back.

Fair enough. "Maisy Harrison," I said, offering him my hand. It wasn't really a shaking-hands kind of place (it had more of an air kisses/fist bumps vibe), but my mother had been deeply committed to proper manners. He gave me an amused smile and shook it. His fingers were calloused on the pads, letting me know he really played.

"Diego." He paused as if he didn't want to continue, and I realized why. "De Luna."

They were family? Brothers? Cousins? I couldn't help it. I compared the two men. Diego had a darker skin tone, black hair, and the darkest-brown eyes I'd ever seen. He had the same cut jawline as Ryan, maybe the same nose. Diego was cute but not in the ground-beneath-me-has-turned-soggy-due-to-inadvertent-drooling Ryan kind of way.

"Basically you're living proof that nepotism works."

That made Diego grin at me, and the similarity to Ryan was even more apparent now. "So if you don't know who I am, you're saying you're not a fan of my cousin?"

"Obviously."

Now he laughed, throwing his head back as if I'd said the most hilarious thing ever. His reaction was loud enough that he drew the attention of everyone in the room, including Ryan. And as Ryan watched me, I couldn't help but watch him back. Like his gaze held me captive and I was too weak to turn away. I forced my eyes down, and it was then that I realized what seemed strange about Ryan and his guitar. He wasn't holding it like he loved it. Like it was a natural extension of his hands. The way I would have held it. The way Diego currently held his guitar.

Instead, Ryan wielded that guitar like a shield against the women surrounding him, invading his space. Like a kid hiding under his covers, hoping his blanket would keep him safe from the monsters.

I almost felt bad for him.

Diego startled me out of my Ryan-centric thoughts, causing my heart rate to increase. "I have to admit, that's a first. Usually that's all the women back here care about. Meeting him."

Was it obvious I had been staring at Ryan? "Not me."

He stopped strumming and laid his hand on top of the guitar. "You're not a typical groupie."

"I'm not any kind of groupie. I have an IQ with triple digits, thanks."

Diego laughed again, and I couldn't help but smile back. After spending a lifetime with brothers who adored me almost as much as they adored teasing me, it was nice to have a man appreciate my humor and not call me a bed-wetting string monkey.

"Then why are you here?"

I leaned forward and told him conspiratorially, "I was coerced by my best friend, who didn't want to come alone. I'm here under duress."

He moved his head toward mine. "Is this like a hostage situation?" he teased. "Blink twice if you need me to call the police."

Okay, he was cute and charming, but I had two life rules:

1.   Never date a musician.
2.   Never have sex with a musician.

My second rule was easily kept by following the first one.

"No need to call out the SWAT team," I assured him.

"So if you're not here to hook up with my cousin, does that mean you're here to hook up with me?" He said it playfully, but I knew that if I said yes, we'd be gone in under a minute.

Because that's how guys in his line of work operated.

"I don't date musicians. Kind of a rule I have."

Speaking of musicians I would not be dating and/or sleeping with, Ryan De Luna appeared in front of me, making my mouth go completely dry. His arms were folded, and he glared down at us. The intense fire in his eyes turned my stomach hollow.

Ryan De Luna had really sexy forearms. I'd never noticed them on a guy before.

And then he spoke. In a husky, deep, thrilling way that made the room so cold that I couldn't help but shiver.

"You know, usually when a girl goes to the effort to sneak in, they at least come over and say hi."

Sneak in? Shivers gone.

Like I was just another one of those girls across the room. So desperate to meet him I'd do anything.

Jerk. I wanted to smack him.

CHAPTER TWO

"Hi," I snapped at him while waving. I hoped he could see the sarcasm in my moving hand. "I didn't sneak in. I was let in." Big difference.

"Who let you in?"

I was about to tell him when I caught Angie's panicked expression. I couldn't get Fox in trouble for doing this. Especially not if I planned on informing Angie that she should love him and get married and make more adorable babies. But Ryan's mesmerizing nearness was messing with my head in a totally bad way, and I had no lies to offer.

Diego rescued me. "I put them on the list. Maisy here and . . ."

"Angie," I added.

"Right, Angie. You know how bad I am with names."

So there.

I expected him to leave, but Ryan stayed put, staring at both of us as if he didn't like what he saw. And every moment that passed made me more and more uncomfortable. Like he could see into my black, orphaned soul or something.

That and the physical awareness of him made me feel panicky. As did how good he smelled. He hadn't showered yet, and I should have been turned off by that. I learned once in a biology class that when women are ovulating, they are more attracted to sweaty men. Like their ovaries have magnificent-male-specimen radar.

I had to be ovulating because I kind of wanted to do nothing else but smell him for the rest of my life.

It freaked me out. "Why are you just standing there? Do you want me to thank you for the partial deafness? Which is kind of a big deal considering I need my hearing for my job. Consider yourself thanked."

"They're called earplugs," he retorted. "You should look into them."

Okay, this celebri-douche was working my last nerve. I gestured to the Martin guitar in his right hand. "So do you actually play that thing, or is it like everything else in your life, just for show?" Because of my brothers, I'd learned quickly that the key to dealing with cocky men was to strike hard if you didn't strike first. (Other things I had learned included eating fast at meals if you wanted to have seconds and, in the middle of the night, always checking the position of the toilet seat so you don't fall in.)

"I play. Do you?"

I couldn't back down from the challenge in his voice. "Of course I play."

He raised one eyebrow as if he didn't believe me. "Are you any good?"

Was I any good? Seriously? "Better than you."

"That's a pretty low bar," Diego added in a joking tone, sending up a chorus of oohs from the other band members.

I had felt good about my attack strategy right up to the moment where I saw the fleeting pain in the internationally famous bajillion-aire pop star's eyes. Then it disappeared. "So play something," Ryan instructed, handing me the precious, snowflake-sparkly unicorn guitar that I wanted to grab and run away with.

I let my fingers drift along the grain of the smooth wood and tested a few chords. It was surprisingly in tune already. I considered being a brat and spending an inordinate amount of time adjusting it to my exact specifications but gave that up when I saw Angie's face. I had promised her I would be on my best behavior, and here I was provoking Ryan instead.

I played the first verse and chorus of my band's most popular (187 downloads to date!) song, "Lost." I hummed along, caught up in the melody, not able to help myself. My sort of twin brother, Cole, and I had written it on a night where we were both really missing our mom. Thinking of her made my throat feel hot. I had to stop playing before I started bawling.

Letting my fingers go still, I realized the room had fallen silent and I had played with my eyes closed.

When I opened them, they instinctively sought out Ryan.

And he looked at me like . . . I couldn't have explained it. There was this connection there, this invisible string stretching taut between us that made my breath catch.

His anger had faded. Music had soothed the savage pop star.

Ryan's expression shifted, and he looked confused. Like I was a puzzle he couldn't figure out.

"I think the lady wins. Definitely better than you," Diego said. Reluctantly, I handed the guitar back to Ryan.

And still we just stared at each other. I think Diego asked me if I'd written it, and I might have said yes, possibly adding that I was part of a band my brothers had started five years ago, but every cell in my body was focused on the man standing in front of me.

I didn't understand why.

"Usually when girls play, it's some indie-folk thing." Diego nudged me. Like he was trying to get me to stop looking at Ryan.

It didn't work. "I like rock. I was raised well."

"What about Angie?" Diego asked, nodding his chin in her direction. "Is she part of your superhot all-girl group?"

"It's not a 'girl' group, it's a band." I hated when guys said stuff like that. As if a woman being in a band automatically turned it into something else besides just a band. And hadn't I just said my brothers started it? Listening obviously wasn't one of his social skills.

In the middle of my indignation, I realized I had totally forgotten about Angie and why we were here. I jumped to my feet, miscalculating Ryan's proximity. We lined up perfectly, nearly touching, and my pulse throbbed so hard and fast that I worried somebody would be carting my never-fainted-before self off to the ambulances.

"Have you met Angie Villanueva?" I asked, my throat dry and my voice scratchy. "She's a widow. Her husband died last year in combat. And she's also a big fan."

He heard my unspoken implication. "And you're not?"

Like that wasn't allowed or something. I so wanted to say, "No, your music blows," but I would be good for Angie's sake.

When I didn't respond, Ryan shot me a perplexed look and turned away, stepping back so I could finally breathe again. I sucked air into my lungs, trying to calm down. Ryan shook Angie's hand and thanked her for her husband's service and her sacrifice. I could tell from the twist of her mouth that she didn't like that I'd played the widow card, but it had been worth it since Ryan was being an absolute angel to her, despite being a despicable devil with me.

A red-hot, breath-stealing, fiery, despicable devil.

"Would you like to get a picture with me?" I heard him ask after they'd made some small talk that consisted mostly of Angie telling him how much she loved his so-called music.

"I would love that." She beamed at him and pulled out her cell phone. "Oh no. I filmed the concert, and my phone died. Can we use yours, Maisy?"

"Yep." My hands shook as I slid my phone out of my back pocket. Ryan put his arm around Angie's shoulder, and they both faced me, smiling. I willed myself to relax or else the picture would be blurry and then Angie would kill me, and I totally wouldn't blame her.

"Say 'cheesy music,'" I instructed.

They both ignored me and just said "cheese." I snapped about ten shots of them. There would have to be some out of that bunch that would work. "All done."

Ryan didn't move. "Do you want to join us? How about a group shot?"

Something about his tone and word choice bugged me. "No thanks. I'm good."

"Diego can take the picture." Ryan kept talking like I hadn't said anything. I glanced at his cousin and saw a mutinous expression on Diego's face that quickly dissolved. This was one of the reasons why my Rule #1 existed. Sensitive *artiste* types were seriously moody. Like they had unending PMS.

"Come on, Maisy, I want to memorialize this night!" Angie waved me to her. I could say no to Ryan De Luna all night. Angie? Not so much.

As if everyone knew I would cave, Diego came over and grabbed my phone.

"This one's going on the website. Ryan's number-one fan," Diego murmured teasingly, and I shot him a dirty look.

I lined up next to Angie, but she wasn't having it. "No, on the other side of Ryan."

Why did it matter? I sighed softly but moved over to Ryan's left side and stood as far away from him as I could.

"Scoot in, Maisy." Diego made a motion to punctuate his request. "Closer. Closer. A little bit closer. I promise Ryan's had all his shots."

Now it was Ryan's turn to sigh. He put his arm around my waist, pulling me to his side. The entire right half of my body went up in flames, my skin igniting like a million Roman candles all exploding at once.

"Say 'cheese'!" Diego directed. "Stay there. Let me make sure the lighting is good on this one. We can't have a bad picture of Ryan floating around out there."

Now he was just torturing me. He probably thought it was because I didn't like Ryan. I was sure Diego had no idea how my entire being feverishly reacted to touching his cousin.

Then Ryan made it a million times worse. He turned his head toward me, his breath hot against my earlobe, and I almost collapsed.

Until I heard what he was saying.

"Flirting with and using my cousin is not the way to get my attention. I don't appreciate your antics."

I pulled back to look him in the eye. I had really tried. Well, I had sort of tried. But Ryan De Luna had just reached the end of my very short tolerance rope, and I was done. "You are seriously the most arrogant, self-centered, douche-iest jackhole I have ever had the misfortune of meeting. And I live in Los Angeles and work in the music industry, so that's saying a lot."

I jerked away, freeing myself from his grip. "Just so you know, I'm not even a little bit interested in you. Like, at all. I was just hanging out with Diego while Angie got her chance to meet you. I know you're a celebrity, and you haven't been friends with reality in years, so here's your long-overdue check—I'd much rather date Diego than you. And I don't date musicians!"

Then Ryan did the most shocking thing yet.

He laughed.

He laughed and laughed like I was some toddler having a tantrum and he thought I was just adorable.

My chest was heaving, my face flushed. I wondered whether Fox would get fired if I smacked Ryan. Angie stepped in front of me like she knew what I was contemplating. She somehow managed to look both horrified and proud of me. "Let's go. Nice to meet you, Ryan. Thanks for the picture."

Before he could respond, I said, "Thanks for nothing, you, you . . ." Angie didn't let me finish and literally pushed me away from the room made of curtains and out the locker-room door. There was a different guard posted outside, which was good because I might have had some things to say to Fox about his poor job-choosing skills.

Angie kept quiet, clear up until we got to the parking lot. "Do you really still have that rule about not dating musicians?"

It was highly satisfying to slam my car door after we got in. "Yes. Now more than ever."

The one consolation? I'd never have to see Ryan De Luna again.

⛵

The next day, despite being exhausted, I made my weekly visit to see Cynthia. After signing in, I followed the orderly out to the gardens. "Maisy's here to see you, Cynthia," he said with a calming smile. I thanked him, and he said he'd be nearby if I needed him, but I had this down to a science and didn't foresee any trouble.

"Hey, Cynthia. Remember me?" I asked, sitting down next to the box where she was planting daisies, her favorite flower. I don't know why I asked her that every time. The answer was always no.

She frowned, her brows furrowing over her chocolate-brown eyes. "I don't, I'm sorry. Do I know you from school? They said I had an accident, and I have a hard time remembering things."

"It's okay. I brought you some brownies." I offered her the covered plate and was rewarded with a huge smile.

Cynthia took off her gardening gloves and dropped them on the grass. She took the plate from me. "I love brownies! They're my absolute favorite. My mom seriously makes the best ones. She said someday she'll share her secret recipe with me." She pulled back some of the tinfoil and broke off a small piece of a brownie to try. "Yours are pretty good. I don't want to eat too much, though. Prom's coming up soon, and I think Scottie Weinstein is going to ask me, and I've already picked out the cutest dress to wear. I just can't put on any weight."

Every time I came to visit, the doctors instructed me to play along, to not remind her that there would be no prom. That unless she had a miraculous recovery, she'd never leave this facility again.

"That sounds like a lot of fun. What is Scottie like?"

"Tall. Cute. Funny. But most important, he's a drummer. In a band." Despite her protests to the contrary, I noticed she had polished off an entire brownie, one tiny piece at a time. "I love musicians."

That made one of us.

"And . . . music. I love music. I mean, have you ever listened to *Abbey Road*? That album seriously changed my entire life."

"I have. It's cool."

"Totally." She nodded. We talked music for a while, which was what we usually did when I came to visit. It was a safe subject, something that didn't agitate or upset her. Other acceptable topics included prom and how excited she was for it, or her gap year and how she planned on backpacking all over Europe. How her parents wanted her to go to Yale, but she wanted to attend Sarah Lawrence. It was exciting how well she communicated today. How smoothly our conversation flowed. That wasn't always the case.

I glanced at my watch. Trial and error had taught me that even though she seemed perfectly fine, half an hour was about all she could tolerate. "It's been great chatting with you, but I've got to get going. I'll see you next week, okay?"

"Okay. Thanks for the brownies. Hey, what did you say your name was again?"

"Maisy." The word caught in my throat because I knew what she was going to say next.

It was what she always said.

"Maisy? Really? That's so random. That's my mom's name."

"I know. You named me after her." I whispered the words, not wanting to cause another meltdown where she would have to be sedated. There was nothing worse than seeing your own mother being held down, screaming hysterically, and not being able to do anything to help her.

"What?" she asked.

"I said that is random. And a fun coincidence. I'll see you soon."

I had to hurry up and walk away before I started crying in front of her. That usually set her off, too.

My mother had been diagnosed with a severe traumatic brain injury after she'd run her car into a telephone pole when I was fifteen years old. When she woke up from her coma, she thought she was eighteen years old and still living at home. She didn't recognize her own children. Initially she was diagnosed with transient global amnesia. A woman in England had gone through something similar. She thought she'd gone to bed as a fifteen-year-old and woken up in a thirty-two-year-old's body, but that woman had eventually recovered. The hope was that Mom would do the same.

My three brothers and I took her home, told her who we were. She didn't believe us. She didn't remember us. Seeing her reflection in a mirror spun her out of control. Fitz had just turned twenty-one, Parker was nineteen, and Cole and I were fifteen. We were all so young. None of us knew what to do, how to help her. Nothing worked. Not the psychiatrist's visits, the medicines, multiple trips to the ER. The part of her brain that allowed her to form new long-term memories had been irreparably damaged. She was diagnosed with early-onset Alzheimer's, in part caused by genetics and partly due to the accident. When she was lucid, she was Cynthia van der Bos, the year before she met my father. The psychiatrist suggested that her teen years had become a refuge for her mind, a safe place to forget about the horrific accident and what my father had put her through.

When it became clear she wouldn't get better, we were advised to put her in an assisted-living facility where they could watch over and help her. We were able to afford it only because my maternal grandparents had been really well off. My father had never contributed a single penny in child support; our mom had used her inheritance to take care of us. She'd paid cash for the Craftsman-style cottage in Venice Beach where I still lived with my siblings. We'd never gone without.

Until recently.

Because inheritances didn't last forever.

"How's your mom?" Angie asked me as I stepped inside the main building. She wore her favorite lavender scrubs and handed off a patient file to a coworker at the nurses' station.

"Good. This was a good day." This facility was how Angie and I had met. She had started working at Century Pacific Assisted Living three years ago. I had come to visit my mother on my nineteenth birthday. Cynthia couldn't talk, couldn't stay still. My being there only made her episode worse.

Angie found me sitting in the lobby, crying uncontrollably. She put her arm around me, told me everything would be okay. I wasn't upset that I couldn't talk to my mom. I was upset because now I was officially "older" than she thought *she* was. In her mind she would stay young forever, like some kind of YA vampire, while I kept aging and aging. For some reason, that broke my heart. Angie promised she would keep a special eye on my mother and would be there anytime I needed to talk.

She'd been my best friend ever since.

"I'm glad she's doing well. It's time for my break. Want to do a lap with me?"

I nodded, and we went outside. The grounds had a large, looping asphalt path enclosed by high honeysuckle bushes and the fence they covered up. Sometimes I walked here with my mom, if she was feeling up to it.

"How is Hector Jr.?" I asked.

Her whole face lit up. "He is the cutest toddler in the whole world. Even when he gets up five times in a single night because his mommy went out and he didn't like it."

"Poor baby." I wondered if now would be a good time to mention my plan to marry her off to Fox so she could have his babies. What do they call fox babies? Kits? Then she wouldn't have to go out at night and could stay home and be a boring married person—making herself, Fox, and Hector Jr. extremely happy.

"But I don't want to talk about my lack of sleep. I want to talk about whatever was happening last night with you and Ryan De Luna."

CHAPTER THREE

I actually tripped over my own feet. "What?"

"There was something there last night. With you and Ryan."

"You are certifiable. Which is probably okay, given that you're currently surrounded by doctors who can treat you."

She nudged me with her elbow. "I'm being serious. There was this, I don't know, fiery spark or something. Like if you'd been alone with him in that room, the whole place would have burned down."

Angie always had been prone to romantic delusions. "If it had burned down, it would have been because I was trying to destroy the evidence and the body. The only thing between us was a mutual disgust and animosity."

I could see I hadn't convinced her, so I pressed on. "Why are you even bringing it up? It's not like we run in the same social circles. I won't see him again."

"Not unless it's meant to be."

My best friend fervently believed in "meant to be." I blamed her mother for all the telenovelas.

It didn't help things that Angie's own love story had started because of "meant to be." She'd recounted it a dozen times. She'd been late to an interview. Her alarm didn't go off. The water in the shower wouldn't turn on. Her dog threw up all over the outfit she'd chosen to wear. Just one delay after another.

And then, right as she was turning into the parking lot of her new potential employer, Hector ran into her, giving her a mild case of whiplash. I'd told her more than once that I didn't think bodily injury via vehicular accident was particularly romantic, but Angie insisted it was. That if she hadn't been late, if so many things hadn't gone wrong, if she'd been just ten seconds earlier or ten seconds later, they wouldn't have met. Hector felt so bad about her injury that he stayed with her in the hospital until her family arrived and then came over to check on her every day for a week. By the end of that week, they knew they'd be together for the rest of their lives.

But neither of them had known just how short that would end up being.

"Not everyone can have love at first crash. Which is another reason to never fall in love. My insurance rates wouldn't recover." Parker had a nasty habit of parking in illegal zones whenever he took the van out, and we had a small mountain of unpaid tickets. "Last night was not 'meant to be.' Last night was only about you meeting him. Nothing else."

"Well, I thought Ryan was very charming. Didn't you think so?"

See? Moonstruck. "No. He was a punk."

"Only to you. I wonder why?" Her voice sounded sincere, but I saw the mischievous twinkle in her eye. Like his punkness had meant he liked me.

But this wasn't elementary school. We weren't six years old, and he didn't pull my pigtails.

I tried a different tactic. "We don't have anything in common."

Angie started ticking off fingers. "You're both beautiful, you both love music, and you both lost your moms."

"His mom died. Mine's still here."

She squeezed my forearm, not saying what I knew we were both thinking. That in a way, my mom had died. Physically she was here, but mentally she hadn't been herself in almost seven years.

One last-ditch effort. "Can I again refer you to the disgust and animosity part?"

Angie shrugged one shoulder, as if that didn't matter. "Musicians are passionate people."

"I'm not passionate. I'm the Ice Queen." A name bestowed upon me by Chuck Glass senior year when I'd punched him in the esophagus after he'd lured me under the bleachers. (Another thing brothers are good for—teaching you how to throw a really effective punch.) Chuck had told anybody who would listen that I was so frigid I'd give *Frozen's* Elsa a run for her money. The nickname had stuck, in part because Cole thought it was hilarious and encouraged it. He shortened it to IQ, which he pronounced *ick*. He especially liked that it made the guys at school leave me alone. "Keeping them away from you is a full-time job," he'd muttered. I'd angrily told him I didn't need a chaperone and then demonstrated my throat-punching skills on him, which he rated as two thumbs-up after he stopped writhing around on the floor.

"You're not the Ice Queen. You just don't know it yet." Angie checked her phone. "We should probably head back."

Despite me repeatedly explaining my rules to Angie over the years, she didn't seem to believe me when I said the musician thing would never happen. Especially Rule #2.

We turned around, and I wondered whether anything she'd just said had merit or if she was such a hopeless romantic that she saw potential even where none existed.

"If Ryan's not happening, I noticed you did seem to like the guitar player. Which I get. What is it about guys in a band that women like so much?"

"I actually know this." It was something I'd researched because I didn't understand how a bunch of gross nerds like my three brothers had a line of pleeches waiting backstage after every show. One blog I read suggested that it was because musicians knew they could get who-ever they wanted, making them generally disinterested, detached, and noncommittal, which women apparently found irresistible.

A study found that musical ability had a high correlation with levels of prenatal testosterone. Which meant musicians were more athletic, healthier, and more likely to create a baby. Something apparently no woman's ovaries could resist. "Some of it is social proof. When a guy is onstage performing and every woman around you wants him, that makes him valuable. If you're the one who gets him, you win. We're a generally competitive animal." Which was how I explained my reaction to Ryan last night. It had been all the screaming groupies who wanted him. That was why I had been attracted to him until he opened his mouth.

That he was retina-melting hot had nothing to do with it.

Not wanting to dwell on my mental image of him, I kept talking. "Charles Darwin said musical ability came to be only in order to charm the opposite sex. A caveman who learned to sing and make music was so superior at basic survival skills that he had free time to become artistic. Which made him more attractive as a possible mate."

"Huh." Angie seemed to be weighing my overexplanation. "I thought it had something to do with their innate rhythm onstage, trans-lating to other areas." She laughed while I blushed and continued on. "Sorry! Didn't mean to scorch your virgin ears. But if it's an evolution-ary thing, that means you can't do anything to stop it. You have to be with Ryan. For the good of the species."

Now I giggled, glad I could dismiss my physical reaction to him for what it was—pheromones and cavewoman instinct.

Even if my lizard brain wanted him for his baby-making ability, it didn't matter. It wasn't like I worked with the guy or something. I thought I'd never see him again.

If only I'd known then what was about to happen.

It wasn't until later that evening that I realized I couldn't find my cell phone.

"Parker, have you seen my phone?" I pulled my bed away from the wall, thinking the phone might have slipped down the side. No luck.

My second-oldest brother paused at the doorway, putting on a jacket. The smell of his cologne filled the room. He'd put on too much, as usual. "Your room looks like a crime scene. Why would I have seen your phone?"

"I don't know. I can't find it."

"You say that like this is the first time that's happened."

"Shut up."

He laughed. "Awesome comeback, Maze. Where's the last place you had it?"

"If I knew that," I muttered through clenched teeth, "I would have it back already." I was forever losing my phone. I had thought seriously, more than once, about supergluing it to my hand. If I didn't love playing my guitar so much, I probably would have.

There was no money to buy a new one, so I had to find it.

"Hey, how's your friend Angie doing?" Despite the fact that he was a total computer geek, Parker was a capital-P player and had his own personal harem—an ever-rotating roster of women who would drop everything just for the chance to hang out with him. He'd recently decided he should add Angie to that list. I think he did it mostly to annoy me.

It worked. "You stay away from Angie."

"She's hot." He made that statement as if it excused any dog behavior on his part.

"I'm serious. Leave her alone. I found her future husband." When I said that, Parker's face turned pale. The thought of commitment freaked him out even more than it did me, and that was really saying something.

He held up both his hands like he was surrendering. "Okay. I'll stay away from Angie. For now."

I threw my pillow at him, which he easily sidestepped while laughing. My aim was pretty bad.

Which was probably a family trait, given the current urine-splattered state of our bathroom.

"If you're done hurling things at me, I'm going out for a few hours."

Given that he was near my room, that meant he was sneaking out. "Through the back door?"

The always upbeat, always happy Parker actually frowned. "Fitz is stressing, and I don't want to deal with him right now. See you later."

I heard the back door close quietly as he left. I should have reminded him not to park anywhere stupid, as he typically did.

Well, I had officially ransacked my own room and come up short. Parker said he hadn't seen it. Maybe Cole had.

I went across the hall and knocked on the door of his room. No response. I opened the door and stepped into the darkened bedroom. "Cole?"

He was already asleep, snoring softly. He worked the early-morning shift (starting at 3:00 a.m.) at the bakery around the corner. Which meant that he usually went to bed early. On nights we had gigs, he would leave straight from the show and go to work. Doing my best not to disturb him, I looked around for my phone.

There was one recharging on his nightstand, but it was Cole's phone. I picked it up and used the flashlight app to search his room.

I noticed a picture tacked to his bulletin board of Cole and me when we were seven years old and had both lost our front teeth. We'd shared a room when we were younger, and even though we were way too old for that now, I missed him being close by. Everybody had called us the twins, despite the fact that we were born nine months apart and had different mothers and were different races.

But even then, people could tell we were brother and sister because of my father's stupid genes that seemed to dominate every one of our DNA strands. We all had his musical talent, dark caramel-colored (as my mom had liked to say) hair, and high cheekbones. And even Cole, who was half-black, had our dad's pale-green eyes. I'd read once that green eyes were one of the rarest eye colors. Something like only 2 percent of the entire world had them. (Given my father's favorite pastime of creating offspring, that 2 percent was probably related to him in some way.) It somehow seemed fitting that my father's DNA took over everything and dictated how things would be for us, even at a molecular level.

I hated that I had to be reminded of him every time I looked in a mirror or into the faces of the people I loved best, or every time I sang or played. That I had talent because of him.

After I closed Cole's door, I went to find out if my oldest brother had seen my phone. He sat at the kitchen table, which was papered with bills and a single calculator. Fitz had his hands fisted in his hair, his head bowed, his shoulders caved in.

"Is everything okay?" I asked.

He jumped as if I'd startled him. "Maisy. Hey."

Usually Fitz was the most mellow person in the world. He took whatever obstacles came his way and didn't worry about getting past them. It made him the perfect guardian when our mom had to leave. Things didn't worry him.

But now? His feathers looked seriously ruffled. "What are you doing?" I asked.

He let out a world-weary sigh. "I might as well tell you. I can't protect you from this much longer. I think we're going to have to sell the house."

"What?" I couldn't keep the panic out of my voice. This was not just a house. This was our home. The only home I'd ever known. Fitz couldn't sell it. "Why?"

"Because Century Pacific has raised their rates again, and the money is almost gone. I don't know how we're going to make next month's payment." He handed me a piece of paper. It was a bank statement.

Showing an almost zero balance.

I sank down into the chair next to him, dumbfounded, and stared at the statement. I'd known for a long time that things were not great, that we had to tighten our belts, but I had no idea we were at "sell the house" bad.

Especially because Fitz had always been so responsible. He'd created a strict budget for us, and we'd stuck to it. We didn't go on vacations; we didn't have big Christmases or birthdays. We bought only necessities.

We all had day jobs—at our mother's insistence. Although she had encouraged our musical aspirations and put us in lessons when we were kids, she told us we had to have something to fall back on just in case. Fitz had gone into carpentry, Parker did graphic design, Cole baked, and I cut hair. I really hated cutting hair, which is why I never made much money doing it, but I contributed to the household finances.

It still wasn't enough.

"I can't believe the entire inheritance is gone." It felt surreal.

"Mom never wanted us to touch the principal. She always supported us off the interest. But that facility costs so much that I didn't have a choice." We had maxed out Mom's long-term disability and her health insurance about two years after the accident.

"How long do we have?"

Fitz rubbed the dark stubble along his jawline. "A little less than a month. We should probably get the house ready to put on the market."

We wouldn't have to do much. We lived in a really desirable location. It was only a five-minute walk to one of the most famous beaches in the world. Which meant that even if the entire house was repeatedly flooded, festered with termites, and declared an annexed protectorate of the Cockroach Kingdom, we would still get millions of dollars.

But how long would that last? Our mom was only forty-eight years old. She would hopefully be around for a long time.

I racked my brain, trying to think of solutions. We didn't have anything of real value except the house. "Maybe we can bring Mom home, and we can take care of her."

"She needs round-the-clock medical supervision, Maisy. None of us are qualified to do that. She's also much happier there than she was here."

"What about government assistance?" Now that we were officially superpoor.

"I don't want Mom to end up in a government-run facility. Not if we can prevent it."

He was right. Angie had told me horror stories about state-owned institutions. Fitz was always right.

"Earlier—was there something you wanted to ask me?"

Now was not the time to mention my missing cell phone, when my brother was already drowning in financial woes. "Do Cole and Parker know?"

"They know. They're not happy about it, either."

I tried not to get upset. Of course I was the last to know. My brothers thought it was their job to protect me from everything in the world, including bad news.

"Don't worry, Maisy. Things will work out." He leaned over and patted the top of my hand. "I'm going to turn in. Good night."

"Night," I mumbled, chewing on the end of my hair. It was something I did when I got really stressed.

This was the worst thing that had happened to us since the night of Mom's accident.

This house allowed us to live together while we pursued our dreams of making it big as a band. It made it so we could work menial jobs that freed us up to practice and perform. Now what would happen? We'd probably all go our separate ways. Fitz would most likely marry his on-again, off-again highly religious girlfriend and start his own family. Cole had talked a lot about moving to New York, wanting to meet his biological mother's relatives. Parker would probably get an STD and die without me around to remind him to get annual physicals.

People would say it was past time for us to move on with our lives. I was almost twenty-two years old. I should have been living on my own. With an actual career, like Angie.

I should stop pretending this band thing really had a chance of happening.

In a daze, I went back to my room and closed the door behind me. I absolutely had to find my phone now. I'd seen for myself that there was no money to replace it. I pulled up the phone-finder app on my computer. It took forever to start up and pinpoint the location.

I'd expected to see a glowing dot at the location of my house. Instead, my phone was in Calabasas.

Which was an extremely upscale, ridiculously expensive place to live.

Why was my cell phone in Calabasas?

I sorted through my memories, trying to figure out when I could last remember having my phone. I hadn't used it when I'd visited my mom. In fact, the last time I had it was . . .

When Diego took a picture of me, Ryan, and Angie.

Diego had my phone.

I wasn't sure how to feel about that.

Now I had to contact him and get it back.

Since this wasn't my first rodeo, I knew what I needed to do. I ran into Cole's room and quietly grabbed his phone. I texted my number.

> The password is 12569

If my phone was on, it should buzz, and the message would be visible on the locked home screen. That would mean somebody had to be standing by my phone, ready to answer. Which was why I alternated my texts with calls. Call, text, call, text. Losing my phone so often had made me something of an expert on strangers and cell phone behavior. Talking on a random phone completely freaked out some people, but they had no problems texting. It was why I alternated, not knowing who would be on the other end. If they were weirded out by talking, hopefully the ringing would get them to pick up. Once I had texted and called my phone for two hours straight until somebody responded.

I tried to do a search for "Diego De Luna" and "Calabasas" on my computer. If he didn't get my texts, maybe I could find his address and drive up there. Unfortunately, we had the crappiest internet service known to man, which made the page just hang and not load a response. It seriously would have been faster to drive to Google and ask them my questions in person.

Thankfully, ten minutes later Diego answered my text.

Hello?

CHAPTER FOUR

> Hey, this is Maisy. From last night. You have my phone!

> Maisy? The banshee/harpy who plays guitar like an angel?

How quickly I'd forgotten that he thought he was hilarious.

> Thanks for the insult/compliment. But I'm not any kind of supernatural creature. Just the owner of the phone you're currently holding.

I saw three dots scrolling while he typed his response.

> How do I know this phone is yours?

Was he serious?

> Duh, I gave you the password.

Maybe you tortured the rightful owner to get the password.

> Yes, I tortured someone to get the code in order to steal a slow, always out of memory six-year-old phone.

I can hear your sarcasm all the way over here.

> Good. Because I'm laying it on pretty thick. Why would I lie?

I don't know. You're the evil mastermind, not me.

I always liked sparring with someone who could keep up with me. And despite his ridiculous assertions, Diego was staying with me, quick with his retorts.

> It really is my phone. Also, for future reference, you should just assume every text or email you get from me is sarcastic and/or snarky. It makes my job much easier.

I was enjoying this way more than I should, especially given Rule #1.

> Noted. Hmm. How to prove the phone is yours? Where's your diary app on this thing?

I would never keep a diary on a device I lost on a regular basis. I quickly racked my brain, trying to think if there was anything mortifying on there.

> Why is your phone so slow?

> I told you. No one would lie to get that thing back.

> It's so outdated I feel like I should have R2D2 plug in just to communicate with it.

> Ha-ha. And you're not allowed to open up any apps.

Especially because I couldn't recall everything I stored on it. Did I have sappy song lyrics on there? Pop songs in my library that I hadn't yet deleted? I really should pay more attention to the kind of stuff I put on my phone.

> Whoops. Sorry! My finger just slipped and I opened up your Facebook app. You should really post your pictures from last night. The world has to know about your devotion.

My devotion? What was he doing?

I opened Facebook on Cole's phone and searched for my name. There at the top of my page was a picture of Angie, Ryan, and me. The caption read:

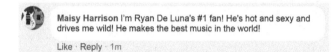

Maisy Harrison I'm Ryan De Luna's #1 fan! He's hot and sexy and drives me wild! He makes the best music in the world!

Like · Reply · 1m

He'd followed it with a bunch of heart emojis. I would lose what little street cred I currently possessed, and my brothers would never let me hear the end of it. Like if I died before them, they'd make it a point to drive to the cemetery and hang Ryan De Luna posters on my tombstone.

> OMG, take that down right now.

Hang on, I'm watching something.

What could he be watching? I'd never once taken a naked or risqué photo of myself, and since I hadn't slept with anyone, there obviously wasn't a tape that could be leaked, but I found myself strangely apprehensive all the same. What was he looking at?

So Maisy Harrison of the band Yesterday--what's this YouTube clip of you singing "One More Night"?

Ack! There *was* something completely humiliating on there! I typed quickly.

> Nothing! It's nothing.
> Move along. Absolutely
> nothing to see here. Did I
> mention it's nothing?

He didn't respond. He wasn't typing. He just left me hanging, not knowing what he would do next.

The reason I'd created that clip was because I had noticed that other singers had success by doing covers of famous songs and earned a decent income through YouTube. I'd thought maybe we could do the same. So I had uploaded all our original songs and done a few solo covers. I kept trying to get my brothers to do a song alone or a duet with me, but they just mocked me instead.

Anyway, I'd turned Ryan's dance/pop hit "One More Night" into a slowed-down acoustic version. Even though the lyrics were about a girl staying at a club to dance one more night with the guy singing, I sang it thinking about my mom. How I wished I could have one more night with her.

But the videos made us only a few bucks a month. Nothing that would help, especially given our current situation.

> Wow. You're good. And a
> total liar. You are a HUGE
> fan of Ryan De Luna, you
> Luna-chick, you.

> Um, no.

> And yet…you sang his
> song. Explain that.

I could explain it easily. My fingers flew over the buttons.

> He has a massive fanbase and I'm pandering to it.

> Bzzz. (That was the sound of a buzzer, not a bee.) Because…lie. This song means something to you. I can hear it in your voice.

What could I say? That it was the song I put on repeat when my musician father permanently walked away from us and my mom stopped being my mom? That I wanted something happy and upbeat to counteract my sadness? That I desperately wanted to believe in fairy-tale romance and love at first sight? That when I finally felt like I could get out of bed and face the world, I never wanted to listen to another false, lying pop song ever again?

I finally settled on:

> Very long and complicated story.

Then I added:

> Have I sufficiently proven that's my phone?

> I don't know. Your texts say you're Cole. Who's Cole? A boyfriend? Did you mention last night whether or not you have a boyfriend?

I didn't.

Do you think you could mention it?

Possibly.

Could you mention it now?

Why did that make me smile?

No boyfriend. But I don't date musicians, remember?

Right. But why not? Who would understand you and your love for music better? The way it consumes you? How you can lock yourself in a room and forget to eat because you're so caught up in creating the perfect sound? How much music is a part of you, like your arm or your leg?

It was true—I'd seen many a failed relationship between a musical person and a nonmusical person. They didn't get the drive, the need to create, and how that usually came first before everything else.

But I was not going to be my mother and blindly devote myself to an unreliable, cheating musician, ruining my life and the lives of everyone around me. I had to draw a line in the sand somewhere.

43

> I'm a musician and so I'm surrounded by musicians constantly. I know what they're like and how for so many of them the goal of getting a record deal is not about the music, not about the fame, not about the money, but about seducing groupies.

He seemed to think about that one; it took him a bit longer to respond this time.

> So what you're saying is you're out seducing groupies? Since you're a musician and all.

> Of course not.

> Beg to differ. What do you think you're doing right now?

Why did that make me blush?

> Are you the groupie in this scenario?

> I am the one expressing admiration for your talent. And I would not mind being seduced.

Ha. I just bet he wouldn't.

I'll have you know that real groupies show up for concerts. You haven't been to a single one of mine.

Tell me when and where.

I don't know when the Ryan De Luna circus heads out to the next city, but we play every Wednesday night at nine at this little club in the Valley called Rodrigo's.

The owner of the club, Rodrigo Sanchez, had taken a liking to us. None of us knew why, but playing at Rodrigo's was the only gig we could consistently count on. Unfortunately, it didn't pay a whole lot. Just a little bit more than what it cost us in gas and repairs on our dilapidated van.

We're in town for a week before we head out to Vegas, so I can definitely come.

With my phone?

Depends on how good your band is.

I didn't need the winking emoji to know he was teasing. I knew I really should put a stop to all this flirting we were doing.

> Although, I don't know how you're going to go three whole days without your phone. I'd go into withdrawal. It would be worse than when I gave up caffeine. Anyway, how do you plan on repaying me for my gallantry?

What was he expecting? Was he still on that "We should hook up" thing from last night?

> By saying thank you.

That should shut him down.

> So...no peeling grapes and feeding them to me? No going out to eat where I pay for the privilege of you judging my personality for a couple of hours? You're not planning on rubbing my feet while whispering sweet nothings in my ear? Not even signing my chest (which I think I deserve since I'm your favorite groupie)?

At least he wasn't acting like every other shocked and outraged musician who had ever hit on me and expected me to swoon at his feet. It was refreshing that he could joke about it.

> None of that will be happening. Please remember my no dating musicians rule, which now extends to include grape peeling, foot rubbing, sweet nothings and chest signings.

> You can't hear me, but I'm sighing with disappointment. Okay. Friends it is. See you Wednesday.

> With my phone.

> Maybe.

I had thought Diego was cute, and although I'd enjoyed chatting with him backstage, this entire exchange made me like him even more. His sense of humor was like mine. He'd made me laugh several times. He was quick and clever and fun. My brothers might even like him and possibly wouldn't punch him if he tried to hold my hand or kiss me.

Cole's phone buzzed. Another text from Diego.

> Maisy?

> Yeah?

> I just wanted you to know...rules were made to be broken. And I'm very, very good at breaking rules.

Why did that make my heart pound and my skin flush?

And why was I picturing Ryan De Luna saying those words to me instead of Diego?

I hadn't expected to hear from Diego until I saw him in person on Wednesday. But he texted me the next morning, asking who my favorite guitar players were.

Which I found out only after Cole came storming into my room to show me his screen. "Who is this fool texting you on my phone?"

I explained the situation to him, but it didn't do much to calm him down. "Diego and I are just friends. It's not a big deal."

"Whatever. I read your texts. This dude does not want to be 'just friends' with you." Cole handed me his phone. "Give him your email. Because if he sends you a picture of his junk on my phone, I'm not going to be responsible for what happens after that."

I pressed my lips together so I wouldn't laugh, and I told Diego to email me instead, giving him my address.

Then, sadly, I sat and waited for my in-box to load. It took so long that I nearly died of boredom.

But there it was! An email from forever99@rdl.com with just one question:

Who are your favorite guitar players?

I hit the REPLY button and wrote:

> Joni Mitchell, Lita Ford, Christa Harbinger. Also,
> Bonnie Raitt is a goddess. What about you?

I pushed SEND, but I knew it would probably be a while before I got his response. I left my room and made myself some toast while I waited. Just as I sat back down at my computer, I had another email from him.

> Hendrix (obviously), Jimmy Page, Muddy Waters,
> and Johnny Ramone are my favorites.

Most guys would say Eddie Van Halen or Keith Richards or Slash when you asked them. They were the more obvious choices. I liked that his picks were a little offbeat.

His next line asked:

> Why don't you have any men on your list?

I responded:

> Why don't you have any women on yours?

He replied:

> Touché.

Back and forth we went, talking about our top five bands and singers, favorite albums, best live concerts. It was slow going because of my machine and the connection. Like Pony Express slow. I wondered if he was playing me. I knew from experience that the way to a musician's heart was to ask him or her about their musical influences or why they'd written a certain lyric, or to tell them how much you loved a specific melody. I'd watched my brothers fall prey to many a girl who'd focused all her attention on just the music instead of gushing about how hot my brothers were. To make it seem like she was different from the others.

They fell for it every time.

Even after I pointed it out.

Our online flirtation continued until Wednesday evening finally rolled around and my brothers and I headed to Rodrigo's. Despite Rule #1, I was strangely excited to see Diego. We unpacked our van, which was currently leaking coolant. Another expensive problem we couldn't afford to fix. Our instruments were arranged in the back like pieces in a *Tetris* game, but we'd been doing this so long it was easy to extract them in the right order.

We went inside Rodrigo's and got set up. I plucked at my vintage Martin Dreadnought. I'd found it at a garage sale a couple of years ago and had seen that the woman selling it had no idea how much it was actually worth. She had put a five-dollar sticker on it. Part of me wanted to pay the money and run, but my conscience wouldn't let me. When I told her she was really underselling, the woman said her husband had left her for her sister, and the judge had ordered her to sell their assets and split the proceeds. She apparently had a trust fund he couldn't touch, thanks to an ironclad prenup, and she didn't need this money. She was very happy to sell me the guitar for five bucks.

Sometimes I played my Dreadnought onstage; other times it was the Gibson Les Paul that had been passed down to me. Fitz had given it to me, but I suspected that my father had initially owned it (and most likely paid for it with my mom's money), but I didn't ask because I didn't want to know.

I didn't want him tainting my guitars, too.

He'd ruined so much of my world already. Like how I disliked performing in clubs. My childhood memories of my father centered around how he smelled after a show—stale cigarette smoke, cheap booze, and even cheaper perfume. Every club we ever played in specialized in that particular aroma combination.

I despised the smell of coffee. He'd drunk coffee around the clock, and every time he'd deigned to grace us with his presence, the coffeepot would be on day and night.

"Hey, Maze? Have you seen this?" There was a weird tone in Fitz's voice.

"Seen what?" Knowing him, it was probably some clip of a bunch of guys burping and farting that he thought was hilarious. I put my ear closer to the guitar string as I slightly turned one of the top tuning pegs, finally satisfied with the sound.

"This." He shoved his phone in front of my face. It was the YouTube video of me singing "One More Night." He asked, "Did you know about this?"

That was a stupid question. "Yeah, I know about the video. I'm the one who filmed myself singing it."

"I'm not talking about the video." He scrolled down slightly, and the first thing I saw was the number of views.

Just a little over one million. "A million views?" I gasped, grabbing at his phone, wondering if I was hallucinating.

"Really? A million views?" Parker asked, coming to peer at the phone over my shoulder. "How much money is that?"

"I can't math that high right now!" My brain was too excited to figure it out. It was probably only a few thousand dollars, but it was more than we'd ever earned from an upload before.

"That's why Mom wanted you to go to college. So you could math," Fitz teased me, apparently enjoying my mental freak-out.

"You mean like *you* did?" I quickly retorted. "Before you dropped out your junior year to pursue your lifelong dream of paying back student loans?"

"How did we get so many views?" Cole asked, coming over to stand next to Parker.

"Keep scrolling down," Fitz instructed.

The very first comment I saw was from Ryan De Luna, and he'd posted it twenty-four hours ago.

 RyanDeLunaVEVO 1 day ago
Beautiful. Now I'm the one who is #moonstruck.

REPLY   1536   👍   👎

View all 363 replies ⌄

CHAPTER FIVE

So many thoughts happened all at once that it was hard to keep track. Beautiful? Who was beautiful? Me? The song? Did he recognize me from his concert? If so, was he being sarcastic? Or did he really like my cover of his greatest hit? If he liked it, was Ryan the one who actually commented on it? If not him, it had to be somebody who worked for him, as the post was from the official Ryan De Luna channel on YouTube. Had Diego shown it to him? Would the views keep going up?

What was happening?

There were more than a thousand replies to Ryan's comment. I didn't bother looking at them because I already knew what they would say. They'd be either some variation of how much that fan LLLOOOVVVEEEDDD Ryan or offering up creative new ways to get rid of me since I'd somehow managed to nab his attention.

"He's also got this video on the landing page of his website," Fitz added. "Didn't you see this guy the other night? What exactly did you do?"

Now all my brothers had their arms folded and were glaring at me. "Oh please, like I'd hook up with this commercialized hack for some views. Give me a little credit. The only thing I did the other night was insult him. Repeatedly. To his face."

None of them looked like they believed me.

"Come on, our fan is here," Cole said. "We should get started."

We often joked about our fan (singular). His name was Joe, and although my brothers had initially suspected him of harboring a crush on me, he just seemed to really like our music and showed up every week to hear us play. Because the rest of this crowd were people who just happened to stop in and get a drink, and girls who lusted after the male contingency of our band. Last and definitely least, you had the guys smart enough to have figured out that hot chicks showed up to hear Yesterday play, and they came to hit on the women.

So yeah, we didn't make much money from playing music. If any of us had been able to quit doing it, we would have. But the love of music, of performing—it's like an infection that seeps deep into your soul, becoming a part of you. Even if I decided to walk away—no more band, no more uploads, no more performances—I would still play. Still write. It couldn't be stopped; it was too much a part of me. Same for my brothers.

I slung my guitar strap over my left shoulder, standing in front of the microphone. When we'd started out, I'd suffered from crippling stage fright. The kind that had me puking for about ten minutes straight, right before the show. But we'd been at it for so long that now being onstage felt normal. I belonged here, performing. Sometimes I had to force myself to concentrate on what I was singing because I'd done the same songs so many times that my mind could drift. I would think about what I wanted to eat when the show was over. But that could ruin the performance, so I tried to stay focused.

Which was harder than usual, considering the YouTube views and the fact that Diego had promised to come tonight.

We ran through our set. Cole played keyboards, Fitz was on bass guitar, and Parker played drums, while I was on lead guitar. We took turns singing our songs, but I did most of the singing. That was because Fitz had talked to somebody in the industry ages ago who'd told him that girl-fronted bands tended to make more money. I don't know if that was an actual fact, but my brothers treated it like gospel truth even though they all sang just as well as I did.

I couldn't see very far past the first row of tables because of the stage lights, but I had hoped Diego would sit right in front. I wondered if he'd made it.

We finished our final song of the night, "Yesterday" by the Beatles. It was our signature song, and at each show we performed it differently. Sometimes we stayed true to the original. Other times we did a fast-paced rock version, a ska-sounding or punk-inspired one, a cappella—whatever we were in the mood for. Tonight we kept it old-school.

Fitz thanked "everyone" for coming out, and we started breaking down our equipment to haul it back to the van. No roadies for unknown bands.

I hummed to myself as I packed up. I never felt more alive than I did after a performance. My skin hummed; my heart pounded like a snare drum in my chest. There was something about getting up onstage and singing your heart out that gave you this absolute rush of adrenaline. It made you totally wired, and it took a while to come down from that high.

Which meant that after a show, we basically kept vampire hours.

After we'd loaded everything, we went back inside. Rodrigo always fed us the most amazing quesadillas as part of our payment. I looked everywhere for Diego, but I didn't see him. It bothered me. I was the kind of person who kept my word. I found it annoying when others didn't.

"Did you see the redhead at the bar?" Cole asked, holding his hands out in front of his chest. "With the big . . ." His voice trailed off as he looked at me.

"I'm not a child. I know how that sentence ends."

"The redhead with the big brains was what I was trying to say."

I couldn't hold in my derisive snort. "Yeah. I'm sure you could see her brains all the way over here."

"Where? I love big-brained girls," Parker said, his head swiveling back and forth as we sat down at an empty table.

"She must have gone to the bathroom or something," Cole responded.

Seriously . . . men! That woman could have all the personality of a wooden plank and my brothers would still want her. Which I knew because of all the planks of wood they'd previously dated.

"There she is. Dibs!" Cole called out, giving the redhead a wink.

"You can't call dibs!" Parker protested, elbowing Cole in the ribs.

I tried to help them out. "Just so you know, women really dig it when you reduce them to objects you can call dibs on." They ignored me.

"You know the band pecking order. Men with picks and sticks get first shot. Which means Cole's out of luck," Parker informed us. Both of my brothers stood up and tried to look like they weren't running toward the bar, but they were jostling and attempting to trip each other on the way. I hoped the redhead liked her men with a side of immaturity.

Fitz stayed put at the table, drumming his fingers against the top. Heather, the waitress who usually worked nights at Rodrigo's, brought a tray of quesadillas and set them down in front of us, along with four sodas. I thanked her, and she said to let her know if we needed anything else.

"You're not going to throw your hat in the ring?" I asked Fitz after I'd polished off my first quesadilla. Not only did performing make you energized, but it also made you ravenous.

"Not tonight." His ex-girlfriend had done something to Fitz that made it so he couldn't let go of her and couldn't move on. I didn't get it, but to be fair, I didn't ask. I'd found that guys didn't much care to talk about stuff like that.

But I should probably try. "Did something happen with Miranda?"

He shrugged a shoulder. "Women should come with instruction manuals."

"Why? That would be totally pointless. I've lived with three men my entire life, and I've never once seen you guys read instructions."

That at least made him smile, which made me feel better. He polished off his entire Dr Pepper in one gulp and then asked, "Weren't you supposed to meet a guy here tonight?"

"Looks like he didn't show." It was probably for the best. But why keep in contact with me, promise to come, and then just blow me off? It was really rude.

"Don't forget we have to vet him before you go out on an official date."

It would probably be bad if I threw my half-empty mug at Fitz. "No, you don't. I'm an adult who can make her own choices." I grabbed his empty glass and my mug. "I'll get us refills." And would refrain from spitting in his drink, which I thought was very big of me.

I made sure to go to the opposite side of the bar from where my brothers were attempting to lure the big-brained redhead with their smooth-talking game. Or shiny objects. Whatever worked.

Rodrigo stood a couple of feet away, talking to a guy in a hat seated on a bar stool. I walked toward them and waited for a break in the conversation. I'd never seen Rodrigo look so serious before. Usually he joked around with my brothers and teased me.

When they finished, I called out, "Hey, Rodrigo, another Dr Pepper and root beer, please?" I passed the empty glasses to him and noticed what looked like a Korean newspaper folded in half on top of the bar.

"Sure thing, Maisy."

"Thank you!"

The man with the hat spoke. "So you are capable of being nice."

That voice. It seemed familiar. I noted his glasses and ball cap, and then he turned.

Ryan De Luna.

"What . . . who . . . what?"

He reached into his pocket and pulled out my phone, then slid it along the bar. "As promised, your phone."

I just blinked at him, then at my phone, then at him again. "Did Diego send you?"

Ryan frowned. "What does Diego have to do with this?"

A rushing sound filled my ears as I realized what had happened. "Wait. You're the one who's been texting and emailing me the whole time?"

"Yes."

"I—I thought you were Diego."

Some movement and female voices murmuring behind me drew Ryan's attention. "Could we move this someplace else? I'm parked out back." He grabbed the Korean newspaper, threw a hundred-dollar bill on the bar, and without even looking to see whether I followed, he left.

Part of me wanted to let him walk out of my life and pretend none of this had happened, but the rest of me demanded answers.

When I went behind the club, Ryan stood next to a silver Prius. He opened the passenger door for me, and I got in without saying a word. He made his way to the other side and sat next to me, causing the temperature to rise about ten thousand degrees. He took off the glasses and hat and threw them in the back seat.

I felt kind of rebellious doing this. On the list of Things Maisy Should Never Do, sitting in a parked car with a boy was pretty high up there. If my brothers saw us, they might possibly pull Ryan through the windshield.

"Why did you think I was Diego?" he asked. Ugh. Even his profile was handsome. I forced myself to look straight ahead so he couldn't confuse me with his good looks.

"He had my phone."

"You mean after you insulted me and stormed off?" He actually sounded amused. Had it been such a novel experience for him that he didn't know he was supposed to be offended? Because I happened to be excellent at offending people.

I couldn't help it. I had to look at him, if only for the chance to try and figure him out. He flashed me the biggest, most sincere, blinding smile. I wanted to melt.

"Diego threw your phone on the couch. I've had it ever since."

The question explosions returned. Why did Diego toss my phone? He knew it belonged to me. It kind of seemed like he was hitting on me. Why would he throw it away like it didn't matter? Not even try to get it back to me? And what had possessed Ryan to pick it up, especially given how I had talked to him? Had I really been chatting with him this whole time? This guy I was relating to, starting to like from our texts and emails . . . was Ryan De Luna?

Angie's head was going to pop like an overinflated balloon when I told her.

"Have dinner with me."

It took me a second to make sense of his sentence. Was he . . . asking me out on a date? "What?"

"Have dinner with me," he repeated, slower this time.

"No, I heard you. I just couldn't believe you were serious. Because I'm not even a little bit interested in signing up for the Ryan De Luna Conquest and Bedpost Notch Tour."

He smiled again, and there was so much charisma behind it I felt dazed. "This isn't about notches. I'm currently notchless at the moment."

"Ha. I don't follow you or read tabloids, and even I know that's not true."

"I can tell you only the actual truth. What you choose to believe is up to you. And I wasn't asking for a date. I have something else in mind."

Then he put his arm around the back of my seat, and I was slammed with a cacophony of sensations—my heart raced, I couldn't breathe, my neck flushed, my skin prickled. I knew what he had in mind, and despite my body's reaction, I wasn't interested.

"Um, thanks for returning my phone. I should probably get back." Before my overprotective idiot siblings organized a mob and/or I did something I'd completely regret.

"Wait. I have a proposition for you."

My stomach lurched and twisted. My brothers had warned me not to get into a situation like this! If Ryan's proposition included any of my body parts that were currently covered by clothing, I'd tell my brothers' mob where to find him. "Proposition?" I hated how my voice squeaked at the end.

"I need an opening act for the rest of my tour."

Why was this both a relief and a disappointment?

"You have an opening act." I distinctly remembered them. A group called For by Four, which I told Angie was either a spelling mistake or grammatically incorrect. They were a bunch of girls from a reality talent show that had been put together as a group and had a couple of Top 100 hits. They had lip-synched their entire set list.

Now Ryan looked uncomfortable. "There was ... a misunderstanding."

"What kind of misunderstanding?"

"The kind where Leilani told the world we were in a relationship even though we'd barely even spoken."

I had a vague recollection of Angie saying something about them dating. "You can't really blame people for believing her. You do, um, date a lot."

"I thought you didn't follow me and didn't read tabloids," he teased, his eyes laughing, which caused a yanking sensation just below my stomach.

"That's how bad it is. Even I know you're a manwhore."

"I've had maybe one serious relationship in my life that ended when I found out she was selling private pictures and texts to the highest bidder. Anything else is either publicity or lies. It's not easy to find someone you can trust. Most women don't want me. They want Ryan De Luna."

He led a charmed life. He didn't need my pity. I didn't want to feel bad for him, even though when his voice cracked a little, I considered hugging him. "If nothing happened between you two, then why would it matter if Leilani said it did?"

"Because when I confronted her about it, she offered to, you know, notch me to make things better. And didn't want to take no for an answer."

It took me a second to realize what he meant. "I'm not a spinster schoolmarm. You can use the actual word."

"Not according to Rodrigo."

Rodrigo? "How do you know Rodrigo?" I felt like my whole world was spinning crazily out of control, and nothing made sense anymore.

"He used to be a studio guitarist. He went on my mom's last tour. When you told me this was where you played, I got in touch with him and asked about you and Yesterday. He said you were a really good girl and that I should be a gentleman."

Next time I saw Rodrigo, I was going to punch him for not telling me he used to play and then let him know I was full up on older brothers and not holding auditions for a new one.

"That doesn't explain why, out of all the bands in the world, you would choose us to open for you."

Ryan sighed, drumming his thumb against the steering wheel. "There's a few reasons. The first is that you and your guys are good. Really good. You're actual musicians who play actual music. I want to move in a new direction with my sound. I want it to be more like what you're doing. And Rodrigo told me I'd be a complete idiot if I didn't have you opening for me. I kind of owe him." He let out a little laugh. "There're some other reasons, but I don't know you well enough yet to tell you."

He was serious. I thought it had been some kind of move or ploy. That maybe he never had a woman not show interest in him so he was going to extraordinary lengths to move me into Luna-chick territory.

He wasn't done. "There're about thirty stops left on the tour. You'd earn $15,000 per show, plus whatever merch you sell."

That . . . was a lot of money. Two seconds ago my decision was a vehement no, but that made me reconsider. That kind of dough would pay for Mom's bills for a long time. "I can't just make a unilateral decision. I have to talk to my bandmates. We'll have to vote."

"What if there's a tie?"

"Oh," I said with a wave of my hand, "then they wrestle or do some kind of complicated boy ritual to figure out who wins."

He laughed, shifting closer to me. The arm on the back of my seat brushed against my shoulder, and goose bumps broke out on my flesh while tiny little shivers wrapped icy fingers around my nerves.

"Tell you what. There's a diner two blocks from here. Brown Bear something. You go talk to your band, and I'll wait there for half an hour. If you don't show up, I'll have my answer."

Tonight? I had spent the last ten minutes trying to figure out how to put distance between us and never see him again because a teensy bit of me thought my rules were totally stupid and should be abandoned. Especially as I studied his strong, cut jawline and firm lips. The windows around us had started to fog up. Like we'd been in here making out.

As blood rushed to my cheeks, I realized I *wanted* to be in here making out. "I don't know. It's late. We'll probably head home and go to bed."

He leaned his head to one side. "Bzzz. Lie. I know you're completely wired right now. Is this why you don't date musicians? Because they see through your musical excuses?"

I didn't date musicians because they were unreliable and thoughtless and ruined families.

Ryan seemed to edge closer to me. "Come on, you know opening for me would do great things for your career."

"You should stick to stroking your ego in the privacy of your own home," I shot back, not sure I would react appropriately if he moved even an inch nearer.

Ryan laughed, turning my resolve to mush. "Ego aside, you know what I said is true."

"Do you really think you can just sit there and brag about how great you are while being all nice and helpful and attractive—"

It slipped out. It literally just slipped out.

"You think I'm attractive?"

"What? No." Yes. "No."

He moved closer again. "Who are you arguing with? Me or you?"

"I'm not arguing with myself." Yes, I was.

"You said no twice."

Desperate, I started grasping at straws. "That's because I doubly mean it."

"I don't think that's why you said it." It was like his voice slowed and dropped with each movement, hypnotizing me.

I looked down at the floor, trying to break the spell. "O-oh? Then why did I say it, Mr. Knower of All Things?"

I gasped as his calloused fingertips gently brushed the underside of my chin, sending burning waves of want and frosty spikes of need through me. He raised my chin, making me look him in the eye.

Oxygen had ceased to exist.

"You said it because you're fighting the fact that you're attracted to me. I can feel it every time I get close to you. The way I make you shiver. I like it." That last part came out as a growly whisper, and I shivered all over again.

He released me and leaned so far forward that although some part of my brain objected to the idea of him kissing me, every other cell in my body told it to shut up. His chest and face moved closer to mine, and he reached out his left arm.

Only he didn't kiss me. He just opened my car door. It took a second for my legs to work, and even then, they still wobbled as I got out of the car.

"Half an hour," Ryan said when I went to shut my door. "Don't disappoint me, Maisy."

I watched as he drove off and realized one of us was going to be very disappointed.

I just had to make sure it wasn't me.

CHAPTER SIX

"Where were you?" Cole asked in a teasing tone when I found him at the bar. "Let me guess. You found the man of your dreams but were too aloof for him to notice you. That's my IQ. Nobody scares men off the way you do."

I hated when he called me IQ. I was about to tell him as much when I was interrupted.

"What? Maisy was roofied?" Parker repeated, obviously mishearing the word *aloof*. "Who do we have to beat up?"

"I am fine! All of you calm down!" I loved my siblings, but they needed to stop acting like we were living in the seventeenth century and they'd been personally enlisted by the king of England to guard my virtue.

"All joking aside, you know how dangerous clubs can be," Fitz added, his worried expression making me feel a little guilty for not telling them where I was going.

"I'm fully aware of the dangers, thanks to your many hypocritical lectures." How was I supposed to tell them what had just happened outside? I hardly believed it myself. "I think you guys should sit down. There's something I need to talk to you about."

They warily did as I asked.

I stood silently for a moment, not sure what to say or how they would react. Better just to rip off the bandage all at once. "So this random thing happened. Ryan De Luna came to see us perform tonight. He liked what he saw, and he asked if we wanted to be his opening act for the rest of his tour."

My brothers just gaped at me. Like I'd announced my recent return from exploring the planet Mars and discovered a new humanoid species there that made me their empress.

I told them the financial details and how Ryan was waiting to hear from us. "If we don't meet him at the Brown Bear diner in half an hour, he'll assume the answer is no."

"Ryan De Luna was here. Tonight. He listened to us play, and now he wants us to open for him? The biggest tour of the year?" Parker said each word slowly and carefully.

I nodded. "That's what I just said."

"And he's at the Brown Bear diner right now, waiting for us to say yes or no?"

"Do you guys have a hearing problem? Yes, he wants us to open for him, and yes, he's waiting for our answer."

All three brothers exchanged glances and without another word jumped to their feet and sprinted for the back door. Fitz grabbed my wrist, pulling me alongside him as they ran.

When we were all in the van and Parker had somehow coaxed the beast into starting, I asked, "Does that mean you're interested?"

Fitz looked at me like I was especially dumb. "This is the biggest opportunity we've ever gotten. We'd have to be total idiots to pass it up. I just don't understand why he'd want us to open for him. We're not going to bring in any new fans. Everybody in the audience would be there just to see him, and we'd get to benefit from it."

"Yeah, and what he's offering salary-wise is really generous, given where we're at in our career," Cole added. "He could have paid us a lot less. Why would he pay us so much?"

"Maybe he's just a nice guy." It was something I had been considering since I left his car. I had initially assumed he was an arrogant, playboy douchebag, but maybe I'd been wrong. Fitz often told me I should give people the benefit of the doubt, that I was too quick to jump to conclusions and didn't let them explain themselves. Maybe I'd done that with Ryan.

We were stopped at a red light. All of my brothers turned to stare at me, and I could see the moment when all three light bulbs lit up over their heads.

"He wants you," Parker said, forced to face forward as the light changed. "This is about you."

"No way. This is not about me. I have made it very clear to him that I'm not interested. At all. The night I met him backstage? He was a total jerk to me. I called him names. The only reason I didn't hit him was because he has big, scary bodyguards. And I really laid into him. You guys would have been proud."

"Maybe that's what he's into," Parker murmured to Cole, who nodded.

I threw up my hands in exasperation. "You guys are seriously the stupidest people ever."

"The thing is, Maze, someone like Ryan De Luna is not like the guys around here." Fitz's eyebrows knit together, concern showing all over his face. "You would be really out of your depth with someone like him."

"If I wanted to date him, there's nothing any of you could do about it. But I'm telling you I don't, and you should listen to me and believe me."

"Even if he tries to make a move on Maisy, and we have to rough up his pretty-boy face"—Cole kept talking like I hadn't even said anything—"it wouldn't matter. This will get our name out there in a big way, and if people like what they see, we'll book new tours and sell our songs. We might finally be able to make a living as artists."

That hadn't occurred to me until he'd pointed it out. That opening for Ryan might mean opening for other acts. That we would get to travel all over the world, performing for thousands of people, building a name for ourselves, gathering a fan base that would actually buy our music.

Ryan was offering to help us start down the path that would lead to everything we'd ever wanted.

It seemed too good to be true. "Do I get a say in this? Like always, you guys have decided what we're doing without even asking what I want."

"Okay, IQ, what do you want?" Cole asked.

"Don't call me that. I don't know what I want. But what if I say no, I don't want to tour with Ryan De Luna?" I couldn't imagine months of my brothers jumping to idiotic conclusions where he and I were concerned.

"We need the money." Parker looked at me in the rearview mirror.

I let out a big sigh. My siblings loved deciding things for me, which I hated, but this was one situation even I knew I couldn't refuse.

Cole seemed to sense my acceptance. He patted me on the knee. "You can say no if you want, but then we'd always think less of you."

We pulled up in front of the diner. I felt both relief and a bit of panic when I saw that Ryan's car was there. As we climbed out of the van, I was hit with the smell of pumpkin pie, my absolute favorite. It had been so long since we'd stopped by this diner that I'd forgotten they served it year-round. I worried a bit about how the introductions would go but stopped with my hand on the front door when I realized my brothers had stayed on the sidewalk, near the van. "What are you doing?"

"Go on ahead of us. We're going to have a discussion on how to handle your new boyfriend," Cole said.

If I kept rolling my eyes this hard, I was going to permanently detach them from my eye sockets. "He's not my boyfriend. He's not even boyfriend-adjacent. We're not going to date, and the quicker you Neanderthals get that through your furrowed foreheads, the easier your lives will be. Now I'm going in not because you told me to but because I really want pie."

Holding up my head, I marched inside. Just as I remembered it. Black-and-white-checkered floor, a long Formica counter running the length of the restaurant, and booths with black vinyl seats. There weren't many people in the diner, and Ryan sat all the way in the back, near the bathroom. He had his hat and glasses on. "Hey," I said, sliding into the booth.

He sported that bone-melting smile again. "I didn't know if you'd come."

"Here I am." Yeah, this wasn't at all awkward. How was it possible for one person to be this good-looking? He sat there looking like a half-Latino Clark Kent. As if it wasn't bad enough that he was so handsome he could have been a movie star, he had this . . . power. This draw that made it so you didn't want to look away from him. Like he was the sun and you were the planet formerly known as Pluto, desperately wishing you weren't so far apart but knowing he would burn and consume you with just one touch if you altered your orbit to get closer.

He was so gorgeous he made you think inappropriate things.

Not that it had ever happened to me.

"What about the rest of the band?"

"Outside, acting like morons." I pointed at them as a waitress approached. I asked for the pumpkin pie and told her to bring some for Ryan as well. He started to protest, but I insisted she bring it.

"I don't really eat processed sugar," Ryan said. "I'm into the whole clean-living thing."

"Me, too. Although sometimes my clean living includes eating a pound of fudge at midnight."

He nodded seriously. "Sometimes you just have to eat a pound of fudge at midnight."

"You say that like you've done it."

"Oh no, I don't have food issues."

Without thinking, I leaned over and smacked him on his manly forearm. "I don't have food issues!"

He laughed. "The pounds of fudge consumed at midnight would suggest otherwise." Which made me laugh, too.

The waitress returned with our slices of pie, topped off with Cool Whip, and we both thanked her. I immediately dug in and couldn't help but let out a little moan when the combination of pumpkin, ginger, cinnamon, and nutmeg hit my tongue. "This is seriously the best thing that has ever happened to my mouth."

"That's sad."

He was such a flirt. And I had the racing heart rate to prove it.

"It's not sad. It's amazing. Try it."

Ryan took one tiny bite, just enough to taste it. "It is good. But I can say with all confidence that it's not the best thing that's ever happened to my mouth." The fiery intensity of his stare was enough to make my Cool Whip melt.

I swallowed hard. He was making this difficult. I was going to go on tour with him unless my idiot brothers were outside coming up with a way to ruin that, and I didn't know how I would be able to handle a sweet, nice, flirtatious Ryan De Luna.

Maybe it was just a waiting game. If I gave him enough time, he'd go back to accusing me of using his cousin to make him jealous. Or bragging about how great he was or how women worshipped him. Something.

Then I could get over this teeny physical crush I had on him.

Okay, this King Kong–size physical crush I had on him.

Trying to look away from him was like trying to pry two really powerful magnets apart. There was a lot of resistance. I somehow managed it, though, averting my gaze down. I saw the same paper he'd had at the bar.

"What's with the Korean newspaper?"

"It's a little trick I learned from a story about David Bowie. He used to walk around New York and never be approached. He said it was because he always carried a Greek newspaper. Like people would see him and think, 'Is that David Bowie?' and then they'd figure it couldn't be and that he was a Greek guy who just looked like him."

"Except for the fact that nobody reads real newspapers anymore. You'd think it would actually draw more attention to you." I didn't get how other people could stop staring at him. So far I hadn't figured it out.

Ryan shrugged. "It mostly works. That, and people tend to overlook you if you're somewhere they don't expect you to be. Like this diner."

Stop staring at him. You've seen good-looking men before. Why are you acting like this is the first time it's ever happened?

I couldn't stop. I didn't know what was wrong with me.

"So, tell me the names of the other guys in your band."

That startled me and let me know how long it had been since I'd last spoken. So long he felt like he had to keep moving the conversation forward. "Um, the tallest one is Fitz, the one in desperate need of a haircut is Parker, and the one waving his arms around is Cole."

"Since you don't date musicians, do you just hook up with them instead? Any history there I should know about? Touring with exes can get complicated."

I choked on my pie and tried very hard not to gag. "Ew. Gross. Zero history. They're my brothers. And the no-dating thing includes hooking up. I don't, how did you put it, notch with musicians, either. That's also a rule."

"So, what, you notch nonmusicians?"

I could feel the flush burning its way through all my layers of skin, setting my cheeks on fire.

"No."

His eyebrows flew up. "Seriously? You've never—"

"Not that it's any of your business, but never. It's something I plan on waiting for. Until I get married." After watching my mother throw away her entire adult life, I had no intention of following in her footsteps. I would never give that much of myself to just some guy. Especially some musician guy. The only way I could imagine it ever happening was if I was so committed to someone, and so trusted him, that I was willing to marry him.

Marriage was something else I didn't imagine myself doing anytime soon.

But it wasn't really appropriate diner conversation.

Thankfully, he changed the subject. "They're all your brothers? Even . . ."

"Even Cole," I said firmly, not willing to explain our sordid family history at this point in our professional interaction.

Because that's all this would ever be. Strictly professional.

He got the hint. "Is Fitz short for something?"

"Fitzgerald. Our father wanted to name us all after famous jazz musicians. Cole is short for Coltrane, and then Parker couldn't really be shortened."

Ryan ate another tiny sliver of pie. "I don't know anyone in jazz named Maisy."

I pushed down the lump in my throat as I thought of my mom. "My mother insisted that I be named after my grandmother. So my middle name is Ellington. When I was little, my mom used to call me Maisy Ell. Have you heard that old song about Daisy?"

He shook his head, so I hummed a few bars and sang the chorus.

> Daisy, Daisy, give me your answer do
> I'm half-crazy all for the love of you
> It won't be a stylish marriage
> I can't afford a carriage
> But you'll look sweet upon the seat
> Of a bicycle built for two

"That sounds familiar." Ryan nodded.

"Anyway, most people don't know this, but for the rest of that song the girl is referred to as 'Daisy Bell.' My mom used to sing me that song all the time but used Maisy Ell. For most of my childhood I thought it had been written about me."

"Do you get your talent from her?"

"No. She couldn't have carried a tune in a bucket. She used to swear that my first word was *shubbup*. When she sang me to sleep, I would tell her to shut up every single time." I would have given just about anything to have her sing it to me again, though.

Ryan laughed at my story, and it warmed me inside not only to hear it but also to share this good memory of my mom. I had actually forgotten about it. "Does your mother like jazz, too? Is that why she went along with the jazz-musician names?"

No, she'd gone along with it because she had absolutely no self-respect or pride where my father was concerned. "She was more of a Beatles fan. If she'd had her way, we'd be John, Paul, George, and Ringo."

He gave me a serious nod. "I can see you as a Ringo."

Now it was my turn to laugh.

"Is that why your band is called Yesterday?"

"Yep. It was her favorite song."

Ryan pushed the Cool Whip off his pie and looked like he wanted to say something but wasn't sure if he should. "You talk about your mom using the past tense. Did she pass away?"

I let out a shaky sigh. "No . . . but it's hard to explain." Especially without curling up into a ball and sobbing.

He tapped his fork against his plate. "Maybe you'll tell me the story someday."

"Maybe I will." Where had that come from? I hadn't planned on telling Ryan De Luna anything personal about myself at all, and here I was ready to spill my guts to him.

"I do find it interesting that you've named your group after a song from one of the biggest pop bands ever, given how much you hate pop music."

This was not the first time I'd had this argument. "They were a rock band, not a pop band."

He leaned back in the booth and rested his arm across the back of the bench. He looked like he was enjoying himself. "They started as a pop band."

"They were the freaking Beatles. They defied labels."

"Hey."

I had been so caught up in my conversation with Ryan that I had completely forgotten about my brothers. Now all three of them stood next to the booth, glaring at us.

"One question, dude," Parker said, taking a step forward. "Are you asking us to be your opening act so you can bag our sister?"

CHAPTER SEVEN

"You did not just ask him that!" I gasped. It was like I had three living chastity belts.

Ryan looked . . . pissed. He cleared his throat. "I'm trying to find an opening act. If you're not interested . . ." He stood up, and all three of them spoke at once.

"Whoa!"

"Hang on a second."

"We were just worried."

Ryan slowly sat back down, then turned his face toward me. "I think your sister is beautiful and talented and funny, but as I've repeatedly been told, she doesn't date musicians. So I don't think you need to worry."

As if what he'd just said about me wasn't enough, that flashing, fiery, intense gaze of his caused my stomach to do flips and my pulse to frantically throb, and I thought my brothers probably should worry.

Just a little.

Okay, a lot.

Fitz, Cole, and Parker climbed into the booth, and both Ryan and I had to scoot down to make room. Fitz told Ryan that we didn't have the money or the ability to travel around.

"We have over fifty crew members traveling in seven tour buses, and eight semitrucks carrying full production. I have room on my bus. You guys can travel with me and my band."

Ryan's gaze flickered back to me, and ice solidified in my veins. I was going to be sleeping near him and traveling around with him and basically living with him?

Other people would be there, including the Dating Police trio, but still.

When Fitz brought up production costs, Ryan offered the use of his touring production crew. They would be able to take care of everything for us, including setup and takedown. "Brad is our production manager. I'll get you his contact information. I'll send you Piper's information, too—she's our tour manager and will tell you everything you need to know."

"Is all the traveling done by bus?" Cole asked, and I felt bad for him. He was prone to vehicle motion sickness.

Ryan's face turned pale, and his mouth became a thin line. "Yes. No planes."

When I'd been obsessed with Ryan as a young teen, part of what had made him so romantic was his tragic life story. I'd watched a documentary about Ryan once or twice. (Okay, five times.) His mother, Sofia De Luna, was a girl from New Mexico who wanted to be a singer. She kept being told the same thing—because of her name and appearance, she should go into the Latin pop market. Problem was, she didn't speak a word of Spanish (her own dad had died when she was young). But she quickly learned how to sing Spanish phonetically and became a huge success.

Ryan's father had worked at one of the biggest American record labels, and he saw her perform at the Grammys. He asked if she'd be interested in crossing over, as so many Latino artists were doing at the time. He'd been excited to find out she spoke perfect English. He had her record a demo and convinced his label to sign her.

They fell in love, got married (at a wedding that ran into seven figures), and had Ryan.

A year later the marriage fell apart. His mother took Ryan on tour with her, hiring tutors when he got to be school-age. Sofia became a massive pop star in America as well, in part due to her relentless touring. Her first English album had four number-one hits.

When Ryan was seven years old, they were on their way to a concert in Puerto Rico when they ran into a terrible storm with hurricane-level winds, and the plane crashed.

Only three people survived, Ryan being one of them. They said Sofia wrapped Ryan in pillows and blankets and then protected him with her body.

I didn't blame him for avoiding planes.

They all started discussing terms and contracts and agreements. My brothers grilled him like it was their last day on the police force and they didn't care if they got in trouble for being overzealous because they were about to retire.

I finished my pie and then reached out to slowly slide his barely touched slice toward me. It seemed like a waste not to finish it. As I did so, Ryan shot me one of his patented Ryan De Luna winks that made my knees feel like they were made out of whipped cream.

There had to be a way to stop this. To stop reacting this way, to logically tell myself he was the kind of guy who had to kick girls out of his bed. He didn't need to chase after someone who had repeatedly told him she wasn't into him and it wouldn't happen. Maybe he saw me as some kind of challenge, but he couldn't really be interested.

If I could just remember that nothing physical would ever happen between Ryan and me, maybe I could control myself.

As I sat and listened to them talk, I felt more and more guilt over how I'd talked to Ryan the night we met. I had been horrible to him, and here he was doing something completely amazing and life-changing for us. He was going to make it so that we could keep taking care of our mom and keep our home. I felt like I didn't deserve his kindness.

The conversation wound down, and Ryan said he had an early interview in the morning. Fitz got up to let Ryan slide out of the booth.

"It's been . . . interesting meeting you all. I'll see you bright and early Friday morning. The bus leaves at eight a.m. sharp, and Piper has no problem leaving anyone behind."

He looked at me as if he wanted me to say something.

Instead, he got out his wallet and put another hundred-dollar bill on the table to pay for our pumpkin pies. As he headed for the door, I started pushing at Cole. "Move. I need to walk him out."

Cole shook his head. "He's a big boy. He doesn't need you to walk him out."

"I'm not going to get pregnant between here and the sidewalk. Don't follow me," I growled, standing up in the booth and walking across the table. Parker yelled something at me, but I tuned him out.

Ryan must have seen me coming after him because he was waiting outside.

As the diner door swung shut behind me, I suddenly felt shy and idiotic. "Um, hey."

"Hi. So your brothers seem . . ."

"Overprotective? Completely insane? One banana shy of a bunch? Yeah. That's them. They're so annoying. Can't live with them, can't dispose of their bodies without drawing suspicion."

He put his hands in his pockets. "It must be nice to feel loved like that."

"I feel smothered. Or, more accurately, brothered."

That got me a small smile, but he fell silent. Where he'd pretty much driven our conversation earlier, now he was waiting to hear whatever I had come out here to say.

Problem was, I had no idea what I should say.

"How did we get here?" I finally asked.

"Well, I drove my car, and I'm pretty sure you came in that thing that at some point was a van."

As if it wasn't bad enough that he was literally the most handsome man I'd ever met in real life, he had to be witty, too. It would have been so much easier to ignore him if he'd been dumb and not funny. "No, I mean how did we go from me being horrible to you and yelling insults and now I'm your opening act?"

He took a step toward me, and my body swayed in his direction. Like it wanted to ignore my head and do whatever stupid thing it wanted to.

"I think you and I remember that night differently. You weren't horrible to me."

"I was. I apologize."

Another step toward me. "I'm the one who should say I'm sorry. I thought you were using Diego to get to me. It's happened before. I shouldn't have assumed you wanted me or that you were playing some game. You've made it pretty clear you're not interested."

My confused, raging hormones and I decided it was a very bad thing we'd made him think that.

Now he was so close that I feared slightly for his physical safety, seeing as how we were in full view of my siblings. My chest felt so tight, like all the air in my lungs had turned solid, and I could no longer breathe.

"When you confronted me, I couldn't remember the last time anyone had ever spoken to me that way. I wasn't upset. I thought, 'Here's a real person who is treating me like a real person.' You made me feel like a human being again."

Ryan reached up to tuck a strand of hair behind my ear, and when his fingers brushed the top of my earlobe, I felt the molten lava of his touch everywhere—even in my ankles.

"You're shivering again." He whispered the words close to my mouth, and I wanted nothing more than to close my eyes and let him kiss me.

Which was dangerous. "Don't," I said, stepping back. "If I'm going to go on tour with you, no more talking about shivering or being beautiful or anything like that." My voice shook, along with the rest of me. "We have to be professional colleagues. Nothing more. I—I have rules. Important rules. That are important."

"Okay. If that's what you want. We should shake on it." He held out his right hand, but I knew what would happen if I touched him. Spontaneous combustion, most likely.

"No thanks."

That made him smile like he knew something I didn't, and whatever he knew was hilarious.

"Good night, Maisy."

"Good night, Ryan."

I had just opened the door to the diner when he spoke.

"Before you go, I did want to tell you that I enjoyed our first date."

"What?" Was this some kind of reverse psychology? Act like we'd already dated so I'd go on a real date to prove we hadn't?

"I asked you to come eat with me. You showed up. We ordered food. I paid for it. We talked and got to know each other better. Date."

"That was not a date," I responded, but realized he was kind of right. He had ninja-dated me, and I hadn't even known it!

"You've already broken your rule. You should try breaking it again." He turned off the alarm on his car, and it chirped in response.

"That's a very bad idea." A very, very bad idea. Although for the life of me, I couldn't remember why.

He walked backward to his car, grinning at me. "Just because it's a bad idea doesn't mean we won't have a good time. You've got my number. Call me if you need anything." Then he got into his Prius and drove off.

I didn't even get the chance to figure out how I felt about any of this because my brothers came outside and ushered me into the van. Where I tried very hard not to think about Ryan De Luna.

And failed.

"We'll have to get a lawyer to look over the contract," Parker said, and then he and Cole started talking about the money.

Even if I didn't date Ryan, what if I wanted to kiss him a little? Would that be so bad? "I have a condition," I announced. "For doing this tour."

"Like only pink Starbursts kind of thing?" Cole asked.

"No. Like you guys are going to acknowledge the fact that I am a grown woman who can make her own decisions. You won't intimidate anybody who speaks to me or threaten any guy who looks my way. I'm perfectly capable of taking care of myself, and you're going to respect that."

I was met with a deafening silence.

"Promise me—a Mom promise—that you guys will do that, or else I'm not going."

"I promise to back off," Fitz said, and although I could tell it killed them to do it, Cole and Parker also promised. Cole then turned on the radio, even though we got only AM stations, muttering something about how he was promising only because of the money.

"Will it be enough?" I asked Fitz. "The money? Can we keep the house?"

"I don't know, Maisy." He put his arm around me and squeezed. "It doesn't solve all of our problems, but it's going to help a lot. In a couple of weeks, we'll be able to catch up on some bills and pay others off. Let's see how things go before we make any major decisions, okay?"

For the first time since Fitz had told me about the money situation, I felt hopeful.

It was all thanks to the world's biggest pop star. Who, no matter what I told him or myself, I was most definitely attracted to.

And who might have me possibly reconsidering my stance on Rule #1.

The first thing I did the next morning (afternoon) when I woke up was call Angie. Her side of the conversation was basically a series of shrieks and screams and "Are you kidding me? Are you kidding me?" She promised to take extra good care of my mom. I tried to visit my mother at least once a week, and I wasn't sure how often I'd be able to see her while we were touring. Even though she wouldn't remember whether anyone came to visit her, I would know.

I briefly wondered what Angie would have said if I'd told her my initial response to Ryan's offer was to decline. It probably would have involved some veiled threats about kidnapping me and leaving me on the tour bus. I promised to send Angie lots of pictures. Although she didn't know it yet, I planned on including quite a few of Fox.

"You also have to tell me every single detail about what happens with you and Ryan De Luna," she instructed.

"Nothing's going to happen with me and Ryan De Luna."

"We'll see."

I decided to leave her to her delusions and misplaced optimism.

The second thing I did was go into my current place of employment and tell them I was leaving. Permanently. Nothing in the entire world had ever given me more joy than to say those two beautiful words: "I quit." Honestly, I hated only three things about my job at the quickie haircut place—the people, getting out of bed to go there, and the work. I had been so miserable I remembered thinking once that if I died and went to hell, it would take me at least a week to realize I wasn't at work anymore.

Of course none of my now-former colleagues believed me when I said I was going on tour with Ryan, but I didn't care.

The contracts arrived, and after finding an attorney who Parker had gone to high school with and getting his input, we all happily signed.

Fitz found one of his more responsible friends to watch the house while we were gone. He also chatted with Piper, the tour manager, and got the details of where we should meet the bus, and she told him to get there early so she could show us around. The expression on his face after that phone call was kind of goofy and endearing. It made me hopeful that he might be ready to move on with his love life. Because it occurred to me while he was talking that if Fitz had someone to focus his attention on, he might be less inclined to worry about me.

When early Friday morning rolled around, I was completely packed and too excited to sleep. With nothing else to do, I went into the kitchen to try and re-create my mother's brownies.

My mom's famous brownie recipe, the hit at any gathering, was handed down to her from my grandma and from my great-grandmother before that. Mom always promised me she'd give me the recipe when I graduated from high school. I'd turned the house upside down looking for it, but if she'd written it down, she'd also hidden it really well.

After spending so much time trying to figure out the ingredients, brownies were basically the only thing I could make. I was useless in a kitchen; Cole was the baker of the family. He'd half-heartedly tried a few times to help me in my quest, but he said it made him too sad.

So it was left to me to figure out how to carry on this family legacy. I kept downloading recipes for brownies and chocolate frosting, ever hopeful that I'd find the right mixture of taste and consistency.

This batch turned out like all the others. Delicious, but not Mom's.

Eventually my brothers got themselves out of bed, and our Uber arrived to take us to a nearby shopping mall. At seven in the morning, the parking lot was empty except for the buses covered in Ryan's latest album art and the name of the tour—*Moonstruck*. How did I not realize this before?

"He named his tour after a word his fans use?" I asked.

"He did. And the fans love it." A young woman appeared on my right. The first thing I noticed was her bright-purple hair, pulled back into two buns at the base of her head. She was about my height (five feet eight) and very pretty. She sported black glasses, a headset, and a big smile. "Hi, I'm Piper. The tour manager. You guys must be Yesterday."

She was a lot younger than I had expected. Early twenties, definitely. We introduced ourselves by name, and I saw that same goofy look in Fitz's eyes when he shook hands with her.

Piper didn't seem to notice. "Thanks for coming early! Whatever equipment and instruments you want to be packed up, leave them here, and I'll have one of the crew grab them. If you'll come with me, I'll show you to your home away from home for the next few months."

We followed behind her toward the huge, shiny buses. There were dozens of people milling around, talking and laughing. I saw Fox and waved to him enthusiastically. He gave me a slight head nod in return.

I wondered if that meant Ryan was nearby. Just thinking his name set me off, like some kind of conditioned response. My heartbeat elevated, my stomach dropped down to my toes, and breathing became complicated.

If that was from just thinking about him, what would it be like when I saw him again? What if he kept flirting with me and then tried to kiss me? What if he still wanted me to break my rules?

Would I be strong enough to resist him for weeks and weeks?

I suspected the answer was no.

CHAPTER EIGHT

Piper led us to the bus parked farthest to the right. "This is your first time touring, right?" We told her yes. "Awesome. I'll try to make sure I cover everything about the bus and the rules. If you have any questions, ask. First, this is your bus, #304. Be sure to check the numbers because they all look the same. We've had more than one mix-up before. You'll be sharing it with Ryan's band. They're around here somewhere."

A middle-aged man sporting salt-and-pepper hair and a friendly smile came down the bus steps toward us.

"This is Vincent, your driver." He wore the same black polo as the security guards, with the word *Moonstruck* over his left breast. How had I not noticed that the other night at Ryan's concert?

"Bus driver and sometimes zookeeper. You can call me Vince." We all introduced ourselves, and then Vince said to bring only a carry-on with us and that he'd be sure to get all our luggage put in the storage under the bus. Piper had mentioned this in her phone conversation with Fitz; space was limited, so we all packed carry-ons that had our necessities, including a few changes of clothes and something to sleep in. We could swap things out from our suitcases when the buses stopped.

Piper told us to follow her, and we went up the steps into the tour bus. I was shocked when I reached the top. It was all buttery leather and chrome and rich dark-wood walls. On the right side behind the driver's seat there was a large wraparound couch with a table in the middle. I placed the plate of brownies I'd baked that morning on the table.

On the left side there were a couple of freestanding chairs next to the mini kitchen. Along with the sparkling quartz countertop, there was a sink, a small refrigerator, a toaster oven, and a lot of cabinet and drawer space. It didn't look like a place where you could really prepare a meal. A big flat-screen TV hung just above the two chairs, and a bunch of gaming consoles were plugged into it.

"This is the lounging area. It's a good place to hang out, watch movies, play video games, get a snack. We have satellite TV and Wi-Fi. As you can see when we're parked, the walls can be extended on both sides for more room. It's a tighter fit while we're traveling. Please remember that you're sharing this bus with eight other people, and your mother's not one of them. Clean up after yourself, and be considerate of others."

At the mention of our mom, my hand tightened on my bag, and it reminded me to send Angie a text later on to check in and see how things were going. Piper opened a door leading to a narrow hallway. There were four columns of three beds. "This is the bunk alley. It is a designated quiet zone twenty-four/seven. If you remember to keep the doors shut, it should keep out the sound from the other areas. This bottom bunk here is being used as a 'junk bunk.' It means it doesn't belong to anyone, and people will put their extra stuff here. Feel free to use it if you'd like, but know that things get ruined that way."

"Why is it so cold?" I asked, and this time my shivering really was from the temperature.

"All the buses are set to sixty-six degrees. We've found that warmer temperatures make smells worse and basically turn the buses into mobile petri dishes. Keeping it colder keeps everybody healthier."

Piper walked to the bunks farthest away, near the back. The hallway was so narrow we had to go single file. There was an entire column empty on the right side, and the top bunk across the way also had its curtains drawn back. "These were the ones used by For by Four. They're all yours now." She tugged on me and whispered in my ear, "Since us girls have to stick together, I'd suggest getting the middle bunk. The bottom one vibrates a lot from being closer to the wheels, and the top bunk tends to sway more."

While my brothers were busy rock/paper/scissoring over who got what, I claimed the only free middle bunk by putting my stuff on it.

"Thanks for the tip," I told her as they grabbed the other beds. "If we're going to be looking out for each other, you should probably stay away from anybody related to me."

"No warning necessary. They all look like trouble," she told me with a conspiratorial smile, and I liked her even more. "Each one of your bunks has a flip-down TV and a DVD/CD player, along with power outlets for your phones, tablets, or laptops. And I'm sure you've all noticed how narrow this hallway is. If you ever find yourself going one way and somebody else is going the opposite, the preferred passing method is rear end to rear end."

I had to twist my lips together to keep myself from laughing. For some reason that struck me as really funny. That there was a rule about how to pass people in a hallway.

My brothers lacked my maturity, and they all started to snicker.

Piper either didn't find it amusing or didn't care. "It also means you can't leave your shoes, instruments, or any other crap on the floor because somebody will trip over them in the middle of the night, and a fight will break out. Again, be considerate. Your bunk should also be the only place you sleep. If you pass out in a public space, you will not escape the wrath of a Sharpie marker. Unless your lifelong dream is for a photo of your face covered in obscene drawings to be posted online, always sleep in your designated bunk."

She started to walk down the hallway and suddenly stopped. I only barely missed crashing into her. "One more thing—always sleep with your feet facing the front of the bus. Accidents aren't common, but if it does happen, you'll save yourself from a neck injury."

Great. Now I'd be stressing about getting a neck injury and/or the bus getting into an accident.

"Let's keep going." Piper opened the door at the end of the bunk alley. There was a much shorter, skinny hallway with a door on the left, a door on the right, and a door at the far end. Piper opened the door on the right, showing us a clean, nice-looking bathroom. "There are two bathrooms here. Trust me when I say you don't want to ever use bus water. It comes from holding tanks at truck stops, and that should tell you all you need to know. There's plenty of bottled water to drink and to use for brushing your teeth."

"So we shouldn't shower here?" Parker asked. That put an image in my mind of Ryan De Luna, his hair wet from the shower, his sculpted chest glistening with drops of water—

Piper answered, interrupting my brain's idiotic tangent. "Definitely not. Whenever we arrive at the city we're performing in, you'll have hotel rooms for however long we're there, and you can shower then. The buses are just for traveling. Anytime you get an opportunity to shower, do laundry, eat, or take a nap, you should always take it."

"But the toilets are okay?" That question came from Fitz.

"The toilets work fine. But the number-one commandment of every tour bus for every tour of all time is this—thou shalt never, ever poop in the bathroom. Ever. For any reason. The smell is horrific, and it costs a lot more money to take care of fecal matter than just urine. If you're desperate, ask Vince to find a gas station as soon as possible. If you can't hold it, you're going to have to learn how to take a dump in a Ziploc bag. Same goes for puke."

There was no way I could poop in a Ziploc bag. To distract myself from how gross that was, I decided Piper probably should have added "Go poop" to her list of opportunities we should never turn down. "What about the door at the end?"

"On the other buses, it's another lounging area. On this one, though, it's Ryan's bedroom."

Now I had an image of Ryan sleeping in a big bed, which sent prickles all over my skin and caused a sensation in my gut that felt like ribbons curling and twisting.

"Let's head back to the front," Piper said, and I felt actual disappointment that I wouldn't get to see Ryan's private sanctuary.

Something was seriously wrong with me.

When we got to the lounge, Piper took out a piece of paper from a plastic sleeve that was hanging next to the TV. "This paper will change every day. It will tell you when your sound check is, your set time, and the bus call time. Don't ever be late. Time, tide, and tour bus wait for no man."

She put the paper back in the sleeve. "I know this probably all seems fun and cool, but honestly, tour buses are difficult. It's kind of like being in a marriage with a bunch of other people without the benefits. You need to learn to give and take, communicate, and be respectful, and know that some battles aren't worth fighting. They're not paying you the big bucks to perform. You'd do that for free. They're paying you the big bucks to ride this bus."

If that's what I was getting paid for, it didn't seem all bad. There were worse things in the world than getting to ride in a luxury bus that would take us all over the country and let us perform in front of thousands of fans. That giddy, excited feeling I'd had since talking to Ryan at the diner resurfaced, despite Piper's warnings. This was what we'd always wanted. We were going on tour. We were being paid good money to play our music. Nobody could ruin that for me.

"Do you guys have any questions?"

"I have a question," Cole said with his flirtation smile, and I shook my head in anticipation of whatever stupid thing he was about to say. "When are you and I going out?"

Piper waited a couple of beats and then said, "I have a lot more to do before we leave. Give me a buzz if you have any real questions. Fitz has my number. And Cole? I *never* crap where I eat."

She walked off the bus, and Cole ran to the steps and yelled out, "I don't crap where I eat, either! See? That's something we have in common!"

"Where do you think that saying comes from? Do you think at some point in time there was a major issue with people crapping in their kitchens?" Parker asked, completely missing the upset look on Fitz's face. If Fitz thought Cole was interested in Piper, there's no way he'd make a move.

What Fitz had failed to take into account was that both Cole and Parker were interested in every female with a pulse in the entire world.

"This is it," I said, sitting down on the couch. "Bus sweet bus." Fitz nodded and sat next to me while Cole and Parker messed around with the Xbox, trying to see if they could get it to turn on.

In an effort to cheer up Fitz, I took the tinfoil off the brownies and offered him one. "Brownie?" Just as he took one off the top, the sounds of laughing male voices and stomping came from the bus steps.

Ryan walked in the room, and my heart jumped into my throat with excitement. His eyes landed on me, and his feet followed until he stood directly in front of me. "I'm glad you guys made it! Hey, let me introduce everyone. The aloof Russian wearing headphones who is just passing through is Anton. Best DJ in the world, but he's also part hibernating bear. When we're not performing, he's sleeping."

Anton, dressed in all black, made a small hand wave before heading into the bunk alley.

"Maisy already knows Diego, but for everybody else, he's my cousin and guitarist." Diego smiled at me, and where the first night we'd met I thought he was cute, now he was just like this nonentity. He'd gone from the Guy I Could Possibly Be Interested In category to whatever category my brain put my brothers in.

But Ryan had thought I was hitting on Diego. Did Diego think the same thing? Would I have to fend off his advances for this entire tour?

I hoped not. Maybe I shouldn't have made my brothers swear to back off guys they thought were hitting on me.

"Deshawn is our drummer, and Marcus here is on keyboards, and that's Billy, who plays guitars and is our music director. He makes us sound amazing every night. Guys, this is Fitz, Parker, Cole, and Maisy of Yesterday."

Everyone went around the room saying hello and shaking hands. I offered everybody a brownie, and it turned out to be a good icebreaker. Ryan's bandmates talked with my brothers about how good they were, and then it was like people just paired up. Billy sat down next to Fitz and asked him about his sound plot so they could submit it to their sound engineer, Santiago.

Cole started talking to Marcus about what kind of keyboard he was using onstage. "I've got Yamaha's Montage 8 as my main one right now." Cole's eyes seemed to turn even greener with envy.

Parker and Deshawn were bonding over jokes about lead singers. "How do you know when a lead singer's at your front door?" Deshawn asked.

My brother already knew the answer. "Because she can't find the key and doesn't know when to come in!"

Which left me with Ryan and Diego. Which wasn't at all awkward. I was about to ask Diego if he wanted a brownie, but he stared at me for a few seconds and then sat down with Billy and Fitz. I let out a sigh of relief at not having to deal with whatever that situation was yet.

Ryan still stood in front of me, shifting from one foot to the other.

"Brownie?" I was doing super great on the conversational front today.

"No thanks."

I put the plate down on the table. Only two brownies left. Sad and forlorn and out of place. Kind of like what was happening to me right now with Ryan.

"Did Piper give you the full tour?" he asked.

I nodded. "Everywhere except your room."

"Oh." He seemed to consider this. "Do you want to see it?"

One part of me was like, *Yes, yes, yes, I want to see where you live,* and the other part was like, *Why does this feel like a setup?* I blamed my siblings for my overly suspicious mind.

My brothers were all deeply engrossed in conversation, which was good because promise or no promise, Ryan might be lying flat on the floor right now.

Especially if they'd heard my answer. "Okay."

I followed behind him, admiring his broad shoulders outlined in his dark-blue T-shirt. It wasn't my fault; they were right in my eye line. I heard Anton snoring as we went down the bunk alley. Each doorway we walked through felt important, like it was offering me one last chance to say no, to turn back and not do anything foolish.

Instead, I made sure to close the doors behind me.

Every step caused blood to rush through my ears and my hands to tremble in anticipation. Obviously, nothing was going to happen, not with my brothers on the other end of the bus. Even though I was too old to feel this way, the nervousness was because I'd never been in a guy's room before.

Let alone with Ryan De Luna.

He opened his bedroom door, and it just looked normal. There was a queen-size bed with a gray quilt and some massive black-and-gray pillows. His bed was surrounded by multiple built-in dark-wood cabinets and drawers. One of his custom Martin guitars stood upright on a guitar stand in the corner. There was also a desk with a mirror, a flat-screen TV, and a black overstuffed armchair. That seemed like the safest bet, and I sat in the chair while he jumped backward and sprawled on the middle of his bed.

"What do you think of my room?"

Ryan seemed totally at ease and comfortable, while I was having a mild heart attack. There was such a vast difference in what was going on right now for both of us. Something new, thrilling, and slightly forbidden for me. For him? Having a girl in his room was probably so routine it didn't even register. "What do I think? To be honest, I'm kind of surprised there's not a stripper pole back here."

He laughed and turned on his side, propping up his head with his hand. "I could get one installed for you."

It wasn't an offer. "Pass."

Now that we were here, I wasn't quite sure what to say or do.

Thankfully, as had been the case several times now, Ryan filled in the void. "This is the quietest place on the bus. If you ever need a place to escape or you want to compose or maybe need more room to sleep, you're always welcome. I know how tiny those bunks are."

"Where would you sleep?" I had a pretty good idea where that would be.

Predictably enough, he patted his bed. "I'm excellent at sharing."

"Say that where my brothers can hear you and you'll lose the ability to father children." He didn't need to know that they'd said they'd back off. I didn't know what was worse—that he was such a dog or that part of me wanted to accept.

"You can trust me." It would probably help his cause if he hadn't winked at me while saying it.

It would probably also help if I could stop picturing it. "Really? You must think I'm so naive," I said, shaking my head, telling my excited hormones to knock it off.

"I mean that totally innocently, I swear." He even made the crossing motion over his heart while he grinned, and his hazel eyes danced.

I wanted to be sucked in by the lie. I wanted to believe Ryan De Luna and I could date and maybe fall in love and possibly live happily ever after. I wanted to believe he wasn't like every other musician I'd ever met.

To believe I meant something to him. That this wasn't about the conquest or notching or adding another stupid girl to his total.

That he was nothing like my father.

But I happened to live in the real world. I couldn't even guess how many other women had been in this room before me.

I stood. "Thanks for showing me around. My curiosity would have killed me."

He sat up on his bed, seemingly surprised I was going. "I was serious. Anytime you want, you're welcome to hang out back here."

Nodding, I quickly left, shutting his door behind me. The door between the bathrooms and the bunks was open, and Fitz stood in the doorway, looking at me sadly.

Since he blocked my only escape route, I had no choice but to walk toward him.

When I reached him, he gently touched my shoulder to stop me. "I know what I promised. I know you're an adult, and I know you can make your own decisions," he said quietly, probably so as to not disturb Anton, "but you were there. You know I promised Mom I would keep you safe. That guy's going to break your heart, Maze. And when it all falls apart, we're going to lose the best thing that has ever happened to us. Please stop this before it starts and we all get fired."

Then he left me alone with my guilt and fear that he was right.

CHAPTER NINE

I rejoined the other guys in the front lounge. I hoped I looked nonchalant and like I didn't care about Ryan or anything related to him. A few minutes later, Fox got on the bus, followed by Vince, and it was time to head out. They gratefully accepted the two remaining brownies, and I found a trash can in the kitchen area for the paper plate and aluminum foil.

The bus rumbled to life and then made beeping sounds as Vince backed up. Finally, we were officially on the road to Las Vegas.

I looked out the window, watching as the other buses started up and followed us, like a massive metallic caravan. I couldn't help but grin. It was happening!

Ryan came into the lounge, and it was like somebody dumped a bucket of ice water on me. Fitz's words echoed in my brain. I didn't want to be the reason we lost this gig. But at the same time, I was still drawn to Ryan. I wanted to talk to him. To sit by him.

It was going to take a few hours to get to Vegas. I decided the best way to deal with my Ryan issue was to just stay away from him. I headed into the bunk alley and settled into my bunk after putting on the clean linens and blanket provided. I climbed into my new bed and realized it was a good thing I wasn't claustrophobic, as the bunk had the look and feel of a coffin.

The previous tenant had left some Command hooks on the wall, and it ended up being a good place to hang up things I needed close by, like my toiletry and makeup bags. I tried to read one of the books I'd brought with me, but my jumbled, confused mind wouldn't allow me to concentrate.

I made up my brothers' bunks as well. Not because they weren't capable of doing it themselves but because I needed a reason to stay out of the lounge, and I needed to keep busy. I even tried taking a nap, but that was an epic failure. Mainly because some kind of video-game playing was happening in the lounge. I knew this because of the excited, muffled yelling I heard from their end of the bus. Someone would shush them, and then it would happen again.

I knew what a mistake it would be to date a famous musician. And I had to keep reminding myself that my family's entire future depended on my staying away from Ryan De Luna.

More whooping and yelling. Now, somebody was singing about an after-party. It sounded like Cole.

This was going to be excruciating.

Somehow the hours passed, and we finally pulled into the parking lot of the Palazzo in Las Vegas. I grabbed my carry-on and headed for the front, careful to avoid eye contact with Ryan. A flustered Piper came on the bus. "There's been some kind of a mix-up, so there will be a slight delay before we can get into our rooms. Irene's made everyone lunch. She's setting up outside."

"Irene?" I heard Parker ask as we filed off the bus, and I hoped for her sake she wasn't young and hot, or she was about to get some serious attention.

"I have a pretty strict eating regimen, and even though the venues would provide catering, I've found that it's easier to have my own gourmet chef." Ryan said it apologetically, almost like he was embarrassed. I didn't know why. If I could afford it, I definitely would have my own personal chef. "Her bus has fewer bunks and a huge galley kitchen, so she can cook while we're traveling. She also has a mobile kitchen she uses at the venues. She's amazing. There's a lot of fighting to be on her bus."

Even though I'd been reminding myself for the last four hours why Rule #1 existed, just being a few feet away from Ryan was enough to make me forget. I wanted to make him laugh. For him to turn and smile at me. To tease me.

I was only halfway through Day One.

I was so screwed.

"You're the new opening act, right?" I turned to see who had spoken, and it was the woman just behind me in line for lunch. She had well-defined arms and braids down to the middle of her back.

"Yes. I'm Maisy." I offered her my hand, and she shook it.

"I'm Ashley. I'm one of the backup dancers. You should come eat with us."

Maybe this was what I needed. To hang out with the women on the tour.

Ashley scooped up four additional boxes for the other dancers, and I offered to help carry them. We made small talk on the way back to her bus. She was from Chico, California, and she'd been on three of Ryan's tours.

The first thing I noticed when I boarded was the overwhelming smell of incense. I was getting secondhand hippie from it. Their bus looked exactly the same as mine, only with a lot more purple and animal-print pillows on their couch.

"Y'all, this is Maisy. And this is Monique, Britt, Megan, and Mariette."

Then I shared this brilliant observation. "Wow. That's a lot of *M* names." They all smiled at me politely, but there really wasn't a good response to my comment. I immediately felt stupid.

We passed out the boxes, and I sat down at their table. Inside the box was a delicious grilled flank-steak salad with mixed greens, walnuts, and other vegetables I couldn't identify. Which probably meant I was not eating enough vegetables in my regular life. I seemed to be the only one actually eating. As best as I could tell, the dancers were simultaneously discussing the merits of nearby clubs, their current favorite music video, the best shade of lipstick from a particular company, and which TV show they should binge-watch next.

It was almost like being in a foreign country with a culture I didn't quite understand and a language I didn't speak. I'd never spent much time with groups of women. There were a couple of girls I hung out with during the day in school, but I was always so focused on music and then my mom that I hadn't made the time for friendships. Angie was the first close female friend I'd ever had.

"What about you, Maisy? Do you want to come dancing with us tonight after the show?" Ashley asked. "And bring those fine bandmates of yours?"

Of course, I immediately wondered if Ryan would be going out dancing with them. If he flirted with these beautiful women the way he flirted with me.

If I was just one of many.

I was not into clubbing. "The guys in the band are my brothers. Who you might want to avoid if you're into commitment and relationships. I'm not sure what my band is doing tonight after the show. Maybe I can go? One of my brothers said something about an afterparty." I hoped that wasn't hurtful or offensive.

Ashley shook her head. "Girl, whatever you do, do yourself a favor, and do not go to Ryan's after-party in his room. Don't get me wrong; he's better about some things than he used to be, but that boy is a heartbreaker."

This was something I already knew and kept reminding myself about, but my body apparently didn't care. My brain tried to tell it that even strangers were warning us away. "What do you mean better than he used to be?"

"He used to be really bad about starting shows on time, partying too much. Nonstop women. Then something changed. He seems like he doesn't really do that kind of stuff anymore, but I wouldn't take the risk. People don't fundamentally change who they are."

It made me wonder what had happened. Why he'd changed.

And if he would change back.

"Yeah, I haven't seen him hooking up with a random girl or groupie in a long time," Britt said. "But aren't you traveling on his bus? He might try to get with you."

"I am. Maybe I should move in here with you guys." I said it in a joking manner, but I was ready to grab my bags if they'd have me.

"We're full up. For some reason, the crew thinks if we live in close proximity with them, we'll suddenly fall in love," Ashley said with a laugh. "If anything, it has the opposite effect. Boys can be kind of gross to live with."

"I'm used to living with a bunch of men." That was the result of being raised with all boys. I was accustomed to the smells and the humor. I'd found that men were usually easy to understand, and so, usually easy to live with. Most of their motivations were based in something physical, like food, women, or sleeping.

A loud whistle sounded outside the bus. "What is that?"

"Piper," Ashley explained. "She loves that stupid whistle. It means she wants everybody to gather together."

I finished up my lunch and followed the dancers off the bus, throwing away the box. I told the girls goodbye and went off to find my brothers.

"When are you going to introduce me to your new friends?" Parker asked as I came to stand beside him.

"I was planning on never."

"Spoilsport."

Piper used the whistle again. "Okay, the hotel situation has been fixed. We have a private elevator for our use only. You must have your key card to make the elevator function. We have access to the Prestige lounge, which means free breakfast, drinks, and appetizers, as well as concierge service. We'll be passing out your key cards and today's PD. Once you get them, you can head up to your rooms."

"PD?" I repeated.

"It means per diem. Money they give us that we can spend on whatever we want every day. Food, transportation, that kind of stuff. It's meant to cover basic personal expenses," Fitz explained.

That seemed generous, but Fitz told me it was pretty standard. Piper handed us our key cards and envelopes. "Don't forget your sound check at five o'clock today. There will be a car waiting for you outside the lobby at four thirty to drive you over."

I thanked her and then checked out the envelope once she'd left. Wow. There was seventy-five bucks inside.

Vince had already off-loaded our instruments and our luggage, and there was a fleet of bellhops with baggage carts waiting to help. Fitz took over, getting everything organized. As we went into the lobby, I looked for Ryan.

To my disappointment, I didn't see him.

Which almost made me miss out on how extravagant and beautiful the lobby was. The high arched ceilings were held up by white columns, and there was a center rotunda over a fountain, flowers, and trees. For a second, I wondered what it would sound like to play in an area like this one.

Our bellhop led us to the elevator and took us up to our floor. My room was next door to Fitz's, and Cole and Parker were directly across the hall. I opened my door while my brothers tipped the bellhop and sorted through our stuff.

"We're going to drop off our suitcases, and then we'll meet up in Maisy's room to go over our set list for tonight," Fitz instructed, but I was too busy trying to take everything in.

I had expected a standard hotel room. Bed, TV, bathroom.

What I got was a full-on luxury suite. A set of double doors as I first walked in led to a bathroom tiled with off-white and black marble. Past the bathroom was the sleeping area, with a king-size bed made up with white linens, a textured beige satin headboard that went all the way up to the ceiling, and a gray velvet bench at the foot of the bed. I dropped my carry-on there.

Because there was still more to see!

I stepped down into a sunken living room. There was a huge wrap-around couch that could have easily sat my entire family, a fully stocked minibar, and a view that seemed to overlook all of Las Vegas.

My brothers and I could have shared this room. There were even two televisions. It felt like too much space for one person.

I'd left my door slightly ajar, and I heard my brothers come in.

"Not too bad, right?" Parker asked, looking out at the view with me.

"I can't believe we're here," I told him.

"Come on, let's get to work," Fitz called out, ever the voice of reason.

Parker sat down on the couch, and Cole had his phone out. Fitz started spreading out a bunch of papers on the coffee table.

When he had sufficiently organized them, he cleared his throat. "If you guys are okay with this, I was thinking we should add Maisy's version of 'One More Night' to our set list. It's a song the audience already loves, and maybe they'll look us up online. Get us more views on our videos, more downloads of our songs."

"That's a great idea, Fitz," Parker said, and Cole nodded his head.

Logically, I could see the wisdom in it. But did I really want to sing that song over and over again? I was trying to distance myself from Ryan, not do things that would make me think about him.

I decided I needed a short mental-health break. "I'm going to use the bathroom," I told them. "Be right back."

After taking much longer than was necessary, I returned to the living room, where my brothers all stared at me.

For a second, I worried I had toilet paper attached to my shoe or something. "Why are you all looking at me?"

"Because we were just talking about you, so when you came in, we stopped." Cole never could lie to me.

My other brothers responded to that with "Seriously, dude?" and "Way to go, WikiLeaks."

Something was very off. "I thought we agreed I was an adult and should be treated like one. What's going on?" We hadn't been out of California long, but my thoughts immediately turned to my mother, and fear clung to my heart like plastic wrap. "Is Mom okay?"

"Mom's fine," Fitz said. "I mean, I'm sure she's fine. I haven't heard anything. It's just . . . remember how I told you about our financial issues? There was something I didn't tell you."

A brick formed in my throat and slowly drifted down until it settled deep in my stomach. "What?"

He exchanged glances with Parker. "We're three months behind in paying for Mom's facility. And if we don't come up with the money by next Friday, they might kick her out."

"How could you not tell me about this?"

"I thought getting this job would solve all our problems." Fitz looked down at his hands, not making eye contact. "But because tonight is our first performance, we won't see a paycheck for at least two weeks. I've been trying to work something out with the facility's administrator, but he's not budging."

It would make more sense to ask the tour manager for an advance. I could see why Fitz wouldn't want to do that. It might make us seem like more trouble than we were worth.

So maybe I could talk to Piper.

Or Ryan.

If they would be willing to give us an advance, everything would be okay.

"You don't need to worry about it," Fitz continued. "We're going to get the money. I just have to make the administrator understand that."

While the money situation was certainly stressful and worth freaking out over, that wasn't really a reason to be talking about me. Cole had specifically said they were talking about me. This was some kind of diversion. I faced Cole. "What were you really talking about?"

Cole let out a huge sigh, like he didn't know what to say. He stayed quiet for about a minute, shrinking under all our gazes. Then everything came out in one breath, as if he couldn't hold it in any longer. "Dad just announced on his Facebook page that he had another baby."

Rushing wind filled my ears, making me temporarily unable to hear. My chest constricted, and I could literally feel the rage bubbling up inside me, along with the beginning of an anxiety attack.

I wanted to break something. I wanted to punch a wall.

I also wanted to curl up in a ball and cry until my heart stopped hurting.

Parker reached for me. "You can talk to us, Maze."

I didn't want their sympathy right now. Or them telling me how they understood.

I was pissed off at Cole for being Facebook friends with our father.

"I'm going for a walk to cool off," I told them, grabbing my key card off the dresser. "Don't follow me."

I left the room and headed for the elevators, not knowing where I could go to be alone. But I saw the backup dancers all laughing and talking as they waited for the next elevator. I could not make small talk and jokes and smile with the tsunami of grief that had welled up inside me.

So I walked the opposite way, tears blinding me, pain in every step. What was wrong with my father? Why did he keep doing this?

He'd abandoned our family after finally confessing that he'd cheated for the entirety of his relationship with our mother. She'd thought Cole was a onetime deal. She had no idea he was impregnating and carrying on with women all over the country as he toured. He told her he couldn't help himself. That he loved who he loved and didn't like using birth control. He literally had dozens of children.

And now he had one more.

At the end of the hallway was a staircase with a notice that an alarm would sound if I opened the door. I noticed a small hallway off to the left leading to a set of double doors recessed into the wall. If I sat here, even if my brothers went looking for me, they wouldn't be able to find me. I slid down the wall, laid my head on my knees, and let myself sob.

But because this was me, of course one of the doors opened.

"Maisy?"

Three guesses as to whose room it was, and the first two don't count.

CHAPTER TEN

There I sat, face all red and puffy, snot running down my nose, eyes bloodshot.

And Ryan freaking De Luna looked like a fallen angel sent to tempt all earthbound women to fall desperately in love with him.

"Are you okay?"

Oh yes, Ryan, I'm totally fine. That's why I'm curled up in the fetal position wailing like a banshee.

I tried to say something, but the words stuck in my throat.

"Do you want me to get your brothers?"

That was the last thing I needed. I shook my head violently. "It's . . . it's a really long story."

He crouched down on the floor next to me so that we were eye level. "I'd like to hear it if you want to talk about it."

An overwhelming need to do just that filled me. I did want to talk about it. I wanted to tell him.

I didn't know why.

So I nodded.

"Do you want to come in?" He pointed behind him with his thumb.

Still not trusting myself to speak, I nodded again. It probably wasn't a good idea to go into his hotel room, but I didn't want to take the chance, however slight, that someone might stumble upon us. Especially somebody who shared my DNA.

Ryan stood up and offered me his hand. After a moment of reluctance, I let out a big sigh and accepted. And remembered why I hadn't wanted to shake hands with him that night at the diner. Because everything I thought would happen did. As his warm hand wrapped around mine and our palms pressed together, every nerve ending in my hand lit up like the Las Vegas Strip at night. That electrical explosion traveled through my entire body, stealing my breath, forcing my heart into overdrive.

I wanted to touch him. For him to touch me. To be held by him.

That one action made everything a million times worse. He made me want things I shouldn't want.

Not shouldn't. Didn't. He made me want things I didn't want.

Shaking, I tugged my hand away from his and folded my arms against my chest. As he unlocked his door, I wondered if he could sense the way I trembled. Which was not due to my emotional upheaval but just from standing this close. Ryan went inside and held the door open, allowing me to enter first.

His room was about five times the size of mine, and it was decorated in a modern European way in grays, burgundies, and blinding whites. I noted he had a huge balcony with trees and furniture before he led me over to the couch. I sat and felt surprised when he plopped down right next to me, considering there were roughly four hundred other places to sit in this one room.

"Tell me." He put his arm around the back of the couch, and I fought the desire to snuggle in close to him and let him soothe away my hurt.

What was wrong with me?

I cleared my throat. "I may cry a lot." It always made my siblings supremely uncomfortable when I cried, which was why I usually tried to keep my tears to myself.

At that, he leaned forward, grabbed a box of tissues off the coffee table, and handed it to me. "I can handle it."

I took two tissues. I used one to blow my nose and the other to wipe my eyes. Despite my warning, it felt like I had dried myself out. There were no more tears to cry. "My mom met my father when she was nineteen. He was ten years older, and the piano player in a jazz band. She fell hard and fast. She had planned to become a neurosurgeon, but she dropped out of college and followed my father around the country. Until she got pregnant with Fitz. She wanted to get married and start a family, but my father said he was too much of a free spirit to settle down. So my mom went back to California and bought herself a home with her inheritance."

I had to blow my nose again, and I thought about how gross Ryan probably thought I was now. "My father kept touring with his band, but whenever he came to Los Angeles, he stayed with us. He got my mom pregnant with Parker and then with me. She didn't know it at the time, but he was cheating on her constantly. He had dozens of women just like my mom stashed around the country. She found out, though."

A concerned look crossed his features. "What happened when she found out?"

"The first time? Nothing. The doctor had just told her she was pregnant with me, and my father brought Cole home. Cole's mother had died giving birth to him, and my father got on an airplane with a newborn and flew from New York to California to see if my mom would take him." I couldn't help but smile as I remembered the way my mother described that moment. "She took one look at Cole and fell head over heels in love with him. Because we were so close in age, he and I were always in the same grade. Some people assumed we were twins or that my mom must have cheated on my father. She didn't care what people thought and ignored the rumors. Sometimes I felt like Cole was her favorite. Like she had to make up for how he'd started out in life by loving him even more."

Ryan shifted beside me, and I couldn't tell, but it felt like he'd moved a bit closer. "She sounds like a great woman."

"She was."

"Was?"

Ryan had already asked me whether my mother had passed away. A legitimate question, considering that his own had and that I spoke about my mom in the past tense. "Later she found out there were more women and more children. It broke her." My voice caught, and I held my breath.

"What is your dad like? He must have some good qualities for your mom to put up with his cheating." It was like Ryan sensed how close I was to falling apart and changed the subject so I could pull myself back together.

My parents' relationship had been hard for me to understand growing up; it didn't surprise me that other people wouldn't get it, either. "He was not a great guy. I don't really remember ever spending time with him or even talking to him. It was like we were nonentities in the household. What I do remember is how he smelled. Like a club. Cigarettes and booze. And that he drank coffee constantly. To this day I loathe those smells because they make me think about him."

"That must really work out well for you, given that you've been playing in clubs."

I couldn't help but laugh at his wry observation. "That was our lives. My father didn't contribute to our care in any way. He didn't pay child support, didn't really interact with us. Showed up when he wanted and left when he was done. When I was fifteen, he did something that ruined my entire life."

My voice broke again, and even though there were no more tears, I still wanted to cry. "He came home for another short visit. At the end of it, he went into the kitchen, where she was making dinner, and told her he wouldn't ever be coming back. That he had impregnated his nineteen-year-old girlfriend with their second child and, as even more of a slap in the face, that he planned on marrying her. I didn't know it then, but the women in our family have always dealt with severe anxiety and depression issues. My mother just . . . snapped. Something happened to her as he explained all the affairs and all the children. Like her mind couldn't handle it, and she had a total mental breakdown. She started throwing things at him and screaming. Fitz was twenty-one at the time and happened to be home that weekend from college. He physically removed my father from the house. Then my mom locked herself in her bedroom for hours."

I had to swallow down the knot that had formed in my throat. "When she came out, she made us her famous brownies. Then she called all of us into the kitchen." The memory of that night was so clear that if I closed my eyes, I was fifteen years old again, sitting at that kitchen table. I could hear how her voice sounded different. How she wore a wild expression I'd never seen. The combined aroma of burned food and the coffeepot still brewing on the counter. The taste of chocolate in my mouth. "She said she would be going out for a little while. She made Fitz promise to take care of us. She told Parker to always be happy and bright. She reminded Cole that he was her best kitchen helper and to never let anyone else's words affect him. She told all three of my brothers that they had to keep me safe. Then she said I should never fall in love with a musician and always be a good girl. She said she loved us and that someday we were going to change the world with our music. She hugged us and left."

My chest hurt, like it was being squeezed by a vise. "I didn't realize at the time that she was saying goodbye. That night she got into a horrible accident. Head-on collision with a telephone pole. She sustained a severe traumatic brain injury. She was in a coma for weeks. When she woke up, she thought she was eighteen years old again. The doctors assured us it would be temporary and she'd regain her memory. She never did. Now they think it might be something psychological combined with early-onset Alzheimer's. She has to stay in an assisted-living facility. I go and visit her every week, and she has no idea who I am."

"That's why you talk about her in the past. Because she's not really there anymore."

I nodded, my throat aching. "I found out later that there weren't any skid marks near the pole. She ran into it deliberately. Because of the accident, everything she said that night has taken on these mythical proportions with us. If she'd said something stupid, like 'Figure out a way to naturally turn your skin purple,' we'd all still be working on a way to make that happen. It's why Cole works as a baker, why they're so crazily overprotective of me. Why we decided to form a band and have stuck with our dream of making it. Why Fitz, even though he's almost twenty-eight, still lives at home instead of moving on with his life."

"And it's why you don't date musicians."

"That's part of it," I agreed. "It's also because of the type of man my father is. Not only was he a terrible father, but he's just an awful person. He uses women like these tissues. He seems to really enjoy getting them pregnant and then abandoning him. Other families have family trees; my father's on a personal quest to create his own family vineyard."

Ryan seemed to consider that for a moment. "Where is he now?"

I shrugged one shoulder. "I don't keep track of him. Last I heard he was in Europe trying to single-handedly solve their depopulation issues by impregnating every woman he meets. He's obviously succeeding, given that my brothers just told me he announced yet another baby. I'm not even sure what number that is. Twenty-two? Twenty-three?"

He let out a whistle. "That is a ton of kids."

"I know I shouldn't hate him. But he left. He gets to go out and make whole new families and forget we exist. He destroyed my mom. He destroyed my family. And he doesn't have to care or be held responsible. He just walked away."

"That's . . . you're dealing with a lot."

I knew it was a lot. But Ryan had said he could handle it. "All I know is I don't ever want to be my mom. I don't ever want to end up with a man like that."

"Not all musicians are like your dad. Not every guy you meet is going to be a bad guy."

I wanted so badly to believe that. But everything I'd ever witnessed, every musician I'd ever met, had been a player like my father. Breaking hearts in one city and then just moving on to the next.

Not wanting to consider Ryan's statement, I went back to telling him why I was upset. "In addition to finding out about the new baby, my brothers also surprised me with the fact that they'd failed to mention we were three months behind in paying for my mom's room and board. Fitz told me a little while ago that we'd probably have to sell our house to continue paying for her medical care. Which I shouldn't care about. It's just four walls and a roof, right? But I can't bear the thought of selling it. If we sell it, then we're admitting she's never coming home. Logically, I know that's true, but I don't want to have to give up hope, you know?" I sighed again, pulling out a new tissue just to shred it apart and give my hands something to do. "Anyway, if we don't come up with the overdue money by next Friday, they're going to kick her out, and I don't know what we'll do then. I hate to ask you, but I was hoping we could get an advance or something."

"I wish it were up to me. But the record label's involved with the payouts, and they'd never allow it. How much do you need?"

I told him, and he immediately got out his phone and called a man named Arthur. He told Arthur to get him a check in that amount.

When he hung up, I said, "You can't. I can't just take money from you. It's too much."

Ryan put his phone on the table, and it made me uneasy that he wouldn't look at me. "There's a way you can earn it, if you're interested."

"Honestly? I'd do just about anything."

He raised his eyebrows slightly at that. "Anything?"

"Obviously, there're exceptions. Given the way you're looking at me, I feel an exception coming on right now."

Why were his little smirks so endearing? "For the last few years, I've wanted to change my sound. I want my music to reflect what I listen to. What I love. Which is hard because my fans, much as I adore them, don't want me to change. It's like they want to stick me in some time capsule where I'm fourteen forever, singing the same songs over and over. Which I get, because when you're at a concert to see your favorite band, the most disappointing words in the English language are 'Here's something from our new album!' But I do consider myself to be an artist. I want to grow. Try new things. Adding you guys to the tour was the first step in moving in that direction. I wanted my audience to hear you, like your music, and then maybe it wouldn't be such a leap for me to change things up a bit."

So far this all sounded okay. Why was my heart beating so hard? And why did he look so uneasy? "Okay. And?"

"The other thing I need to change is my image. You're not the only one who thinks I'm a manwhore. My label thinks I'm immature and not to be trusted. When I said I wanted to make my next album more rock, they said I had to prove myself first. That I take myself and my career seriously. My publicist suggested I accomplish that by having a girlfriend. A fake one so there wouldn't be any public blowups and so it wouldn't end badly." He gave me a pointed look, and all the puzzle pieces fell into place.

Was I understanding this right? "You want to pay me to pretend to be your girlfriend? Why? You can just go downstairs and pick one. They'll all say yes."

"Why? Because I don't need a groupie or someone potentially crazy. I need someone like you. Smart, talented, beautiful, and relatively normal. You need the money, and I need a woman who can be discreet. Plus, you're very convenient."

"Just what every girl longs to hear. That she's convenient." Even though his compliments thrilled me in a way I didn't know was possible, something still felt icky about the whole thing. "But if you pay me to be your girlfriend, doesn't that basically make me a prostitute?"

"Only if we sleep together."

Whoa. "That is not happening."

His smile let me know he'd been trying to make a joke. "I know. Notching is out of the question. We'll obviously take sex off the table."

"Let's take it off all the surfaces because it isn't going to happen." Even if my girlie parts thought it sounded like an interesting idea. "You think you're going to prove that you're more mature and responsible by having a fake girlfriend?"

"They won't know you're fake. Nobody will. We'll have to make everyone else think it's real."

I was a musician, not an actress. But here I was again with Ryan De Luna offering me an opportunity I couldn't say no to. "I'll have to tell my brothers so they don't punch you. But they can keep a secret. A relationship? Not so much. But they can stay quiet."

There was a knock at the door. Ryan got up to answer it, and I did not admire how nice his jeans looked on him as he walked away. Not even a little.

I heard Piper's voice and was glad she couldn't see me. Ryan thanked her and then stopped at a desk to grab a pen. He wrote something and then handed me a check that was about twice the size of normal checks. "Just so you know, I've never done something like this before. I don't have to pay for women."

"You're not helping your case." I took the check from him. He'd made it out to the band. It represented not only security for our mom but also the chance to relax and enjoy the tour, knowing that things back home were taken care of.

It might even mean we'd get to keep the house.

"Be careful with that," he joked, sitting down on the couch next to me. His knee touched mine and sent a jolt through me. "It's pretty much all the money I have in the world right now."

"I don't understand. Don't you make millions of dollars a year?"

An alarm sounded on his phone, and he picked it up. "I'll explain later tonight. At the after-party. Which would be a good time to show everyone we're together."

Despite Ashley's warning, now I would have to go to the after-party. Which I wasn't excited about. At all.

"I really can't take it if this is all your money." I tried to give him back the check.

He put his hand on mine, and that explosive, Vegas-lights, shimmery feeling returned. "This is an investment in my future. Keep it."

I didn't argue. I couldn't. My mom needed it.

"So is that a yes? Will you be my fake girlfriend?"

Fake yeah! my body said. "I guess I have to be."

"That's the spirit," Ryan said with just a hint of sarcasm. "I have to get to sound check, so I can walk you out."

He grabbed a bag, his phone, and a key card, and I followed him out of his suite. "I thought that wasn't for a couple more hours."

"I get to do sound check first. One of the perks of being the headliner."

We walked into the main hallway, and I saw Fox waiting near the elevators.

"This is my room." I came to a stop, and so did Ryan. "So I guess I'll see you later."

"Yep." He shifted his bag from one shoulder to the other. "I feel like we should do something to make this relationship of ours official. Like seal it with a kiss."

At that one word, my entire body melted, throbbing with the need to have Ryan kiss me and screw the consequences.

What I wanted: to throw myself at him and kiss him until the entire world faded away.

What I said in an attempt to preserve even a smidgen of my dignity: "Don't press your luck. I haven't cashed the check yet."

But he must have heard the way my voice shook, witnessed how my body trembled. Because he moved so close that I had to press myself against my hotel-room door to maintain a fraction of space between us. "At some point it will have to happen, Maisy. Nobody will believe it if we don't hold hands." He took my right hand, interlacing his fingers with mine. "If we don't touch each other." He ran the backs of his fingers against my left cheek. "If we don't kiss."

His lips hovered above mine, tormenting me. Breathing ceased to be an option as my entire body turned into a flock of coked-up butterflies. The attraction was so intense it was almost chemical. Like he had scientifically bewitched my hormones. Somehow I felt both hot and cold inside. Like ice and fire froze and burned through me at the same time, even though that was physically impossible.

His touch drove me crazy, and his lips so maddeningly close made me quiver.

And made me ache.

"I know I'm not supposed to mention it," he said in a husky tone that turned my abdomen entirely liquid, his words like sparks that ignited the electricity between us, "but you're shivering again. And I still like it."

He painstakingly untangled himself from me, one epically slow movement at a time. First, he let his hand fall from my cheek, caressing me the whole way. He slid his fingers from mine, and I'd never realized how many touch receptors I had in my hand or that they could all simultaneously combust.

Then, very last, he dragged his mouth away, and I nearly cried out in disappointment and frustration that he'd been so close and hadn't actually kissed me. If I'd been capable of moving my legs, I might have chased after him and demanded he finish what he'd started.

"See you later, Maisy."

He walked down the hallway like he was totally unaffected by what had just happened. After several minutes, I finally had the strength to peel myself off the door, stick the card into the lock, and let myself into my room.

I saw my reflection in the mirrored closet door. My cheeks were flushed, my eyes bright.

Did you forget about Rule #1? my brain asked.

I hadn't forgotten. I'd just found a loophole. We weren't really dating, so it didn't count. Technically, I wasn't breaking my rule.

It was fake. Not real.

But everything that had happened in that hallway was very, very real.

And I wanted more.

CHAPTER ELEVEN

On the drive over to the arena, my brothers had talked solely about the set list. Fitz suggested that we do a couple of cover songs. "We want the crowd to be singing along and excited about us. I think that's the best way." Everyone agreed, and we picked two pop songs that we'd performed before. They'd been in the Billboard Top 100 for weeks, and thanks to nonstop radio play, everyone would know the words. We just made them more rock. We also decided to sing our two most popular original songs, "Lost" and "How You Lie." Along with "One More Night" and "Yesterday," that would be our entire set. We had only about half an hour, which was a generous amount of time for how well known our band was (we were not well known at all).

When we arrived at the arena entrance, a horde of screaming teenage girls lined the walkway, holding up signs and pictures. Fitz opened the door and climbed out, and all the screams died. The girls started texting on their phones and resumed their conversations.

I thought it was hilarious. My brothers were not quite as amused. "I think I feel insulted." Fitz frowned.

A crew member met us and led us out to the stage. "Wow" was all I could manage.

We were set up in the center of the massive arena, meaning we'd need to play to more than one direction.

"Can you imagine if we were the headliners and this many people wanted to see us perform?" I asked, not really able to take it all in.

"Someday it will be," Parker assured me with a grin, twirling his drumstick and then sitting down behind his kit.

Fitz and I had brought our guitars, but Parker's drums and Cole's keyboard had been set up by the production crew. It was so nice not to have to worry about amplifier and speaker locations and not to unravel yards and yards of black cords.

Someone wearing a headset and carrying a tablet approached. "Hey, guys. I'm Kenny. I work with Santiago, your sound engineer. You are in excellent hands. He's one of the best."

"I'm *the* best, thank you." A loud voice boomed over the speakers, making us jump.

"We put your microphones where you indicated you wanted them on your sound plot, and if you'll get your instruments set up, we can start."

I took my Dreadnought out of the case and moved my Epi-Pen aside to get the check from Ryan. I turned to face my brothers. "Before we start, I got the money for Mom's overdue fees."

Given their expressions, it was like I had just announced that I had discovered the cure for cancer while doing the tango with a shark.

"Where?" was all Parker asked, taking the check from me.

"I got it from Ryan because—"

Before I could explain, Cole interrupted me. "What exactly are you doing for that kind of money?"

I would not smash my guitar over my brother's head. I would not. "Oh no, you've found me out. I've decided to become a high-class escort and enter into an indecent proposal with Ryan De Luna."

Did they get my sarcasm? Of course not.

"If that's true, you should have held out for a lot more zeros."

Seeing as how fratricide was still illegal, I told them about Ryan's situation. I swore them all to secrecy and then explained how he needed a fake girlfriend to impress his label and improve his image and that it had to be someone who wouldn't sell him out or write a song about him. "I'm a nice, normal, trustworthy girl-next-door type, not a diva or a psycho."

"He has met you, right?" Parker asked. I went over and took the check back, then stuck it in my bra for safekeeping while we did our sound check. I punched Parker on the arm, as he so rightly deserved. "Ow! I need that to play tonight."

"How long are you planning on pretending to be his girlfriend?" Fitz asked.

"It will be for just a little while." With a twinge of unease, I realized Ryan and I hadn't really discussed terms other than not sleeping together, and a rush of blazing heat reminded me that he expected us to touch and kiss. But I didn't know how long this would last and whether we would date or pretend to date or what he expected from me.

Cole moved his keyboard slightly to the left. "Don't get all Ice Queen and weird on him and wreck it. I don't want to be fired."

"Don't call me that. I've already had the 'Don't get us fired' lecture this week, thanks. And if I'm weird or an Ice Queen, that's your guys' fault."

"How is it our fault?" Fitz protested.

"Two words. Russ Karn."

At that, they fell silent, as well they should have. Russ Karn, captain of our high school football team, had been my prom date senior year, and he had been a very nice boy. A nice boy who was respectful and a gentleman the entire evening—opening doors, pulling out my chair for me, dancing to both fast and slow songs. When he took me home, he confessed he'd been dying to kiss me the entire night. Which I thought was awfully sweet, so we stayed in the back of the limo and made out a little.

Up until the moment my brothers practically yanked the door off its hinges and hauled him out to the front yard.

"What kind of girl do you think our sister is?" Cole demanded while holding Russ by his tuxedo lapels.

I got out of the limo and screamed at them to stop, that they were ruining everything. Fitz dragged me inside without even letting me say good night. Monday morning at school, Russ sported a black eye and never spoke to me again.

Cole looked just as angry as he had been that night. "We didn't tell you this at the time, but Russ Karn had made a bet with the offensive line that he was going to score with the Ice Queen on prom night. Which I didn't find out about until the night of, and I ditched my date to go looking for you. I went home and told Parker and Fitz, and we tried to call you, but you had your phone off. We were all worried he might try and force you to do something you weren't ready for. So when you showed up at home and he was all over you, yes, we overreacted. But he deserved it. You're welcome."

Shock flooded my limbs, making it difficult to blink, chased by an overwhelming sense of guilt. Here I'd been mad for years about something they'd done, but they'd done it not to be interfering or overprotective, as I'd assumed, but because they cared about me and didn't want me to get hurt. I'd rushed to an unwarranted conclusion.

Before I could say that I'd been wrong, Kenny returned with our inner-ear monitors. Santiago worked with each of us to figure out which parts of the band we wanted to hear and which we didn't.

"You mean I can tune out the drummer?" I asked. "Parker couldn't hold on to a steady beat if he married it first."

When my brother smiled and shook his head while Cole and Fitz laughed, I knew things would be okay between us.

Sound check took a while as Santiago learned our preferences, and we learned to trust his suggestions. The music in my IEM sounded off, and Kenny explained that performing in clubs and arenas were two totally different beasts. Not only that, but the arena was currently empty, and Santiago had to account for the bodies that would be there, the sounds they'd be making, the wind currents—all kinds of stuff. If Santiago didn't do his job correctly, then it wouldn't matter how well we played. We'd sound like garbage.

"Which is why it's fortunate for you that I am the best," Santiago intoned over the speakers.

We played through our set list, and Santiago instructed us to play softer or sing louder or vice versa, then checked the levels. About an hour and a half later, we had it all arranged to his satisfaction.

"Next time will be faster," Kenny promised. He got somebody else to show us to our dressing room. We had only about an hour and a half until the concert started. There were assorted snacks and water, juice, and Gatorade waiting for us, along with my carry-on so that I could get ready.

"We never did get a rider," Fitz said, a note of disappointment in his voice.

"Right. How else are the venues going to know I need fresh-cut Casablanca lilies, fruitless baskets, two boxes of cornstarch, imported Versace towels, and a twelve-foot-long boa constrictor before I can even think about going out onstage?" Cole asked as I headed into the bathroom.

I changed into a tight red shirt and black leather skirt that felt more rocklike to me (more binding and less comfortable than my regular clothes) and did my makeup and hair. One of my brothers might have possibly changed his shirt, and that was it.

Totally unfair.

With an hour left, we started warming up our vocals. We'd done this for so long it was second nature—no thought or concentration required. Even though the warm-ups felt comfortable and routine, a nervous energy permeated the room. Parker kept twirling a single drumstick between his fingers while Fitz paced and Cole jiggled his right leg up and down.

Finally, there was a knock at the door telling us it was time. I watched all the people running around, doing what needed to be done to make this show a success. I thought of all the other crew members I couldn't see, all the people who were reliant on Ryan for jobs. I listened to the twenty thousand fans currently chanting his name and thought of all the money they'd spent to watch him perform. He was busy and important, and it occurred to me that what he had done for me earlier was really special. How he had sat and talked to me, let me whine and complain, and then helped me with my problems. It caused a pulling sensation on my heart that I had neither the time nor the inclination to examine too closely.

We went under the stage to where we would be lifted up after we were announced. Kenny helped us with our IEMs. Once he finished, I grabbed Fitz's and Parker's hands, and Parker reached out for Cole, bringing him into the circle. The lift went up slowly, the bright stage lights beaming down on us.

"Ladies and gentlemen, please put your hands together for Yesterday!"

"This is for Mom," Fitz said with a smile.

We walked onto the stage, waving to the polite applause we received. We were not who the audience wanted.

But my brothers didn't care.

I was not the bantering-with-the-crowd type and quietly walked over to where my microphone and guitar were set up. Parker, on the other hand, had no such problem. As soon as he was seated at his drums, he said into his microphone, "Hello, Las Vegas! How excited are you to see Ryan De Luna tonight?"

The entire arena erupted in hysterical screams.

Cole played along. "Will we do until you get to see him?" He even struck a pose, much to the delight of the crowd.

"If Ryan doesn't treat you ladies right, you come find one of the Harrison boys," Parker teased, causing even more shrills and shrieks.

"Yeah, we know what women like," Cole said, and I thought the crowd might actually fall down from the response. Like the walls of Jericho.

A woman near the stage screamed, "I want to have your babies!" and ten seconds later a lacy hot-pink bra landed on the stage. It was like the feminism movement was regressing before my eyes.

I figured somewhere Gloria Steinem had just become violently ill without knowing the reason why.

With the crowd whipped up into a frenzy, Parker hit his sticks together to an eight count, letting us know when to come in.

The adrenaline rushed through my veins, singing as it went. An electric buzz sank into my skin, spreading until it filled my soul. The only thing I could compare it to was when I'd been close to Ryan earlier.

Only more magical.

Our music filled the speakers and shook the stage beneath our feet. I sang the first five words of the cover song we'd chosen, and the crowd immediately responded, singing the next four words back to me without prompting.

It was the most incredible feeling in the world. It would be hard to explain to someone whose life didn't revolve around music, but it was this . . . overwhelming euphoria. Connection to the audience that was connecting with us. As if we'd harnessed some great, inexplicable power and thrown it out to the crowd, and they were funneling it back to us with their cheers.

Not that we were flawless. We made mistakes. Rushed beats, sang flat notes, misplayed chords. Probably due to jitters and excitement, but it couldn't detract from the golden bubble of happy that encased all of us onstage.

When I got to "One More Night," the audience practically lost it. They sang every word along with me, and I had to fight to not get choked up. The music uplifted. It united us and spoke to every person in the arena in a way that no language ever could. I'd never felt so energized, so completely alive.

Like I had been fundamentally changed and would never be the same person again.

This was what I was going to do with the rest of my life, no matter what it took.

We finished with "Yesterday" and thanked the crowd for listening to us. This time, the cheers and applause were real and maybe a little bit earned.

Then we were back under the stage. The audience's response still rang in my ears. I felt hands slap me on the back and heard people say, "Great show!" and "Good job!" I was on such a high that I walked by Ryan without even realizing it.

Clear up to the moment when he slipped a hand around my waist, pulled me in close, and pressed his lips softly against the side of my face. I gasped, my breath sticking in my throat.

"Sorry," he murmured. "Your cheek looked like it was missing a kiss. You were absolutely incredible out there. I couldn't take my eyes off you."

With a wink and a grin, he was gone, and I almost stumbled and fell into a stack of animal props they used for the circus portion of his show.

"Come on, IQ," Cole said as he navigated me toward our dressing room. "Let's get you cooled off."

Not possible.

"I know you said this is all fake, but that looked real to me."

What could I tell him? There was nothing to say, so I just kept walking.

"Don't get me wrong, because I think he's a cool dude, but don't say you weren't warned."

I'd been warned. Repeatedly. By both strangers and the people who loved me best.

I was finding out that it didn't matter. I knew what I should do: what was best for me and my life.

In that moment? I absolutely, 100 percent, did not care.

CHAPTER TWELVE

Fortunately, I did come down from that euphoric high and regained my sanity.

We stayed and watched most of Ryan's show. I was impressed by his energy level and how he seemed to hold the audience in the palm of his hand. Whatever he said or did, they responded at increasingly frantic levels.

Which I got, because all I wanted to do was watch him perform. How had I ever thought he wasn't talented? He sang so well. Unlike a lot of music stars, Ryan sang the songs his audience had come to hear. All their favorites, if their reaction was any indication.

Our driver sent Fitz a text saying he was available whenever we were ready, and we decided to head to the hotel before the traffic got too bad.

I tried to invite my brothers to Ryan's after-party but found out Ryan had already invited them. Cole said he'd had a quick talk with Marcus about it. The after-parties were fairly tame, especially in comparison to other music stars. "Marcus was telling me about when he was on tour with that rock group Wild Stallion. A bunch of press used to tag along, and they'd get ridiculously drunk and put holes in the walls and cause toilets to explode. One time in Florida they even nailed the furniture to the ceiling. He said it was like blowing up a car in a movie—the cost of the destruction was mitigated by the amount of entertainment value it provided."

None of that sounded particularly entertaining to me, but I was not a guy.

Speaking of guys and weird things, despite their usual overprotectiveness, my brothers didn't seem to have any problem with Ryan.

Whether that was because of who he was as a person or because he was the guy allowing us to live out our dreams, I didn't know.

We all went to our respective rooms to shower and change. I felt strangely nervous. Like I was about to be on a different kind of stage and nobody at that party would buy the lie that Ryan and I were together.

Just as I finished fixing my hair, there was a knock at my door. I grabbed the key to my room and joined my brothers for the walk down the hall. They were still on that performance high, laughing and jostling one another. I, on the other hand, feared I might puke from this new kind of stage fright.

Ryan's door was open, with one security guard posted there. He recognized us and waved us inside. The main living room was already full. I saw Ryan's band, and Diego had a group of pleeches surrounding him, vying for his attention. I didn't see Ryan. But I got to meet his three backup singers as well as the lighting supervisor and two other bodyguards.

Then a door opened, and Ryan walked out, his hair wet from a shower, the dark-green shirt he wore turning his eyes that shade. Multiple people murmured his name when he appeared, and I knew they would all want his time and attention. I wasn't sure if I should approach him or wait for him to come over and find me.

His gaze landed on me, causing goose bumps all over my forearms. He smiled—a dashing, brilliant, charming smile—and headed straight to me.

I started to say something when he got close enough, but he grabbed me, pulled me into a hug, and twirled me around. "I'm so glad you're here."

He smelled amazing. Like soap and oranges and something masculine that was just . . . Ryan. My heart pounded in my throat as he set me down. "I'm glad I'm here, too." Strangely enough, I meant it.

"Come with me." He took me by the hand and led me to an empty sitting room. I saw the women who had been with Diego start toward us, but Fox stood in the doorway, not letting anyone inside. Ryan sat us on a white-quilted love seat.

I wondered whether I should sit really close to him or try to retain control over my reaction by keeping some distance between us. I settled on the second choice.

"How was your first show?" He shook his head as if he'd misspoken. "I know it wasn't your first show. I mean, how was it playing to an audience that size for the first time?"

"Pretty amazing, actually. I couldn't stop grinning for half an hour after it was over." I curled my legs up underneath me while Ryan spread out in every direction, legs askew, arm behind me on the couch.

"You played more covers than I was expecting."

"We wanted the audience to enjoy themselves. That's why you brought us along, right? To entertain and warm up the crowd for you. We wouldn't have been doing our job if we'd bored everybody out of their minds."

He looked surprised and then smiled again. "Most opening acts don't do anything like that. They care only about their own self-promotion."

I propped my elbow on the back of the couch and let my head rest on my hand. Super aware the entire time of just how close our arms were now. "I guess we're not like other people."

"I already knew that," Ryan said with a quiet smile, reaching over to play with the ends of my hair. "Your hair is so soft."

My own fingers itched to touch his hair in return. Especially since a song had literally been written about it by reigning pop princess Skyler Smith. If I remembered correctly, they'd dated at some point. I wondered if she was the one serious girlfriend he'd mentioned.

The surge of jealousy I felt bothered me. This was fake. We were pretending. Which made me think of our earlier conversation that afternoon. "I never thanked you."

"For what?"

Out of the corner of my eye, I watched as he wrapped a tendril around his index finger. I gulped. "Specifically for the money to help my mom. But there's a lot I haven't thanked you for. Thank you for bringing us on tour with you. Thank you for listening to me earlier. Thank you for putting up with my brothers."

"I should probably get a medal for the last one," he teased, and that sparkle in his eye made me want to sigh. "But everything else? It was my pleasure."

That he was so gracious in accepting my gratitude made me feel guiltier that I hadn't thanked him before. His hand moved closer to the side of my head, and I fought the urge to lean into it. I was glad we were alone. "I also need to thank you for making this a pleech-free zone."

His hand stilled. "A what?"

"The night we met, you had this mob of women, and they were these plastic, peacocking leeches. Pleeches."

"Now you're just making up words?"

"I am a lyricist, thank you."

"Is that how you write? More lyric-centric?" Musicians didn't write songs with just the lyrics or just the melody. The two came together, but one might come easier than the other. For me it was always the words.

"Yep. What about you?"

"Usually the music first. Sounds like we'd make a great songwriting team." He paused, letting the word "team" sink in. As if we could be more. "I've been working on something. Do you want to hear it?"

"Sure."

Several guitars stood in the corner next to a black baby-grand piano. Like this was his own personal music room. Ryan grabbed one of the Martin guitars and sat down again. This time he twisted his body to face me, and our knees touched. I sucked in a deep breath, ordering my pulse to calm down and my lungs to start working again.

He began to play. It was not so long ago that I'd thought he was a poser and pathetic for holding his guitar like it had a force field that could protect him. But now, as he sat there and played a beautiful tune, solely focused on making his music, I realized it was the sexiest thing I'd ever seen.

My heart beat slow and hard in time to the rhythm of his song.

"What do you think? I'm considering calling it 'Maisy Is Jealous of Pleeches.'"

Ryan laughed when I shoved his shoulder. "I'm sorry you've confused my disdain for jealousy. Although, to be fair, you've probably made a lot of women very jealous." Not wanting to think more about that, I changed the subject. "I bet your fans love it when you sing ballads."

"Do *you* love it when I sing ballads?"

I probably would. "I have no opinion on you singing ballads." I wanted to say I wasn't a fan, but at this moment that wasn't exactly true. "Do you want help with the lyrics?"

"I'm doing okay, thanks. They're probably not very good, though. Lyrics have never been my strong point."

"Duh. 'Hashtag My Heart' wasn't exactly profound."

"Ha. I would bet the rest of my savings that you know every word of that song."

He was right. I did. "Sort of speaking of money, you said you were going to tell me what was going on with your financial situation tonight."

Ryan set the guitar down. "It's a pretty simple story. My manager made a lot of poor investment decisions and wiped me out. I still have assets but not much else."

"Did you fire him? Her?"

"Him," he confirmed. "And I can't fire him because he's my dad."

"That . . ." What could I say? "That sucks. How are you paying for this tour?"

"I took most of what I had left for the initial costs, and we make a lot of money every night in ticket sales and merchandise. I think tonight they cleared almost half a million in merch alone."

Half. A. Million. Dollars. I couldn't even conceive of earning that kind of money in one night!

"This tour will pay off the few debts that remain and help get me back on the right road financially. I'll be okay."

It made me realize what a big risk he'd taken in choosing us as his opening act. If he had hired a more famous band, one that could bring in more fans, it would have helped his bottom line. "Does everyone know?"

He looked alarmed. "Nobody knows. No one on this tour besides you."

The fact that he trusted me with this information filled me with a glowing lightness not unlike what I had felt onstage earlier. "Why not tell people?" I was poor. It wasn't that big a deal.

"When a musician goes broke, it destroys people's perceptions. Think about a musician who lost all of his or her money—that's all you remember about them. Not how many hits they had or how much you liked their music, just that they went bankrupt. It would ruin my endorsement deals. Who would buy clothes from my fashion line or pick up my perfume if I can't even hold on to my millions of dollars? No one would ever take me seriously again. Perception is everything in entertainment, unfortunately. It's also why I had to sign a new three-album deal with my label. I needed the money. Now I'm stuck making the music they want me to make. Although I guess I can't really complain."

"Have you tried?" I asked. "It's literally like the easiest thing in the world to do." That got me a small smile, but I could tell how upset the whole thing made him. I hoped he'd told his dad to get lost. "Does your dad still handle your finances?"

"No." He let out a short, sardonic burst of laughter. "I hired a business manager, but my dad doesn't know about it. His job is pretty much title only these days. Not that he cares. As long as he can convince barely legal girls to go home with him to the house I paid for, that's all he cares about. That and his hair plugs."

The bitterness was evident in his voice, and I couldn't blame him.

Not able to help myself, I reached out, laid my hand on top of his, and squeezed it gently. "I'm sorry. I know what it's like to have a crappy, selfish father."

Then I did something that surprised both of us. I leaned over and kissed his cheek, letting my lips linger longer than what was probably normal. I heard his breath catch when I did it, felt his jaw tighten.

When I started to pull away, he reached out and grabbed my face to hold me in place. "Maisy." He said my name like a plea. As if he was asking permission. The air thickened around us, making my limbs feel heavy, my vision hazy.

He was going to kiss me.

I couldn't let that happen.

"Ryan, wait."

He went still. Waited.

I tried to ignore the lava that bubbled in my stomach, the chills that ran up my spine to my neck and spread out from there.

"I'm not . . . I'm not ready for you to kiss me."

"Why?" The word was strangled, as if it took every bit of restraint he possessed to hold back. He rubbed his thumb against my lower lip like it was some kind of substitute for what he really wanted. The feeling of that slightly calloused skin leaving puddles of fire on my mouth was almost my undoing.

"Because . . ." What could I say that wouldn't make me look like a total fool? That I was afraid of the fact that I was starting to have feelings of the not-hatred variety for him? That I knew the more physical we became, the faster I would fall? That this was supposed to be fake? Pretend. Not actual life. It was a business transaction. That I didn't want to see the look of pity on his face when he realized it had become real for me? Because I knew, deep in my gut, that if we kissed it would be totally real for me.

I didn't want to be the girl who was, as he'd said earlier, convenient. Sure, he thought I was pretty and wanted to kiss me, but that didn't mean I should let him. I had to protect myself. Because the more time I spent with him, the more I got to know him, the more I suspected that if we kissed, I would do nothing but spend all my time thinking about him and wanting to be with him. I would stop caring about everything else that mattered to me in this world—my mom, my brothers, my music. I knew Ryan De Luna would be all I would see. Already, I could barely resist his charm and magnetic pull.

If he kissed me? I'd lose myself completely.

Much as my brothers wanted the job, the only one who could protect my heart was me.

"Because I can't. Not yet."

He swallowed. Hard. "Okay. You tell me when you're ready." He pressed his forehead to mine like he couldn't bear to let me go. That sweet gesture made my heart thump even faster.

This isn't real. This isn't real. This isn't real.

No matter how many times I reminded myself, it didn't seem to sink in.

When we did pull apart, it was slow and gradual.

And totally awkward. "I thought after-parties usually included, you know, an actual party. With other people."

Yep, that didn't make things worse.

Sigh.

"I thought it would appear more meaningful that I wanted to be alone with you."

Because it was me, I had to make it about a thousand times more stupid. "In that case, I'm surprised you didn't bring me into your bedroom."

I could feel the blush start in the general area of my chest, claw its way up my neck, and then settle onto my cheeks, hotter than any California wildfire.

Please don't let him notice.

"Well, I would hate to have to pay for your brothers' medical bills. Because once they kicked the door in, Fox and the others would be all over them."

Whew. He must not have noticed.

"Why are you blushing?"

Oh crap. Yes, he had.

He briefly brushed his cool fingers against my reddened cheek. "You burn so hot."

I did the only thing I could. I laughed.

"What's so funny?" he asked.

"Do you know what my nickname was in high school?"

"Hot Babe? Ryan's Number One Fan?"

"Ice Queen."

Now it was his turn to laugh. "Why? I haven't noticed anything frosty about you."

"Not even my sarcastic retorts and glares?"

His gaze pierced me with its intensity, making even my toes quiver. "I see only fire."

Because you make me burn.

That was about all I could take for one evening. "Let's join the others."

I didn't want to see if he followed me or not. I didn't want any more embarrassment or to say stupid things or want stuff I couldn't have.

When I went back into the living room area, I noticed a bunch of tables set up with food that I hadn't seen before. Including a multilayered chocolate cake. Which I needed more than I needed my next breath.

Ryan came to stand beside me. I grabbed a piece and inhaled the first bite. It was rich, moist, and totally delicious. The second the sugar hit my bloodstream, I instantly felt better. "I take back what I said about that pumpkin pie. This is the best thing that has ever happened to my mouth."

"I offered to show you something better. You're the one who stopped."

There was no way I could retain my composure if he kept saying stuff like that while staring at my lips. "Did it occur to you that I don't want to date a serial kisser like yourself? With multiple victims?"

"You mean multiple prizewinners?" He wiggled his eyebrows at me, and I had to laugh.

This could work. If I just kept it light and breezy and fun, nothing bad would happen. I wouldn't really fall for him, and nobody's heart would get broken.

I saw a flash in my peripheral vision. "What was that?"

"Usually the security guys collect cell phones from outside guests and then return them at the end of the evening. But I figured the best way to spread gossip like this was to allow them, so the word could spread. Quickly and naturally. Since that's the goal . . ."

Ryan again invaded my space. My stomach flipped over; warmth spread all over my skin.

Then he reached up to touch his thumb to my mouth again, taking me back to where we'd just been. I didn't want the tingles of excitement that gathered at the base of my neck.

"There was some frosting on your mouth." He licked the chocolate off his own thumb, and needy fire burned through me so quickly I almost collapsed.

Words were not a possibility.

"Have you rethought the kissing thing yet?" His words were husky and sounded like they were laced with want.

"You mean in the last two minutes?"

"Has it been only two minutes? It feels like a lifetime. Are you sure I can't kiss you?"

I was sure, right? There was a good reason for it. At least, I thought there'd been some reasons why we shouldn't do that. I just couldn't remember them. When he looked at me like that, with hazel fire burning in his eyes, I couldn't remember my own name. I was pretty sure I had one of those.

What I did know was that I couldn't stay. I needed some distance from him, and that, hopefully, would give me some perspective. "I should probably go."

"Okay."

My feet weren't cooperating, and neither was Ryan. He stood there, immobilizing me with his hotness.

"So, uh, thanks again. Especially for earlier with the shoulder. And for, you know, letting me cry all over it."

"My shoulders are available anytime you want. I've got two of them."

He sure did. Two amazingly broad, well-sculpted shoulders.

That were totally distracting me.

"Right. I'll see you tomorrow, probably."

"Tomorrow," he agreed.

Before I could talk myself out of it, I moved across the room and felt his gaze on me with every step. Like he was touching me even though he was twelve feet away.

As I walked down the hallway, I had a serious conversation with myself. Rule #1—never date a musician. That hadn't changed. I wouldn't actually date Ryan. I could pretend to, for the sake of his career and my mother, but I wouldn't let it be more than that. Nothing deep or real. Just a light, mutually beneficial friendship.

I had to stay strong. Remember my rules. Not fall in love.

And never, no matter what I wanted, let him kiss me.

CHAPTER THIRTEEN

I tossed and turned most of the night trying to figure out what I could do to improve my impossible Ryan situation. I just had to be an adult. Be in control of my behavior. Not turn into a puddle of goo every time I got within a six-foot radius of him. I needed to steer clear of him and remember that there were so many red flags warning me not to date Ryan that he was basically Communist China.

I hoped maybe I could sublimate some of my want for him by doing physical exercise. Like running.

I'd taken up running after my mother's diagnosis. Mostly because it helped me cope with the situation but also because if things like Alzheimer's ran in my family, exercise and eating well were some of the best ways to stave it off. (Even if I didn't quite have the eating-well part down yet.)

At about five thirty in the morning, I headed over to the private gym reserved for the crew. It was empty except for the electronic dance music playing loudly over the speakers. I hated EDM. It sounded like a computer having an epileptic fit. Fortunately, I'd brought my MP3 player, and I turned on some running music and stuck my earbuds in. I got on the treadmill and plotted a course of intermittent running with varying inclines. I really wanted to push myself today.

I got into the groove, rocking along to some of my favorite eighties songs and pouring all my excess energy and worry into the run. I closed my eyes, focusing on the feeling of my feet hitting the machine.

I was so caught up in this little world I'd created that when somebody tapped me on the shoulder, I lost my footing, and like something out of a YouTube video, I fell forward and smacked into the control panel and then onto the running belt. I felt my face make contact with it before I was thrown backward. I landed on my stomach, the wind totally knocked out of me.

Stunned, I rolled over on the floor and tugged my earbuds out, breathing hard.

Ryan hovered above me. "I'm so sorry! Are you okay?"

I blinked a few times, wondering if my imagination had conjured him up. "I don't think anything's broken. I'm fine. But everything hurts."

"Want me to kiss it better?" That's when I knew it was actually him. My imagination Ryan would have offered me chocolate and sung me a song.

"I think I'm okay. But maybe I'll just lie here for a little while."

At that, his teasing expression faded. "Are you sure? Are you not telling me how bad things really are? I can take you to the hospital."

"I'm fine," I told him. "I'm not downplaying anything. Go work out."

He hesitated, like he didn't want to leave me. I waved him off, again telling him I was mostly okay.

"Is it bad that I'm hoping you don't have any visible bruises? Because nobody is going to believe this is how you got them. Not exactly a good way to start our pretend relationship."

Was he serious with this? "Yes, let's make my humiliating injury all about you and your PR. Now shut up and go away before I give you some visible bruises."

That seemed to do the trick. He moved a few feet away from me and faced the mirror behind us. I turned my head to see him stretching. He was spending a long time doing it. "You can stop. You're the fairest of them all."

He grinned. "You must be okay, given the amount of snark you're currently throwing my way." He selected a treadmill two places over from where I'd been running. He warmed up, running slowly, and then pushed some buttons to increase the intensity. I wiggled my toes, making sure I hadn't broken my neck. While I tested each part of me for functionality, I realized Ryan had, to my great delight, removed his shirt.

He had a truly beautiful chest and back. I was fascinated by the way his muscles moved as he ran, expanding and contracting to the beat of his stride. He was so strong. Masculine.

Then I noticed something on the left side of his chest. I realized it was three tiny music notes. I looked in the mirror where his right side was reflected and saw what looked like a small triangle pointing up on his torso. On his left bicep was a single black stripe.

I'd never been a big fan of tattoos. But after seeing them on some of my favorite TV crushes, I had changed my mind a little. Given their location, you'd know Ryan had them only if he had his shirt off. It gave me a secret thrill that I was the one getting to see them.

Even if I'd nearly sustained a concussion to do it.

The fact that my brain was going in that direction was a clear indication that I needed to leave this room.

I was feeling better, so I got up slowly.

"Hey," Ryan called out. He turned off his machine and came over. Gah. His chest was even better up close. I really wanted to do some personal exploration of those bumps and ridges. "Are you sure you don't want to see a doctor?"

"Yep." One-syllable word. That was what I could manage when faced with his glistening abs. Fantastic.

"I could walk you to your room."

"No. Thanks." I had to curl my fingers into a ball to prevent myself from touching him. My heart still beat too fast, but I attributed that to my mishap and not to my current visual stimuli.

"I didn't get the chance to ask you last night, but our call time for the bus isn't until eleven o'clock tonight. What would you think about going out on our first official fake date later on? I can come by your room at six."

"'kay."

"Great! I'll see you then."

Dazed, I nodded and turned to leave. I heard his treadmill start up as I headed for the door. I'd almost made it when I heard his voice.

"Hey, Maisy? For our date tonight, what do you prefer—shirt off or shirt on? Because it seems like you enjoy it off." The jerk didn't even sound winded as he ran, all smug and arrogant.

That I'd been ogling him hard enough to earn an award for it was completely beside the point.

The sound of his laughter followed me all the way into the hallway.

If he had not distracted me with his bare chest, I could have said no to tonight. Made up some excuse, like I was going to hang out with my brothers. I would have been just fine if Magic Mike had kept his shirt on. I would have stayed strong and remembered all the wise choices I'd made very early this morning.

Instead, I was all, *Oh, Ryan, yes, let's go out tonight, and please make me forget all my rules and plans. Tee-hee.*

So much for the hope that physical activity would somehow lessen Ryan's attractiveness.

As I turned on my shower and started to undress, I realized there probably wasn't enough gym equipment in the entire world to make me forget how gorgeous Ryan De Luna was.

I wasn't sure what to wear for our date and ended up calling Ashley's room. After consulting with the other dancers, they decided on a little black cocktail dress that Britt brought down for me after I told them my size. Part of me wanted to be subversive and wear a pair of jeans and a T-shirt. But it was Ryan. If this was our first official pretend date, it would probably be somewhere swanky. I put on makeup as if I were about to go onstage and piled my long hair into a messy, but hopefully elegant, bun.

I packed all my belongings and dropped my suitcases in Parker's room. He promised to have everything brought down to our bus. He didn't seem particularly happy with my outfit choice, but I figured that meant I looked good.

When Ryan knocked on my door, I gulped down my nervousness and took in a deep breath. When I opened it, I was very glad I'd made the effort. He wore a black suit that had been tailored just for him. His hair was perfectly mussed, like he'd just rolled out of bed, and that combination of sophisticated and down-to-earth was more than my senses could process.

"You look . . ." His gaze traveled up and down my body almost like a physical touch. "Wow."

I would not blush. I would not. "Thanks."

"Shall we?" He gestured with his arm, and I joined him in the hallway. I noticed Fox and said hi to him, but he just nodded. It wasn't going to be easy to get him to fall in love with Angie if he didn't ever talk to me.

We rode the elevator in silence, and I tried not to stare at Ryan. Which wasn't easy.

"We're going out the front," he said when the doors opened. "We want them to get pictures. I hope you're ready for this."

I wasn't ready. When we walked through the doors, a crowd of teenagers erupted in hysterical screams around us. Only the security holding them back kept us safe. The constant flashes of light were blinding. Ryan put his arm around me and let Fox lead us to a waiting SUV. Ryan helped me climb into the back and then followed me in. The car door shut, and Fox got into the passenger seat in the front. I heard him say, "Drive."

"That was insane," I said, watching some of the girls chase us as the SUV pulled away quickly from the curb.

"Welcome to my life." He said it in a mocking way, but I could hear the unspoken exhaustion in his tone.

"Where are we going?"

"I asked the concierge for a recommendation. Someplace where we could eat and listen to live music. No smoking allowed."

It touched me that he remembered my preference. It struck me how closed-in the back seat felt. How much room he took up. I scooted closer to my door and looked out the window. Not that it did me any good. It was like Ryan had infected every molecule in the air with his yummy scent and overwhelming maleness.

"You're sitting over there like you think I'm going to pounce on you."

I was practically hugging the door. But I couldn't tell him that the opposite was true—I was afraid I would pounce on him.

"I'm not the kind of guy who would take you out if I wasn't willing to respect the boundaries you've set. In case you haven't noticed, I'm very disciplined."

That much I had noticed. "Anybody who could ignore that chocolate cake last night has to be disciplined."

"I've never really been into chocolate."

I blinked a few times, not certain I'd heard him correctly. "I'm not sure we can even be friends now."

He laughed, and the sound loosened my limbs, allowing me to relax.

"I've found that I don't really miss it."

"Is that part of your clean-living thing?" Because if the price of remaining healthy was no more chocolate, you could count me out.

"It's a lot of work to run around that stage night after night. If I don't eat right and take care of myself, it takes too much out of me to perform. Trust me, I know."

That reminded me of something Ashley had said. "I heard you used to be kind of a punk and into partying."

And women. Lots and lots and lots of women.

A strobe light outside hit his window, outlining his strong profile. "Yeah. I was really selfish. I was late to shows and cared only about having a good time. I wasn't an addict or anything, but I probably took things too far."

"So what changed?"

"I wish I could say maturity, but I was at South by Southwest a few years ago. I was so late they brought out the next performer. I threw an absolute fit backstage when I finally showed up, furious that they'd bump someone of my status. Rick Jovan was standing there."

That would be Rick Jovan, lead singer and guitarist for the rock band Jovanni.

"He told me to stop being disrespectful to my fans, who had given me their time and money. He said I was a cliché and a jerk and that I needed to grow up and act like a man. For some reason, that just clicked. It made something change inside me. Do you know what it's like to find out that you've basically been a huge tool?"

"If it helps at all, I've known you were a huge tool for a long time."

Ryan laughed at my teasing. "I decided not to take my life for granted. I love singing. I love performing. I don't want to do anything to jeopardize it."

"I get that." I was in that very boat. Only the thing that could jeopardize my future was this man, who I felt a strong, unsettling connection to. He knew things about me that I didn't want anyone to know.

"We're here," Fox announced. We had pulled into an alley, and a man in a white button-up shirt and black pants held a door open.

The driver had parked the SUV close to the wall on my side, so I had no choice but to slide over and exit through Ryan's door. Ryan waited for me, holding out his hand to help me down. I didn't need his help, and while I was supposed to remember to be strong, I liked the feel of his hand enclosing mine.

Fox said he'd stay at the car with the driver and to call if we needed him.

"Mr. De Luna, welcome. Right this way." The man at the door led us through the bright lights and stainless steel of the kitchen and into the club itself. It was decorated like a speakeasy from the early twentieth century—lots of red velvet and gold finishes. The club was dimly lit, and we were seated in a quiet booth away from the main-floor tables. It would allow us some privacy.

"This is very cool," I told Ryan with a smile as I unfolded the napkin and placed it across my lap. It was so dark it was a little hard to see the menu. Ryan grabbed a pamphlet from the center of our table that listed the evening's acts. "I think it says Louis something."

Our waitress, also wearing a white top and black slacks, came to introduce herself and take our drink order. Both Ryan and I asked for water.

A spotlight turned on, pointed at the stage. A man walked out in a tuxedo and went to the microphone. "Ladies and gentlemen, welcome to the High Life. For your ear-tainment this evening, we have the Louisiana Trio."

The club patrons applauded as the announcer left the stage. Blood rushed to my ears, blocking out everything else. My heart pounded frantically against my chest. Ice filled my lungs, weighing me down to my seat. I must have misheard.

When the curtain rose and I saw him, I realized I hadn't misunderstood.

The jazz music began, and I stood, looking for the door we'd used to come in. I had to get out. Away from here. From him. I hadn't had a full-blown anxiety attack in years, but it looked like I was about to. I was so light-headed I thought I might pass out. Small black pinpricks began to cloud the periphery of my vision.

"Maisy?" Ryan's voice sounded far away, like he was calling to me from the bottom of a well.

"I have to . . . I have to . . ." My legs started to crumple.

Then his arm went around my waist, the other under my knees, and he swung me up into his arms. I think he carried me back through the kitchen and into the alleyway.

Had I not been basically incoherent at the time, I would have found this extremely hot.

Fox rushed over and opened the SUV door so Ryan could lift me into the car. It became easier to breathe as the blood returned to where it belonged and the air no longer felt too thin.

"Is she diabetic or hyperglycemic?" Fox asked.

"I don't know," Ryan answered, the frustration evident in his voice. "She did hit her head this morning. And she eats a lot of chocolate. I don't think she's diabetic."

For some reason, that struck me as immensely funny, and I started to giggle.

"Maisy?"

"I'm okay," I said, still trying to catch my breath. But the attack had passed. "Can we go somewhere else, please?"

At Ryan's direction, the driver started the car and pulled out of the alley, back into traffic.

"What was that?" Ryan asked, the concern evident.

"That," I told him with a sigh, "was my father."

CHAPTER FOURTEEN

"Your father?" Ryan repeated. "In the jazz band? Which one?"

"He was the piano player." I straightened up, that dizzying sensation from earlier completely gone. "I didn't know he was in Vegas."

Apparently, Ryan had stuck the pamphlet with the bands' names in the pocket of his jacket. He pulled it out. "Louis Harrison?"

"It's the French pronunciation. 'Lew-e.' Not 'Lewis.' People always pronounce his first name wrong."

"Probably has something to do with that *s* on the end."

"Probably," I agreed. His gentle teasing was helping me feel more like myself again. It was something my brothers would have done, and I liked that he did it instead of babying me. "Sometimes I hate that I love music so much because I know I got that from him. It's bad enough that every time I look at one of my brothers, I see his face. When I was younger, every week I changed my mind about what I wanted to be when I grew up. Fashion designer. Interior decorator. Veterinarian. Salon owner. But I kept coming back to music. No matter what I did, no matter how much I told myself I wanted something else, it was always all about the music."

"I get that." Ryan fell quiet for a couple of minutes. "I should take you back to the hotel. Let you rest."

"What I need right now is some really great food. I need loud chaos so I can forget."

"If there's one thing Vegas does exceptionally well, it's loud chaos." He asked the driver to stop. He took me into the nearest casino.

We ate a restaurant where the waitstaff fell all over themselves to serve him. Once we were seated at a table near the door where we could hear the casino, I noticed the menu didn't have any prices listed.

"Don't worry about it." He had to yell when I pointed it out. "This is a date, remember? Really great food is coming your way."

I ordered a steak, and he had some kind of lasagna made out of vegetables. He spent the entire dinner telling me story after story about people in the industry, completely distracting me.

It was perfect.

After Ryan paid the bill, we went to the cage cashier, and he handed me a bunch of chips. I had no idea how much they were worth, as I'd never gambled before. Fox got us into a VIP area. I recognized a movie star seated at one of the tables. I tried to remember his name. Unfortunately, most of my pop-culture knowledge was stuck in the 1980s, along with my mother's brain. He was the one who just got married. Chance or Chase something. The woman he had his arm around had to be his wife. They looked happy and very much in love.

We sat down at the blackjack table with them, and Ryan said hello. He made the introductions to Chase and Zoe Covington. We chatted for only a few minutes. They were in town to do some fund-raising for an ocean-conservation charity they had just started together, and they offered to send some materials to Ryan. They left shortly after we arrived, arms wrapped around each other.

I tried to imagine Ryan and me being like that. Having those kinds of feelings for each other, and I couldn't.

I'd never played blackjack before, so both the dealer and Ryan tried to help me with my cards. He had the waitstaff bring me a big bowl of ice cream, and I discovered that gambling was pretty fun when it wasn't your money you were spending.

Nothing but utterly loud chaos, making it impossible for me to dwell on my father sighting.

Then it was time for us to go back to the bus. We were driving up to Northern California, then on to Oregon and Washington, spending two to three days at each spot.

It was unbelievably awkward when we pulled into the hotel's parking lot, right next to our bus. I'd never gone out on a date before where we both ended up in the same place at the end of the evening.

We went into the lounge, where most of the band and my brothers were watching a movie about giant robots. There were a few strange glances, but we went into the bunk alley, past a snoring Anton, and stopped at my bunk.

"Everybody saw us on our date," I offered. That had to be helpful, especially if they were gossips who would pass the word along.

"They did." Ryan was so tall and broad that he took up the entire hallway. Like there was nowhere for me to go and nothing for me to do but just give in. The temperature rose as he moved closer to me. "Now what?"

The way his gaze dropped to my lips, I knew what he hoped I'd say. I fought off the tingles. "Now bed."

"Excellent idea."

Good grief. "No, me in mine and you in yours."

"That's not nearly as much fun." He looked like a kid who'd been told he wouldn't be getting a puppy for Christmas. I wanted to laugh at his forlorn expression.

"My brothers tend to punch first and ask questions later. Another delightful thing we inherited from our father. They would probably remove all of your favorite body parts."

"That would be a shame for both you and me."

"Somebody should wash your mind out with soap."

He held up both hands, laughing. "Hey, I'm not the one who started it."

"Then I'll be the one to end it. Good night, Ryan." I grabbed my carry-on bag and shooed him away so I could go into the bathroom and change.

As he left, someone grabbed my knee, and I yelped. Cole was on the bottom bunk. "That was . . . disturbing."

"I don't want to hear it," I told him, knowing I was furiously blushing. It was one thing for Ryan to flirt and tease in private; it was a whole different ball of wax to know it had taken place in front of a judgy brother. "Speaking of things I didn't want to hear tonight, did you know our father was in Las Vegas?"

The guilty expression on Cole's face told me everything I needed to know. "How did you find out?" he asked.

"Guess where Ryan took me on our date tonight? To the club he was playing."

"Did you talk to him?"

"Did I talk to him?" Had Cole started taking drugs? "To the man who ruined our family and our mom? No, I didn't talk to him." But the fact that Cole had asked made me realize he probably had. "Have you seen our father?"

More guilt on his face.

"Why would you see him on purpose?"

"He's our dad."

"He is not our 'dad,'" I snapped back. "He's our genetic donor. I can't believe you did that."

"He asked about you, Maisy. Wanted to know how you were doing."

That just made me angrier. "Know what I want? For him to have not left our mother. For her to be whole and not living in some facility because of the accident. You can't always get what you want."

I felt totally betrayed. I went into the bathroom and slammed shut the sliding door. It wasn't nearly as satisfying as slamming a heavy, swinging door.

There was not one part of me that believed my father cared about me. I had too much experience to suggest otherwise. I'd never once felt like he loved me. As a little girl, I was always trying to get his attention. To be pretty enough or talented enough so I'd be worthy of his notice. I didn't know if it was just the basic differences between men and women that made Cole and me see things in such radically different ways, or just our personalities.

If our father cared about us, he would have checked in on our mom. He would have been there after the accident to see how he could help. Instead, he abandoned us and forced Fitz to become our substitute parent. If our father had cared, he would have sent us money. He wouldn't have fathered twenty new half siblings. He wouldn't have put his pathetic music career above us.

I sighed as my anger started to dissipate. The entire evening had been like a roller coaster. High, low, high, low. Thanks to my baggage and dumb family.

All this time I'd been saying I needed to stay away from Ryan so he wouldn't break my heart.

Maybe Ryan should stay away from me and my drama. He'd be better off without it.

I had to call Angie the next day. I didn't want her to get the wrong impression about Ryan and me if she saw something online.

She didn't even say hello. "What's happening with you and Ryan?"

"What have you heard?"

She squealed so loudly I had to pull my phone away from my ear. "Nothing. I was completely speculating. Lurid details now!"

"I need you to be my nurse."

"Why?"

"Nurse–patient confidentiality." I didn't know if that was a thing, but she had to stay silent.

"Okay. What are your symptoms?"

"At the moment? My stomach hurts and my chest aches. I'm making really stupid decisions, risky moves, and I want to forget my rules."

"I am diagnosing you with a serious crush. Which I can't blame you for. Now what's the secret you need to tell me?"

I sat in one of the bathrooms, the only places that had any privacy on this bus besides Ryan's bedroom.

I was not going in Ryan's bedroom ever again.

"Ryan and I are dating."

More shrieks and squeals.

"Angie, Angie! It's fake. We're not really dating."

"Oh. Okay. Wink. Wink. You're not *really* dating."

It might make my life easier if my best friend believed me. "I'm serious. We're just friends."

"Right. I forgot because of how you look at each other and how your voice sounds when you talk about him." She paused. "How many times have you guys kissed already?"

"None." Ha!

"How many times have you almost kissed?"

Uh. Well, that one was a bit trickier.

"I knew it! You love Ryan, and you're completely moonstruck, and you're going to have little moon babies."

"What's a moon baby?"

"I don't know, but you're going to have one! I'm going to be best friends with the wife of the world's biggest pop star."

"Or you're going to be best friends with the lead singer of the world's coolest band."

"Shh," she told me. "I'm picturing your wedding. I've caught the bouquet made out of sheets of music."

"Which means you'll get married next. Speaking of . . . have you talked to Fox lately?"

"Fox?" She sounded completely confused. Maybe I had misread that situation. "Why would I talk to him?"

"That night at the concert, I thought I saw something between the two of you."

Now there was silence from Angie's end. I hadn't imagined it!

"You can marry Fox and become his vixen and have little fox babies. Which are called kits." I had totally looked it up.

"That's not his real name. It was one he got at boot camp because he was wily and devious. His real name is Eugene."

Fox was definitely better. "I love that you know that about him."

"This conversation has taken a turn for the weird. I'll talk to you later."

I got her to stay on for a few more minutes as I asked her about my mom. But my mother was the same. No changes, and she had been calm and contented.

She hadn't missed me at all.

I promised to keep in touch, glad I had at least planted the seed in Angie's mind about Fox.

Keeping in contact became difficult because we were so busy. We did several more performances in parts of the country I'd never seen before. Each time we did a show, it felt just like the first time. I hoped that would stay true. That it would never become old and boring, and I'd be just as excited someday at my last show as I was now.

Our bus was a complete and total bro-zone. Every other occupant of the bus changed wherever, and they were often in various states of undress. Which was fine; I was used to it.

Except for Ryan.

That never failed to make my pulse race and my breathing become shorter and faster.

Which I think he knew.

Like the night I came into the lounge and found him playing video games. He kind of sucked. I said as much.

"See that leaderboard?" He brought up the screen. "Number one, thank you very much."

Then he rested his hand on his bare stomach, and it took all of my willpower not to do the same.

Sarcasm was my only defense. "Against twelve-year-old kids. I'm super impressed."

"You can do better?"

Did he not remember the last time he issued me that challenge? "I don't really like video games."

He tossed me a controller, and, sighing, I sat down.

"What do your tattoos mean?" I asked, maneuvering around a difficult obstacle in the game.

"Checking out my tats? I knew you liked me."

"Shut up. I was just curious."

I easily won the first round, which seemed to throw him.

"Let's go again." We'd been playing for a couple of minutes when he said, "The music notes are obvious. The triangle represents fire. Something I got when they started calling me El Caliente. And the black band is for my mom."

That was really sweet. So sweet I almost considered throwing the game. I didn't, though.

It took only three rounds before he admitted defeat.

"What was that?" he asked just as Parker entered the room. He looked at us and raised one eyebrow.

"Whatever you do, dude, don't play against Maze. She will destroy you."

"Where was that warning five minutes ago?" Ryan turned toward me. "I thought you said you sucked."

"I didn't say I wasn't any good. Just that I don't like them." Apparently, whatever kind of manual dexterity made me skilled at guitar also made me excellent with a game controller. "Three brothers, remember?"

"You're the kind of girl a guy would show off to his buddies," Ryan said in a tone of respect and awe.

Since I had those three brothers, I knew that was one of the highest compliments a man could give a woman. "I could trounce them, too, if you'd like."

"You probably also shouldn't try to argue with her, either," Parker suggested, sitting down on Ryan's other side, to both my relief and disappointment. "Maisy always thinks she's the smartest person in the room."

Before I could protest, Ryan jumped in. "When she thinks this, are you the only other person in the room? Because then she'd be right."

That led to some shoving and laughter, and I was impressed by how quickly and easily Ryan had won my brothers over, especially getting in on their insult games.

He soon found ways to win me over, too.

In Portland, my brothers and I had a fun, amazing performance, and at Piper's invitation, I stuck around backstage instead of returning to the tour bus. I didn't tell her that I tended to stay and watch his concert most nights.

Ryan put on another mesmerizing show, and I found myself humming along to most of his songs. In the middle of his set, instead of running offstage to change outfits like he was supposed to, the crew members brought him a guitar and two stools.

"I know you've already heard a version of this song once this evening, but I thought you might like to hear it again. I need everyone to put their hands together and bring out the lovely Maisy Harrison. Come on out, Maisy!"

The audience cheered and whistled.

Stunned, I stayed put in the wings. I turned to see Piper nudging me, a huge grin on her face. "Go on, Maisy. It'll be fun."

When I didn't move, she took matters into her own hands. She pushed me, hard. Landing me onstage.

"There she is! Everyone welcome Maisy!"

The audience started chanting my name while I was stuck in my deer-in-the-headlights position.

One of the roadies came out and handed me my Dreadnought. I wanted to duck backstage and pretend this wasn't happening, but I couldn't.

What was he doing? Our "relationship" wasn't front-page news, although it had made the rounds. Maybe Ryan was trying to take this thing more public. Which I had agreed to and been well paid for.

So I walked across the stage, waving to the crowd and smiling. When I got close to him, I asked, "What do you think you're doing?"

"Sit down." He nodded at the empty stool, and I sat, putting my guitar across my lap.

"I want us to sing 'One More Night' together. Like your YouTube version."

"But . . . we haven't practiced." The thing with seasoned professionals was that you didn't have to practice for weeks on end to get something right. We could take two or three passes at a song to coordinate our vocals and the music. A rehearsal or two later, we could perform just about any song perfectly. But Ryan and I hadn't gone over the music together or worked out our harmonies or who would come in when.

"Just sing it exactly the same way you did in the video," he said. "I'll take the first verse, you take the second, and we'll sing the chorus and the bridges together."

This had the potential to be a disaster of epic proportions.

Ryan started the intro to the song, and I joined in. Even if our voices weren't compatible, our guitars seemed to love each other.

He began to sing.

> I know you can't stay
> Someplace you gotta be
> Won't stand in your way
> But, girl, you gotta see

Then I joined in.

> We'll make this all right
> Won't give up the fight
> If you give me, give me . . .

> One more night
> Just to be with you alone
> One more night
> Let the music take us home
> One more night
> To pretend we're in control
> All I need is one more, one more, one more night

Nothing stunned me more than how perfectly our voices blended together. As if we'd practiced this song a million times. So much so that I nearly missed when I was supposed to come in.

Tomorrow you'll be gone
Tonight's our last chance
I know you're moving on
I need one last dance

Then Ryan came back in, and again we sang in perfect, flawless harmony.

Like ships in the night
We'll fade in the light
So please give, give me . . .

One more night
Just to be with you alone
One more night
Let the music take us home
One more night
To pretend we're in control
All I need is one more, one more,
One more, baby,
One more night

He looked into my eyes as he played the final notes of the song. That moment, onstage with him, was transcendent. Like my spirit left my body and was watching everything happening from twenty feet in the air. I couldn't feel my arms or hands or face. My fingers played solely from muscle memory because I wasn't controlling them.

When I originally recorded this song, I'd been thinking of my mother. I wasn't now. There was only the music surrounding us, binding us together. Everyone around us faded away. There was no stage, no crowd of screaming women.

Just Ryan and me.

His soul spoke directly to mine, saying, "I found you." Two halves fusing into a whole.

The last note faded, and the audience screamed. I wanted to say something to him. To tell him how important this moment felt. That something had just shifted between us.

When he leaned over, I thought he would say it first. "I practiced with your video." That explained how it had gone so well.

It was not what I had hoped he would say.

I discovered it wasn't what I wanted him to say, either.

Because he hadn't felt it. I'd been alone in what I'd experienced. So I smiled and again waved to the crowd as Ryan said, "Give it up one more time for Maisy Harrison!"

I needed to accept the reality of our situation. I was a paid, fake girlfriend.

But given what had just happened onstage, he made it hard for me to remember.

The next day, just before we reached Seattle, I woke up from a nap with a raging thirst and started for the front of the bus to grab a bottle of water. As I climbed out of the bunk, I heard the far door open and saw Ryan enter the bunk alley.

Which meant I had to pass him. He again had his shirt off. I was starting to wonder if there was some kind of De Luna vendetta against crew necks.

We met in the middle, but instead of turning and passing, he stood in front of me. "Hey."

"Hi. Move, please."

He turned his body to one side, but he took up too much space.

Just as I realized there was no way to move past without brushing up against him, the bus swerved violently to the left. The motion threw me against Ryan and knocked both of us to the floor. Somehow he twisted and took the brunt of the fall, letting out an *oof* sound as I collapsed on top of him.

There was a thumping noise, and I looked up to see that DJ Anton had rolled out of his bed and landed in the alley.

He didn't even wake up.

"What just happened?" I asked, breathing heavily. Whether that was because of whatever the bus had just done or because I was currently flush against Ryan, I wasn't sure.

He didn't help things when he reached up to pull my hair back from my face. It had hung around him like a curtain, but now he wrapped the length of it around his hand. "Vince really loves animals. He swerves for turtles and possums."

Ryan's strong, steady heartbeat pulsed beneath mine, and my entire body lifted and fell as he breathed. "I should get up." My voice was little more than a whisper.

"I don't mind."

Truth be told, neither did I. I liked the way he felt pressed against me, all strength and firm tightness. Muscle and sinew against my curves and softness.

His free hand went to the small of my back, and my shirt must have ridden up a little because I felt his fingertips on my bare, blazing skin.

Too much. Stimulus overload.

I tried to stand up, ignoring the fact that every movement had me sliding against him, but he still had me by the hair. "Ow!"

He quickly let go, and I finally got clear of him. I stepped back so he could stand as well.

Ryan looked far too pleased with himself.

"Was this some kind of trap?" I asked.

"Yes, I arranged for Vince to almost kill all of us just for this moment. I knew exactly when you'd be walking down this hallway and set the whole thing up flawlessly."

Was it wrong that I found his sarcasm sexy?

"But now that it happened, I'm not sorry it did."

Problem was, I couldn't be sorry about it, either.

So much so that after the show in Seattle, I said yes to something I probably shouldn't have. Piper told us we had two days off. Some of the crew planned to fly home. I considered doing that, but Angie assured me she had a handle on things. I also thought about going to see the sights, like the Space Needle.

Ryan offered me something that sounded far more interesting.

"The reason we have time off is that the label hired Baylor Michaelsen to film a music video for me at Olympic National Park. Do you want to come watch?"

I immediately agreed.

Which turned out to be a mistake.

CHAPTER FIFTEEN

Baylor "Bay" Michaelsen was a director whose most popular movies featured constant explosions and scantily clad women. On our early-morning drive to the set, Ryan explained that Bay was trying to get into more indie and artistic films and had offered to direct this video. It would be an attempt to showcase a different side of his work.

Ryan played the song for me that would be featured in the video. Considering it was a two-and-a-half-hour drive, we had plenty of time to listen. The song was called "Be With You" and was about a guy regretting his breakup and wanting to get back to the girl he wished he hadn't left. It was different from the ballads on his other albums. There was a haunting quality to it. He sounded more authentic, more honest. Less synthesizers, more real music. I actually kind of liked it.

Apparently, the label wanted to release the song and the video the same day. The production company had permits to shoot that day and the next, and then the editing would be completed in two weeks. As soon as we got to the set, Ryan asked for a production assistant who would keep an eye out for me. He said he'd see me later and went to get changed.

The PA, a girl named Lauren, explained the concept of the video. It was about a love affair between a knight and a fairy princess. Her father, the king, had threatened to kill the knight if they so much as touched. They couldn't be together, but it didn't stop them from loving each other. Ryan would be singing his song as he searched the fairy princess's kingdom to find her. We were down by the coast, and I could see these tall rocks off in the distance. Fog clung to everything.

Ryan came out of wardrobe, and my heart nearly stopped. When they'd said "knight," I had expected, I don't know, a metal suit of armor or something. Instead, they had him in this black leather getup. His right arm was covered in scales, with small metal rings that went up and formed half a breastplate over his right pectoral muscle. On the left side there were three leather belts, one over his shoulder and two across his torso that held the bulk of his "armor" in place. He had a knife in a leather sheath with two tiny straps on his left arm. Leather pants with a sword scabbard and actual sword, along with matching boots, completed the outfit. They had left him unshaven, his hair wild.

His armor was totally impractical for a real fight.

But any fairy princess who denied him anything was obviously out of her mind.

Lauren showed me to a chair and asked me to turn off my phone and be quiet. Since I hoped someday to shoot my own music videos, I wouldn't do anything to jeopardize being able to stay. I wanted to learn all I could about the process. I did as she asked.

"I'm assigned to you for the next couple of days. Is there anything I can get you? We have a craft-services table set up."

I was too wired to eat anything, so I told her I was fine.

"Is Caryl here yet? Her call time was over an hour ago." A man walked past me yelling in a British accent, followed by multiple underlings, and I realized he must be Bay Michaelsen. Lauren confirmed it a second later.

"Why is he yelling?" I was afraid to ask it too loudly, not wanting to draw any attention to myself.

"They hired Caryl Clausen to be Ryan's love interest." At my blank expression, she went on, "You know, the fashion model? Best friend of

Skyler Smith? Anyway, she's not here yet, and nobody can get her, her manager, or her agent on the phone."

"We'll do some of Ryan's solo scenes first. I need him down by the water and in the boat!" Bay directed, and everyone scrambled to do as he commanded. They loaded Ryan into this rinky-dink rowboat and took him out into the Pacific Ocean. The low-hanging clouds swallowed him up. Bay called "Action," and Ryan rowed the boat toward the beach, breaking through the fog and mist to land on the rocky shore. He jumped out looking determined and mysterious and began walking up the coastline. I could see that the camera angles would catch the snowcapped mountains off in the distance.

I realized I'd been holding my breath when the director yelled "Cut." They made Ryan do the same thing five more times until the rising sun began to burn off the fog.

"Moving on to the next location!" Bay called out.

"The vans are this way," Lauren said, pointing me toward the road.

I loaded up with a bunch of crew members, and the hot topic was the missing model. There was no time to delay production because of Ryan's touring schedule and the song's release date.

We pulled into what Lauren called a "temperate rain forest." The trees were massive and covered in moss, with vines hanging down everywhere. Ferns grew among the trees along with wild grasses. I could see why they'd chosen this spot to stand in for a fairy kingdom. When we parked and got out of the van, I saw a camera already set up and covered in plastic because of how wet everything was. A bright-blue river ran just past the grove of trees, gently rushing over small rocks.

"I have Caryl's agent on the phone!" A woman with a headset rushed over to the director. "She'll be here in half an hour. Apparently there was some kind of mix-up on their end about the correct call time."

"Tell wardrobe and makeup to get ready for her so we can hit the ground running," Bay said. And his expression clearly indicated that he didn't believe there'd been any kind of mix-up.

I again took a seat and watched as the director had Ryan walk through the trees, searching for his lost love. He had Ryan cut through some vines, hack down some ferns, and I realized they'd given him a real sword.

Then Ryan stood in front of a fallen cedar tree, and they blasted the music through a sound system so he could sing through it three times. The director asked him to try some different things while singing, playing different emotions on some of the lines. The music was so loud I couldn't tell if he was actually singing or just lip-synching. Lauren explained that it didn't matter. They would overlay the track while editing. Some stars preferred mouthing the words, and others sang for real so they would match the song's intensity. I knew what she was talking about. There was nothing more distracting than watching a music video and seeing the singer's mouth barely open even though they were supposed to be hitting a high note that I knew took physical effort.

About two hours later, Caryl arrived on set in her costume. They had her in a gauzy pink-and-purple dress with sparkles all over the bodice. She had bright-silver makeup around her eyes. She was blonde, tall, ethereal-looking. I could see why they'd picked her.

"What took you so long to get here?" the director asked.

"Things happen. So sorry," Caryl said with a smile that looked totally fake.

One of the makeup artists stood next to Lauren. "She spent the last hour fighting with me over every product I used and the final outcome. I showed her the concept art, but she didn't care. It's not like she has to worry if I get fired."

"Where are your wings?" Bay barked at Caryl, and she looked supremely bored.

She named a famous lingerie company and said, "Contractually, I'm allowed to wear wings only for them."

This led to more yelling, with Bay demanding that someone get Caryl's agent on the phone. She sat in a chair texting while all this was going on.

"Maybe we could add them in digitally later," the assistant director said to Bay, and he agreed to start shooting. They had created a throne made out of twigs and flowers, and Bay told Caryl to sit in it. With a loud sigh, she went over and sat down.

Bay explained the shot, how Ryan would walk in slowly and then kneel in front of her throne. "Try to look like you adore her."

"That'll be difficult," somebody murmured nearby, and I had to agree. Caryl kind of seemed like a brat.

"Wait, are you filming from this side?" Caryl indicated her right side.

"Yes, because that's where the cameras are," Bay growled, obviously getting more irritated by the minute.

"You can film me only from my left side. That's in my contract. Also, I don't do natural lighting."

Was Caryl saying she didn't do the sun? The light source surrounding us everywhere right now?

"We're already set up," he said through clenched teeth.

"That doesn't really sound like my problem."

Bay's face turned bright red, but he gave in and had the crew carry the camera to the opposite side of the throne. Light panels were brought out for Caryl.

"Don't forget I have to approve the final cut," she said with a smirk, and it almost felt like she was enjoying the chaos and problems she was creating.

At this point, the director just ignored what she was saying. "Play back the music and . . . action!"

Ryan did as he'd been asked, slowly walking up to the throne and bowing to the princess. Caryl looked at him like he was a bug on the bottom of her shoe.

"Cut!" Bay called out, frustration evident in his voice. "Caryl, you have to look at him like you love him. With longing. Let's go again!"

They did the scene over, and her reaction was exactly the same as the first time.

Bay told everyone to stop. He approached the throne. "Do you know what longing is, Caryl?"

"He should just tell her to pretend Ryan's a doughnut or a new Birkin bag. Maybe she'd get it then," Lauren said to the makeup artist, and I tried very hard not to laugh.

"Again!" Bay shouted.

Again, Caryl looked hostile.

"That's not longing!"

"I'm the professional model. I know how my face looks best, and that's what matters in this video. You hired me for how I look. You let me do my job, and you do yours."

"That's it! I am done. You are fired," Bay shouted back. "You are in breach of contract. You were four hours late for your agreed-upon call time. You've done nothing but cause delays. You refuse to take direction and won't wear the wardrobe. I will not tolerate your selfishness and disrespect. Get her off my set!"

"Fine. I will still get paid. You'll be hearing from my people," Caryl said as she sauntered off.

"Yeah, have the head nurse call us," the makeup artist muttered, but I couldn't laugh this time. Now what would they do?

"I can't believe any of that just happened," I said. "How could she be such a jerk?"

Lauren let out an undignified snort. "I've seen so much worse. Once you get enough fame, you can be horrible, and people put up with it. The stories I could tell you . . ." Her voice trailed off.

It made Ryan's down-to-earth behavior even more admirable.

I was distracted by the sound of desperate arguing. I was close enough to the director and his team that I could hear everything they said.

"You have to apologize and get her back. We're in the middle of a national forest in Washington. Who else are we going to get to play this part?"

"Could we have him never actually find the princess? The whole video is about him searching for her?"

"Maybe when we get to LA we can hire someone new and put her in front of a green screen and then add her in to the scenes."

"That won't work. Ryan's supposed to interact with her."

"Why can't Maisy do it?"

That last line was from Ryan.

"Who is Maisy?" Bay asked and turned to stare at me when Ryan pointed.

"She's the lead singer from my opening act. She'll be here today and tomorrow."

The director stood in front of me, studying me. "Do you have any on-camera experience?"

Other than YouTube? Not so much.

"Wait a second. I'm not an actress." I was also not interested in trying to become one. I didn't want to screw up Ryan's video.

"To be fair, and no offense, but neither is Caryl Clausen," Ryan said with a wink.

"People say no offense when what they mean is I'm about to insult you but don't get mad. It's rude." Why my mother's words came out of my mouth just then I couldn't have explained. It was like the main part of my brain was freaking out, and so dumber parts were free to speak up.

"I didn't say it to Caryl, so it doesn't count." Ryan looked as if he was really enjoying himself.

"She could work," Bay announced. "Get her into hair and makeup and then into the actual wardrobe, including the wings. Do you mind if we dye those red streaks pink or purple to match the outfit?"

"Don't I have to agree to it first? Sign a contract?" I asked as some-one reached for my elbow.

Ryan knelt in front of me as he had for the fairy princess. "We'll give you the money we were going to give to Caryl. Please, fair maiden, be in my music video so we don't waste over a million dollars."

I didn't know if Ryan had personally contributed to that amount, but given his financial situation, all the ways I owed him, the offer of even more money, and that he was kneeling—how could I say no? "I'm *really* not an actress."

"You'll be fine," he assured me. "Do you mind if they dye your streaks?"

"No." I could always redo them red later.

"No, you won't do it, or no, you don't mind about your hair?"

"I'll do it," I told him. "And I don't mind about my hair."

Have you ever regretted a decision so quickly that you felt a blind-ing pain right behind your eyeballs?

This is a mistake! kept running on repeat through my brain as the beauty team got me ready. I knew I would go out there and make a total fool of myself. The hairstylist decided on purple streaks, as all she had to do was add some blue to the red. My hair, makeup, and outfit were completed in record time. The dress was too long, so the head of wardrobe slashed off four inches or so, giving it this jagged look that somehow worked. As if the dress had always been that way.

All the same, I felt like a little girl wearing her mother's shoes and outfit. I was a fake and a fraud, and soon they would all know it.

The success of this video now rested on my untrained, unprepared shoulders.

I was glad I hadn't eaten that morning because I seriously felt like I was about to puke.

CHAPTER SIXTEEN

Bay had me go to the throne recently vacated by Caryl. It wasn't uncomfortable, as I'd imagined. There was even a cushion. In fact, it was far more comfortable than the collapsible chair I'd been in all morning. Bay called Ryan over, intending to speak to both of us at the same time.

"This is a song about loss. It's also a song about aching regret. About desire. About wanting someone so badly, but there's nothing you can do about it. You can't even touch each other. You can't change your situation or the fact that you're from two completely different worlds."

It was starting to hit a little too close to home.

"You're a princess, and he's a lowly knight who would do anything for you—slay any dragon, defeat any foe, defend your kingdom. But you'll never be together. It will never be real. It will never work, and it's killing you both."

Now I was sure that Bay Michaelsen was straight trolling me.

"When he kneels, I want you to look at him with longing. Like he's the most beautiful thing you've ever seen, and all you want to do is kiss him and hold him, but you can't. Ryan, when you look up at her, I want to see the same thing on your face."

This was probably the most nervous I'd ever felt in my entire life. They started the music, and Ryan walked through the forest to me, then knelt at the base of the throne.

When he raised his eyes to mine, I gasped and started breathing hard. He looked at me with so much desire, with so much naked want in his eyes, that I had to grip the armrests of the throne to not fling myself at him.

I didn't have to act. No pretense necessary. I only had to let my emotions show on my face. Which wasn't hard because, despite my nickname, I was a fairly emotional and passionate person. I'd never been all that great at lying. I basically had to be myself and let all the things I felt for Ryan show.

Did he do the same? Or was he a much better actor than I'd given him credit for?

"Perfect!" Bay sounded over the moon. "Let's do it again."

Again? I wasn't sure how many times my heart could take it.

It turned out to be a lot of times. A lot.

Every scene that Bay had planned out, we shot at least four or five times. He said it would have been more if this were a movie.

There were some where I watched Ryan walk through the forest looking for me. One where I stood on the opposite side of that river (the Hoh River, I learned), and Ryan couldn't figure out how to cross and get to me.

Then we shot a scene where we walked across an open meadow ringed by trees. We were supposed to walk toward each other, and when we met in the middle, we wouldn't touch, but just stand as close as we could without doing so.

Every time we shot this, every time, I trembled as we stood in the center. To be so close to him, to smell him, to feel his warmth but not be able to do anything about it, was maddening.

I had no idea it could possibly get worse.

As darkness descended, the director told me I was done for the day but to be back at six the next morning. Ryan promised he would get me there on time. He had to stay behind to film some other scenes of him singing in a couple of different outfits: one modern, one a billowy set of clothes they would turn a wind machine on. They had set up a room with a green screen in one of the trailers and planned on filming him there. Ryan asked Lauren to make arrangements to get me to a hotel nearby. "I didn't want to drive another five hours to get to and from Seattle, so I had Piper make some reservations. If that's okay."

It was okay. I also didn't want to be trapped in a car alone with him for two and a half hours tonight and two and a half hours tomorrow morning. Especially not with how I was feeling right now.

He watched me the entire way to the wardrobe trailer, and I wondered if he felt even a little bit the same way I did.

When I changed into my street clothes, it took me a minute to find my phone. I'd had it in my pocket, but it wasn't there now. I eventually found it under some hanging dresses. I texted Fitz to let him know what had happened and that I'd be staying the night near the national park. To ease his mind, I made sure to add that I had my own room.

Lauren found the driver, who took me to the hotel. The lodge was cute and clean but definitely rustic. I wondered if Ryan had ever stayed in a place so . . . not five stars before.

Even though I told myself I wasn't waiting up for him, I waited up for him. I kept checking my phone to make sure it was working. But he didn't call or text, which surprised me.

I spent another night not able to sleep as I ran the events from the day on a continuous loop through my brain. How close we'd come to touching but hadn't. How much I craved his touch. Wanted to be held by him. It was like I couldn't turn off my mind, and it was filled with nothing but Ryan.

I knew I had to get up early to get back to set. I kept telling myself, "If I fall asleep now, I'll get at least six hours of sleep." Then it was five hours. Then four. Then three. I counted all the way down until it was time to get up and get dressed.

When I got out of the shower, there was a message on my phone. I clicked on it eagerly but was disappointed to see it was from Lauren. She said a car would be waiting out front for me.

Just for me, I discovered. Ryan had a slightly later call time and wouldn't be driving in with me.

I wasn't sure what to make of that.

The car brought me to the set and a waiting Lauren. She took me to hair and makeup and then wardrobe. They found a coat for me, as it tended to be cooler in the mornings.

Bay wanted to take advantage of the fog in the forest. A driver dropped Lauren and me off at the location where we would be filming. They had me film some solo shots. They asked me to be sad, and I thought about my mom. They asked me to look like I was in love, something I'd never experienced. So I thought of Ryan and how he made me feel. Bay seemed happy with whatever I was doing.

Ryan showed up about half an hour later. I had hoped I'd be more immune to the costume and how he looked in it today.

I was not.

The director had us stand in front of a wide moss-covered tree. "For this shot, I want you two to stand as close together as you possibly can. Ryan will be singing the words to you, Maisy. You can ghost your hands over each other." He stepped in to demonstrate what he meant. He ran his hand over the curve of my cheek without touching me. "But no kissing or actual contact at all. I want more of that longing, staring deeply into each other's eyes. Okay? Roll the music! Let's give this a shot."

Gulping, I stepped as close to Ryan as I could. If I so much as breathed deeply, I would have touched him.

The intro played, and when the lyrics started, Ryan sang to me.

He sang softly, his voice deep and husky and beautiful. It did something strange to my heart. I felt his hands just above my arms, running from my wrist to my shoulders. It made all the hairs on my arm stand straight up.

Then I tried to look into his eyes. It was too much. My lips parted as he sang the words over them. As if I could inhale his beauty and make it a part of me.

"Perfect! Ryan, move your head like you want to kiss her, but you can't."

His lips above mine, so close but so far, were torture. Exquisite, agonizing, wonderful, terrible torture.

I let my eyes fall shut, feeling his hands now hovering near my waist. Like he wanted to pull me in tightly.

"Open your eyes, Maisy! Really look at him!"

When Fitz was in college in a psychology class, he had talked about this study where people who spent four minutes staring deeply into each other's eyes felt like they were falling in love.

I could now totally attest to the truthfulness of that statement. Especially since I did it for a lot longer than four minutes.

His black pupils seemed to dilate, and I realized that our blinking and heavy breathing had become synchronized.

"Show us how you would touch him if you could, Maisy!"

I had left my arms dead at my sides, too afraid to reciprocate what he was doing. But now I had to. I started at his neck and ran my palms over his chest, wanting to brush my fingertips over his exposed stomach, curling them in so I wouldn't. A feverish chill started in my spine and spread out as I let my fingers drift over his hair, and I wondered again what it would feel like. I saw the muscle in his jaw flex as he stopped singing and just stared.

The music suddenly cut out.

"Give us a second. Stay put. We're having a couple of sound issues."

We probably could have taken some steps back, created some distance, but neither of us did.

I wondered if Ryan knew I wasn't pretending. That I was completely incapable of acting. That everything he saw on my face was real, every reaction, truth. Another desperate pleech who had fallen under his spell. Would he think I was pathetic? Would he feel sorry for me?

I couldn't bear his pity.

"Your eyes," he murmured, his words warm against my skin. "They have pops of yellow in them and a darker band on the outer rings. Is that blue? Green?"

"You have a starburst pattern of light brown with golden streaks around your pupils," I said. It was a relief to tell him.

I felt my body sway toward him, and I pulled back, not letting us touch. "I feel like I'm not in control of myself. Like I don't know what I'll do."

If the confession surprised him, he didn't show it. "Like you might be planning on taking advantage of me?" Somehow his tone was both teasing and serious. "Please say you are."

"We're ready! Let's go again!" Bay called out, interrupting us.

Which was a good thing, because I was about to tell Ryan he could take as much advantage of me as he wanted.

We filmed that scene several more times as the sun lifted the fog. When the forest was clear of the clouds, Bay brought us over to a blanket that looked like it was made of grass and flowers. It was plastic, but the director assured me it would look real on screen. He had us lie down and then arranged us. I had to point my toes, and someone pulled my hair out behind me, I assumed artfully, and positioned my wings. They made sure Ryan's armor stayed in place, and one of the stylists fixed his hair so it wouldn't look flat.

They put our hands on the blanket between us. Totally close, but no contact.

"For this scene I again want the two of you to stare at each other. We're going to be dropping some glitter and flower petals on you. Let me know if it gets in your eyes or mouth."

There was a camera positioned above us high in the air, pointing directly down. Two ladders were set up so that crew members could shower us with petals and glitter. We did this for several minutes. Then we did another take. And another. And another until Bay called for a short break.

I sat up, rubbing glitter off my hands. "It looks like a stripper sneezed on me."

Ryan laughed and sat up next to me, stretching his arms. His big, delicious, strong arms.

I might have sighed.

His lips were close to my ear, sending hot shivers from my ears down to my toes. "Over there."

I looked to where he pointed. About forty yards away, apparently not bothered by the people, equipment, or intermittent music, I saw a mother deer and her little fawn. She paused, as if watching us, then sauntered off, her baby frolicking alongside her.

"So beautiful!" I said with a smile.

I couldn't be sure, but if I'd been asked to testify under oath, I would have sworn that he murmured, "You're beautiful."

I heard his breath hitch. My own breathing had entirely stopped.

The cameras weren't on, so the no-touching rule didn't apply. Even if we were surrounded by people, I didn't care. Apparently neither did Ryan. His palm slid across my left cheek, and I relaxed into it, craving his warmth and the feel of him. "I've wanted to do nothing else for the last two days," he told me.

I reached up to grab his hand and wrapped my fingers around his wrist. All the built-up wanting, teasing, getting so close had driven me insane. I'd never felt so physically frustrated in my entire life. "Me, too."

I heard a buzz, and before I could react, I felt something prick my face. Oh no.

"Careful," Ryan said, swatting his hand. "There's a bee."

"Too late. And I'm deathly allergic to bees."

He started yelling for the medic, and I could feel my face puffing up. There was an itching and burning sensation, like somebody had set my face on fire. I had an Epi-Pen in my purse in the wardrobe trailer. I tried to say as much, but my throat and tongue had started to swell, making it impossible to talk.

Panicking was the worst possible thing I could do, so I did my best to stay calm. Ryan, however, did not.

He yelled at everyone to do something and held on to me tightly. Fortunately, the medic had an epinephrine shot in his bag. He administered it, saying I still needed to go to a hospital. He offered a couple of places. There was a hospital in Forks, but that was about forty-five minutes away. There was also a smaller medical center about fifteen minutes north of us.

Ryan immediately chose the closer medical center.

While we waited for a car, the medic used his fingernail to get the stinger out. He washed the area where the stinger had been, then he put some hydrocortisone cream on it. The car arrived, and Ryan picked me up and carried me over. This time I was aware and awake, and it most definitely was the sexiest thing ever. I laid my still-puffy face against his shoulder. He put me into the back seat, climbed in next to me, and immediately put his arm around my shoulders. As if he couldn't stop touching me.

The medic climbed into the front seat, presumably to keep an eye on me.

During the car ride, I realized I could talk again. "How do I look?" I asked him in a strangled voice, wondering what he would say.

"Like you stared directly into the Lost Ark."

His answer so surprised me that I started to laugh, which hurt my face. "Don't make me smile."

"I'm sorry," he said, his arm tightening around me. "I'm sorry about all of this."

"It wasn't your fault. Not even Ryan De Luna can tell Mother Nature what to do."

"Yeah, she and I would be having some words right now if I could."

When we arrived at the medical center, I guessed that they'd been called and told to expect us, as none of the staff blinked an eye at our costumes.

The medic filled them in on what had happened, and they showed me to a room. I climbed into the bed, and a nurse came in to take my vitals. Another nurse put an oxygen mask on me. Ryan stood at my bedside, doing his best to both stay out of the way and be nearby.

The nurse who took my blood pressure and checked my temperature asked me questions about my medical history, like whether I'd had a reaction like this before. I moved the mask aside and told her I had, once, when I was eight. I always carried an Epi-Pen with me.

"The doctor will be in shortly," the nurse said when I'd finished answering her questions. She closed the door shut behind her.

"Why didn't you tell me you had this allergy?" Ryan had pulled up a chair on the right side of my bed and held my hand.

"When was that supposed to come up in conversation? 'Hi, I'm Maisy. I'm into music and long walks on the beach, and I'm allergic to bees'?"

"I don't know, maybe when we started filming in a forest?"

He was right, but there was no way to explain myself. While onstage in outdoor arenas and stadiums, I kept an Epi-Pen in my guitar case. When I went out, it was in my purse. But I'd taken one look at Ryan in his knight getup, listened to him sing his beautiful song to me, and stared into his gorgeous eyes, and I didn't think about bees even once.

"Did I ruin your video?"

"Screw the video." Only he didn't say *screw*. "They can make it out of what they have now. We were almost done anyway."

"I guess the important thing is that it all worked out horribly."

Ryan shook his head at me. There was a knock at a door, and a second later a harried-looking older doctor came into the room.

"I'm Dr. Martin. I understand you had a run-in with a bee and lost?" She put some antibacterial gel on her hands. Then she took out a penlight and looked in my ears and eyes and down my throat. "Isn't it a little early for Halloween?"

I would have explained, but she was using a tongue depressor on me at the time. She checked out the sting site. Then she had me sit up, and she used her stethoscope to listen to my lungs. When she was finished, she went over and washed her hands. "Given that the swelling has gone down and you seem to be able to breathe and speak, I am going to have one of the nurses bring you a prescription-strength antihistamine, and then you should be on your way."

Lauren came into the room carrying our clothes and belongings. "I have a car out front to take you back to Seattle whenever you're ready. The medic can ride with you if you want."

I was about to tell her that was unnecessary, but Ryan insisted he accompany us. I thanked Lauren for everything, and she left.

"I'm going to get changed in the bathroom," I said. I wanted to get this costume off me.

"Do you need any help?" Another serious/joking question.

"I'm a big girl, Ryan. I can do it myself. I'll be right back."

It was actually a little harder to get out of the dress and wings than I'd anticipated. The wings were completely bent and broken, and I hoped they weren't planning on using them for anything else, as they were now a lost cause. I used the facilities, washed my hands, and did my best to wash my face. A puddle of glitter surrounded me on the floor. I had the feeling that was going to be happening for a while.

When I came out, I saw that Ryan had also changed into regular clothes. Which was kind of a bummer.

A young nurse knocked on the door with a small cup on a tray. "Here you go."

"This stuff always knocks me out," I said before swallowing it.

"You're not driving, are you?"

"No, she's not," Ryan answered.

I saw the moment when the nurse realized who he was. She got really flustered. "Oh. Okay. Great. Well, here's your discharge papers with the instructions for what you should, uh, what you should do if your symptoms return."

"Thanks," I said.

"Please call us if you need anything. Anything at all." Only she said that last part to Ryan and not to me.

He thanked her as well and then took me by the hand to lead me to the waiting car. He kept his head ducked down the whole way, not wanting to be recognized.

I could tell it was too late for that. The allergy medicine kicked in, making my limbs feel lethargic and my mind fuzzy. Ryan had to keep me from stumbling more than once.

We got into the car, and I lolled my heavy head against the back of the seat. "I have glitter in places that do not bear mentioning," I murmured.

I felt him pull me in close and rest my head against his shoulder. "I was really scared today. The thought of something happening to you . . . and there was nothing I could do . . . don't ever do that again."

"I'm not in charge of the bees," I told him in a tired voice, my eyes fused shut, sleep enveloping me.

"I know." He might have kissed me on the forehead, or I might have imagined it. "It just made me realize that . . . Maisy? I think that I'm falling in—"

I passed out before he could finish his sentence.

CHAPTER SEVENTEEN

I woke up on the moving bus, not sure how I'd gotten there. "She's awake!" Cole yelled, and then all three of my brothers stared at me.

Only I wasn't in my bunk.

I was in Ryan's bed.

"Why didn't you have your Epi-Pen on you?" Parker asked.

At the same time, Fitz said, "I'm so glad you're okay."

Cole added, "It looks like somebody took a meat tenderizer to your face."

But no Ryan.

And why did my current location not freak out any of my brothers?

They were all talking at the same time, making it difficult to catch what was going on. From what I could tell, Ryan had brought me back and insisted that I sleep in his bed, as it was the most comfortable and would give me the most room, which my brothers thought was "very cool of him." Then he had a doctor who specialized in allergic reactions come in and check me out, who pronounced me fine despite the large swollen welt over the sting site. The doctor had said that the welt might get bigger over the next two days, but it would go away.

We were almost to the arena in Idaho, but Ryan had found a local band to fill in for us at the show. He hoped I'd be feeling well enough to perform once we got to Salt Lake City.

My face still hurt a little, but I felt back to normal.

Ryan, on the other hand, was anything but. When I found him in the lounge later and thanked him, he grunted out a response, never taking his eyes off the TV screen. It was not how he normally acted with me, and I wasn't sure what to do.

I called Angie to get her advice and was again met with squeals. "I saw the pictures! I need more information! Why did you star in Ryan's new music video?"

"Pictures?" I put her on speakerphone and then used the web browser.

If we hadn't been front-page news before, we were now. Literally the entire world knew.

There was article after article about how Ryan and I were dating.

It was the photo attached to those stories that made me feel like I'd just been sucker punched. Somebody had captured the moment of Ryan showing me the deer. I watched the animals with total delight.

But Ryan didn't face the deer. He faced me. And he looked at me like . . . I had captivated him. Like he wanted me. Like I was the only thing that mattered to him in the whole world.

Or maybe I was projecting, because he certainly wasn't acting like he wanted me now.

I didn't even ask Angie for her advice. I found out how my mom was doing (same) and said I'd call her later.

Was this why Ryan was acting weird? The photos? Wasn't that what he wanted to have happen?

Over the next few days, as we traveled through Idaho and Utah, Ryan stayed away from me. Which wasn't easy to do on a bus that size, but he somehow managed it. His discomfort with me made me completely uncomfortable. Made me not quite myself. For example, on the stage in Salt Lake City, I said, "Hello, Seattle!"

I discovered fans don't like it very much when you call out the wrong name of the city you're in.

During Ryan's show, I stayed in the wings, wondering if he would want me to come onstage again to sing "One More Night."

He didn't.

Thanks to the photo and rampant rumors, I had to stay off social media. Because when Ryan had initially asked me to be his pretend girlfriend, it had seemed like no big deal. I'd thought, what could possibly go wrong?

I quickly found out what could go wrong. The hatred of a million Luna-tics, for one. They attacked me online—all our videos had thousands of hateful comments. Apparently, it was all Parker could do to keep up with the vicious things put on our Facebook band page. He finally had to turn the comments off.

Was that why Ryan had grown distant? Things hadn't turned out the way he'd hoped? Did he blame me for the negative online reaction?

Some other part of me worried that I'd done or said something after I took the prescription at the medical center. Something totally humiliating that he didn't know how to get past. I would have blamed it on the medication, but that wouldn't have been why I did something stupid. My inhibitions had been lowered, and who knows? Maybe I'd tried to kiss him, which he didn't want.

I'd built up whatever things I'd felt at the music video into something they weren't.

I was way too embarrassed to ask.

It didn't help that I kept finding new and terrible ways of adding to that embarrassment. Like after the Salt Lake City show, all the guys went out, even Vince and Anton. I stayed behind, excited to have the bus to myself for the first time ever. I cranked up some loud tunes and danced around the lounge in a T-shirt and shorts.

In the middle of executing a spin, I turned to see Ryan standing near the driver's seat, watching me. I immediately blushed at being caught. I couldn't read his expression. My heart raced, pounding hard against my chest. I took a step toward him, and he left. Just walked down the stairs and out into the night.

Something had definitely changed between us. Ryan wouldn't talk to me. We were never alone. There were no more offers for fake dates or to spend time together.

Fitz even asked me if we were having problems, and he knew we weren't really dating.

Things were so bad that when the bus stopped the next day to refuel at a truck stop, I approached Diego.

Since I'd joined the tour, Diego had kept his distance. I sometimes caught him watching me with a wary expression, like he didn't trust me. Or just didn't like me.

He was smoking a cigarette, and I smiled, trying not to let the smell bother me or make me think about my father. "Hey."

"Maisy." His expression was so cold. His body language screamed that he wanted to be left alone. He held his cigarette out toward me. "You want one?"

Gross. "No, thank you."

He laughed. "I should have guessed. Smoking's prohibited on the bus. I would guess I have you to thank for no coffee on the bus, either."

There was normally coffee on the bus? There hadn't been since the tour started. Maybe that was why Ryan was grouchy. He missed his caffeine fix.

But then I remembered that he said in one of his texts he'd given up caffeine. That didn't mean that it wasn't typically around for the other band members, though.

Was I the reason for that? Had Ryan done that for me?

"The only reason he's interested in you is because you didn't try to have sex with him the first night you met. No one makes him work for it."

"I'm not making him work for it."

Diego let out a little laugh, throwing his cigarette butt to the ground and squishing it with his foot. "Aren't you?"

Was I? Was that what Ryan thought? That I was leading him on?

Diego walked away, leaving me to try and figure out what had just happened. Was he jealous or just not very nice?

The one person I could ask about it unfortunately was the one person avoiding me.

Ryan continued to ignore me clear up until we got to the show in Wyoming. The venue was about half the size of what we'd become accustomed to. As Parker greeted the crowd, before we even started our set, I heard a splat sound on the stage. Another one. What was that? Then something hit me in the head, hard. Pain radiated out from my forehead. I reached up and realized it was an egg yolk. Somebody was throwing eggs at me. Another one hit my chest.

One of the bodyguards leaped down into the crowd and chased down the egg tosser. A teen girl took advantage of this and jumped up onto the stage. She wore a shirt with Ryan's face on it. "Do you think you're good enough for him? Do you think we're going to stand by and let you have him?"

She rushed me, yelling foul things. She grabbed my hair and pulled, so I did what any reasonable woman would do. I stomped on her foot, forcing her to let go of me.

Before I could do anything else, Fox was there, pulling the girl away. My brothers helped me get off the stage.

The girl was struggling and screaming, and Fox handed her off to two other guards. "Take her outside and call the police. She just assaulted Maisy." Then he turned to me. "Are you okay?"

"I'm fine," I said, watching as egg whites dripped from my head to the ground.

Cole went to find me a towel, Parker said he'd find some aspirin, and Fitz just disappeared, leaving me alone with Ryan's bodyguard.

It was the first time I'd been alone with Fox for a while. Even though my head throbbed and that panicky feeling made my throat feel tight, I considered asking him if he knew why Ryan was being so weird. I quickly realized that even if he did, he most likely wouldn't tell me. "Why don't we ever hang out, Fox?"

"We're hanging out now," he said.

"After I got attacked? That doesn't count."

He shrugged one shoulder. "I take a lot of shifts. I'm the only one of the guards without a family. Plus, no one can take better care of Ryan than me."

"Yeah, not so much Ryan's girlfriend, though."

At that, Fox laughed, although he was trying not to. That was what my brothers and I did when times were tough. We joked, and it made me feel better.

"What do you think about Angie?" I don't know if it was the frustration I was feeling over Ryan's behavior or my own inability to figure out what I wanted from him, but somebody should be happy.

"Angie?" Fox's face softened. "She's amazing. She's dealt so well with Hector's death. She's such a good mom and so kind and giving, funny and . . ."

He trailed off when he noticed my grin. "I think you should marry her."

"I think she has to consent first."

I noticed he didn't disagree or tell me I was crazy. "You obviously have feelings for her. Maybe you should let her know."

"Maybe you should, too."

There was a commotion on the stage, and Fox went out to investigate, talking into his headset as he left.

What had he meant? Maybe I should, too? Angie knew I adored her.

Then Fitz was back with a worried-looking Ryan in tow. I realized what Fox had meant. That I should tell Ryan about my inexplicable feelings. Feelings he probably didn't want to hear about.

Was I that obvious? Had everyone figured it out? Was that why Diego was cold and Fox mentioned it so casually?

And why Ryan stayed away from me?

"Are you okay?" he asked.

"I can handle a few eggs. Although I prefer my eggs inside a cake. I also would have preferred them to throw cake at me. It wouldn't have hurt as much."

That made him laugh. Cole returned with a washcloth, which Ryan took from him. Then he sponged at the egg on my head. "Never stop surprising me, Maisy Harrison." His hand moved to where I'd been struck in the chest, and at the last second, he handed me the towel, as if realizing what he'd almost done.

Fox returned with a stricken look. "Maisy, I'm so sorry."

It took a second to register that Fox held the broken pieces of my Dreadnought in his hands. I reached for it, unable to comprehend that my favorite guitar was now in pieces.

Everybody's voices sounded far away, like echoes from the other end of a cave. It seemed like Ryan was saying he was sorry. So, so sorry. Tears filled my eyes, making it impossible to see. My throat tightened as I ran my fingers along the surface. It couldn't be fixed. Someone had totally destroyed it.

"I want more security, and I want you to press charges against everyone who did this!" Ryan yelled. Why did he even care? He'd made it more than obvious over the last few days that I didn't matter to him.

He told Fox to take me back to the bus, and he started arguing with Piper over canceling the show completely.

"It's not fair to penalize thousands of fans for the actions of a few," she said.

Ryan yelled something back, but I cradled my guitar in my arms and let Fox lead me. I still had my Gibson Les Paul, but the Dreadnought had been a part of me and my music for so long. It was like somebody had just ripped off my arm.

"I'm really sorry, Maisy. I have Larry posted at the door. Let me know if you need anything." Fox gave me one last sympathetic look and returned to the venue.

I put what was left of my guitar on my bed, not sure what else I should do. I couldn't bear the thought of just putting it in a trash can. I went into the bathroom and used some shampoo and bottled water to wash the egg out of my hair over the sink. I changed my clothes and lay down in my bunk. I tugged at the loose metal strings on the Dreadnought and felt overcome with the desire to sob again.

First things with Ryan fell apart, and now someone had destroyed my guitar. The eggs I could get over. That damage was already gone. But this? This was permanent.

Was my situation with Ryan permanently changed, too?

I would not lie here and cry about it. I wouldn't.

Even though it was still early evening, I reached into my bag and pulled out the medical kit I'd packed. I took an over-the-counter sleeping pill, wanting this day to be over.

Tomorrow had to be better.

The next day didn't start out great, either. I woke up, got out of my bunk, and used the bathroom. There was a moment when I forgot what some crazed Luna-tic had done to my Dreadnought. When I saw the mangled pieces at the foot of my bed, it all came rushing back.

Fitz leaned out of the top bunk to sleepily tell me we were almost to Missoula, Montana.

I went into the lounge since I was starving, and I found Cole drawing on a sleeping Ryan De Luna with a permanent marker.

"What are you doing?" I hissed.

Cole had the nerve to look surprised. "Piper said it's a rule that if you fall asleep in a common area, you get a Sharpie to the face."

"Not Ryan! He is going to be pissed. Weren't you the one lecturing me about not getting us fired?"

"This is totally different," he said in a loud whisper.

"Why?"

"Because this is funny." He rolled his eyes at my outrage. "We're staying at a hotel tonight. We aren't performing until tomorrow. That's plenty of time to clean it off."

I climbed into my bunk to google how to remove permanent marker from skin. The consensus seemed to be rubbing alcohol. I rummaged through my medical bag, but my bottle was missing. I knew I'd packed it. Bringing along first-aid supplies always fell to me since my brothers couldn't take their health seriously. I could have broken bones jutting through my skin, and they'd still be like, "You're fine. We don't need to go to the hospital." Sometimes I worried that I was the only thing keeping them all from dying due to botulism or a staph infection.

I heard the moment Ryan woke up and the yelling and laughter that ensued. It even sounded like some wrestling occurred.

Cole ran through the bunk alley, yelling, "It'll come off! It'll come off!"

A thudding sound let me know Ryan had tackled him.

I got out of my bunk, and they stopped fighting. Ryan immediately stood up, while Cole lay laughing on the ground. Cole had drawn cat whiskers, a cat nose, and surprised eyebrows on Ryan's face. "Do you see what your brother did?"

He didn't wait for my answer but went into the bathroom. He grabbed a bottle of water and poured it over a washcloth. He then put some soap on it and started scrubbing.

"That won't work. You need rubbing alcohol." I was torn. I wanted to go in and help him, but he'd made it obvious he didn't want anything to do with me.

"There is no alcohol of any kind on this bus," Cole called out from the floor. "Anton drank all of it."

I wondered if that was what happened to my rubbing alcohol. "I can grab some when we get to the hotel." There had to be a lobby with a gift shop.

"I can wash my own face." Ryan let out a growl of frustration since his method wasn't working. He went to his bedroom and closed the door behind him.

Part of me wanted to let him figure it out on his own. The other part of me felt responsible because someone with my DNA had done that to him.

We arrived at the hotel, which ended up being a collection of adorable log cabins with a barn, open grazing fields, and a whole swath of forest.

Which, of course, immediately made me think of the last time I'd been in a forest with Ryan, and my blood pressure spiked in response.

"This resort is a working cattle ranch," Piper told us as she passed out the room assignments. "It's one of the few places that could fit a group our size near the arena. You are welcome to participate in any of the activities during your free time."

I was told I'd be in a two-bedroom cabin with my brothers. I watched as Ryan slunk off, a hoodie pulled up over his face to prevent anyone from seeing what Cole had done. I asked Fitz to take my luggage with him to the cabin and found the main lodge. They did have a small store, and I located rubbing alcohol and cotton balls.

After I paid for them, I tucked them into my carry-on and went over to the cabin I'd seen Ryan enter. He answered the door after I knocked three times in a row.

"Let me help," I said when he answered. He stood in the doorway for a few seconds and then moved aside.

He appeared to have a cabin to himself, and the inside was nothing like the outside. I had expected moose heads, old quilts, and musty corners. Instead, the kitchen was the nicest I'd ever seen. Wooden beams held up a high vaulted ceiling, and the furniture, while comfortable and cozy-looking, was obviously expensive.

Ryan sat down at the small table in the kitchen. I took out the supplies I'd bought.

It was then it occurred to me that in order to clean his face, I was going to have to touch him.

I swallowed hard, dousing a ball in alcohol. He was just like any other guy. This was not a big deal. I could clean him up without freaking out. Then I started scrubbing his forehead, concentrating on my actions and not on how his warm, smooth skin felt beneath my fingertips. As the internet promised, the permanent marker began to lift off. "It's working," I told him.

I tried to keep my breathing even as I rubbed the cotton against the bridge of his nose and across his sculpted cheeks. He really was beautiful.

He carefully watched me the entire time. *Just get the marker off and go,* I told myself.

Finally, it was all gone. "Okay." My voice sounded strained and breathy. "Go and rinse your face with warm water and soap, and you should be good."

"Thank you." He acted like it pained him to say it. The chair scraped across the tile floor as Ryan stood. I gathered up the cotton balls and found a trash can under the sink in his kitchen. I screwed the lid on the rubbing alcohol and put it in my bag.

We both finished at the same time. Ryan came out of his bathroom drying his face off. Part of his hair was wet. He pushed his hair back, away from his forehead. "I need a haircut," he said as if he knew exactly what I was thinking and what I'd been looking at.

I do not know what possessed me to say, "I can cut it for you."

CHAPTER EIGHTEEN

Cutting his hair would be dangerous. Very dangerous. Standing so close, touching him. While my brain malfunctioned over the possibility, my mouth short-circuited and started blathering off nonsense. "It's what I do. Cut hair. Or I did. As my job. Before I came on tour with you and started playing music. My mom insisted we all have fallback jobs, and I didn't want to go to college, and beauty school sounded like the easiest thing. Although I'm sure you don't want me to do it. I'm not all that great, and you probably have someone you pay a thousand dollars an hour to cut it—"

"Sure." Ryan cut off my rambling.

I had expected him to say no. That he had somebody who would fly out and take care of that sort of thing for him. His gorgeous locks were too important to leave in the hands of a semiprofessional such as myself.

"Oh. Okay. Are you sure?" I didn't want to force him to endure my presence.

"Yes, Maisy. I'm sure. I'm getting a little scruffy." A bit of that light was back in his eyes, the teasing, intense one that made my stomach feel hollow.

"You know, we were just on the set of your music video. You could have had the professional hairstylist cut it then." Suddenly my brain shifted gears, and I wanted to cut his hair. To do something nice for him to show him I was grateful. To get the chance to be close to him.

What I didn't want was for him to agree only because . . . I was here. Still convenient.

"They wanted my hair a little longer for the video." But he didn't say anything else to reassure me.

Deciding I was an adult and could handle it, I took one of the kitchen chairs and put it next to the sink. "Sit here. It'll be easier to clean up than trying to cut your hair in the bathroom. Not that you'll be the one sweeping it up. I'm sure they'll have somebody who—" I was rambling again. "I'll be back in a second."

He did as I asked, and I went into the bathroom and grabbed the shampoo and conditioner the ranch had provided. I didn't recognize the brand but figured it would work. I also took a couple of fluffy white towels.

Then I rummaged through my bag to find my special hair scissors, a comb, and clippers. I cut my brothers' hair on a regular basis, so I brought them along in case I needed them on tour.

Ryan watched me as I walked over. "Lean forward," I told him. I stood between his legs, his arms on either side of my outer thighs. My hands shook as I put one of the towels around his neck. "I'm going to, um, wash your hair first. It's easier for me to cut wet hair."

I turned the water on, letting it run until it turned warm. I had him tilt his head back so I could get his hair under the faucet. "Is that too hot? Too cold?"

"It's just right."

I was about to wash and cut his hair. Which meant touching him even more. I let out a sigh and pushed his hair under the water. As I'd imagined, it was really soft.

This was something I had done every day for years. I'd washed the heads of thousands of people. It wasn't a big deal. It was just a job. Totally impersonal.

Unfortunately, nothing about this moment felt impersonal.

I put a small amount of shampoo in my palm and scrubbed it in. I let my fingers gently dig into his scalp, and I lathered up the shampoo. I did it slowly, enjoying the sensation of getting to touch him. The wet, silky threads of his hair slid across my hands, caressing them. I broke out all over in goose bumps.

He let out a soft groan of pleasure. "That feels really good."

My knees buckled. Literally buckled. They smacked into the cabinet under the sink, but I caught myself before I landed in his lap.

Concentrate! Instead of lingering, I tried to be all business. It didn't help that he sighed and relaxed even more, obviously liking what I was doing. I was so intent on trying to finish that I didn't notice when my hair fell across his face until he tugged gently on the ends.

"Sorry for hitting you in the face with my unruly hair," I said. I turned off the water and dried my hands. Then I dried his hair with the same towel. I ignored how close I had to stand to him to do this.

"I don't mind," he said after I finished. "I'm curious. Why do you keep your hair so long?"

"Get up for a second." He stood, and I repositioned the chair in the middle of the room so his hair wouldn't get into cabinets or on countertops. "You can sit." I got my scissors and comb and waited while he sat back down again.

"You didn't answer my question," he reminded me.

That was probably because I had been trying desperately not to make eye contact with him. My pulse still hadn't quite recovered from how much he'd liked getting his hair washed. "It's not even that long right now. I cut six inches off a few weeks ago. Anyway, when I was little, *Rapunzel* was my favorite fairy tale. I wanted to grow my hair down to the floor until Parker pointed out that she grew her hair long to let her kidnapper in and out of her prison. Which sort of ruined the whole thing for me. Then it was because I wanted to be strong like Samson."

My scissors stilled. I'd never told anyone that before. Not even my brothers.

"Why did you need to be strong?"

I pulled up a section of his hair and snipped. Muscle memory took over, making it so that I could cut and chat at the same time. "Because my mom needed me to be. She relied on all of us a lot. She did her best, but in the end, she was devoted to a man who didn't care about her. Or us." My throat felt thick, as if I'd suffered another bee sting. I cleared it, wanting a lighter note. "Now I don't know. It's my best feature."

"As a guy, please allow me to tell you that it is not your best feature."

Blood rushed out of my brain, leaving me light-headed. "Oh? What is?"

"I'm too much of a gentleman to say."

I hit him on the shoulder, and he laughed, and it felt like nothing bad had ever happened between us. We were back to being Maisy and Ryan again. Or Mayan, the couple name the tabloid sites had taken to using.

"I'm messing with you," he said. "Your eyes are your best feature. Not only because they're beautiful, but also because before I met you I didn't know how much eyes could convey. How I've never felt more like my real self than when you look at me."

I was so glad I was standing behind him and he couldn't see me, because I had not prepared snark for that statement. "Trying to write a lyric?" was all I came up with. I cut his hair quickly, faster than I'd ever cut hair before. I needed to be finished and leave.

"Trying to tell the truth."

We were silent as I focused on his hair. I grabbed the clippers and finished the bottom half. I was satisfied with how it turned out, but I kept turning his words over in my head. Why was he suddenly being nice again? Flirty?

Saying things I shouldn't want him to say?

"All done." I began to pack up my stuff, wanting to get clear of his cabin before I did something stupid. Much as I did two seconds later when I asked, "Why would you say something like that to me? You've

spent the last few days doing nothing but avoiding me. People are noticing." I noticed. All the time. And it was making me miserable.

He turned around in the chair so he could look at me. "I feel terrible about everything that's happened. Not only at the concert with the
eggs and your guitar but also what my fans are saying online. I knew
some people would be upset. I didn't think they'd all go crazy. The label's
happy, though. No such thing as bad publicity for them."

"There's something you're not saying." I could hear it in his voice.
He was holding back.

He gulped, looking deeply uncomfortable. "I said something to
you that I shouldn't have."

Ryan had been a total gentleman with me. What could he possibly
be talking about? "When?"

"In the car. After the doctor visit."

"When I was passed out? The last thing I remember was walking
through the medical center."

A dozen different emotions crossed his face. "You don't remember
what I said?"

"What did you say?"

"It doesn't matter."

The thundering in my chest made me think it did matter.

A lot.

"I miss you." I blurted out the words, surprising myself. I didn't
know where that confession came from, only that it was the truth. "I
miss my friend." At some point Ryan had become my friend. My very
hot, very sexy friend, but still my friend. I missed spending time with
him. Laughing with him. Playing music with him.

At that, he stood and pulled the towel away from his neck. He
walked over to where I waited next to the kitchen table. "Maisy, what
do you think is going on here?"

"A haircut?" I asked, every nerve ending tingling in response to
being close to him again.

"I mean between us. What do you think is going on between us?"

I was confused. "You hired me to be your fake girlfriend."

"And the fact that we're attracted to each other means what?" His voice was deep, gruff.

Molten heat filled my veins, making it hard to think. "I'm not . . . you're not . . ." But I couldn't deny what he'd said. I was ridiculously attracted to him. As he was to me. I realized he wouldn't have said "we" if he didn't feel what I felt.

But he was still Ryan De Luna. Still a musician. Still had the ability to shatter my heart. He'd stopped speaking to me for a few days, and I'd totally fallen apart. What would I do if I fell in love with him and he betrayed me? Or walked away?

I wouldn't recover.

"It's just a side effect. From pretending to be in love for the video. I mean, we are in close proximity all the time. Some of your fans think I'm stalking you." My attempted explanation, my stab at saying something lighthearted, fell flat.

"I'm also in close proximity to Piper all the time, but I don't think about her the things I think about you." His fingers went around my waist and pulled me against him, the contact explosive. My breath caught as delicious heat consumed me, the flames licking and biting as they traveled across my skin. I closed my eyes for a second, unable to sort out so much sensory stimuli all at once. My limbs felt drugged, too heavy to move or use.

When I opened my eyes, he stared down at me with his fiery gaze, and my knees threatened to give way again. "I know what I want. But I don't want to pressure you or influence you. Think about what you want. About what this means. When you figure it out, come and find me." He said it with so much confidence. He was so sure. As if he knew something I didn't and was waiting for me to catch up.

Then he released me, walked over to his front door, and held it open. His touch had apparently disconnected my legs, and it took a few moments for my brain to regain possession. When I could move again, I grabbed my bag.

I paused in the doorway, feeling like I should say or do something.

Instead, I just left, my mind and heart jumbled up. What did Ryan want from me?

More important, what did I want from Ryan?

What I wanted and what I needed were two very different things. I had my rules for excellent reasons. I didn't arbitrarily wake up one day and decide I would stay away from musicians. Yes, they were passionate people who loved music the same way I did, but they were flaky and commitment-shy and broke hearts. Women lined up just to breathe the same air they did. Pleeches were willing to do absolutely anything to be close to regular musicians. They were a thousand times worse when it came to guys like Ryan. I didn't want to always feel insecure, to always be wondering if my significant other would be faithful to me.

Rules are made to be broken.

Ryan's words echoed in my head, but he was wrong. Rules were meant to keep us safe. To protect us.

Yes, I was attracted to him. Along with every other heterosexual female on the planet. That didn't mean I had to act on it. We could stay friends. Good friends. Who enjoyed each other's company and did not get physical.

Because if I kissed Ryan, there'd be no going back. I'd cross a line I couldn't uncross. I already felt so many complicated things for him. If I added cuddling, hand-holding, and kissing, I knew it would destroy me.

That's what I would tell him. I would keep pretending to be his girlfriend for as long as he needed me to, but that had to be it.

When I went around a bend to our cabin, I saw two people pressed up against one of the walls seriously making out. Like they'd chosen that spot solely to make a mockery of my decision. As I got closer, I realized it was Fitz and Piper. They were wrapped up in each other, oblivious to everything around them.

My first reaction was a combination of "Good for them!" and "Ew, disgusting."

Then my heart and my stomach ached, wanting that kind of passion for myself. With Ryan.

They didn't even notice as I walked by. So much for Piper never dating someone she toured with.

Rules are made to be broken.

Maybe Ryan was right. And I was wrong. Maybe he wouldn't crush my soul and my heart. Maybe we had a chance.

Maybe, like Fitz and Piper, I deserved some happiness in my life.

The next day my brothers decided to do some of the activities the ranch provided, like horse roping or cattle riding or something. I just needed my steak to be on a plate. I didn't need to know what it did during its downtime.

Although everything Fitz said now seemed suspect. Was he really going off with Cole and Parker? Or did he have secret plans to meet up with Piper? Did my other brothers know about them? I guessed they didn't, because there would be relentless tormenting if they knew.

I wondered what they would do if they found out what I was considering when it came to Ryan.

"What are you going to do today?" Parker had asked just before they left.

"I was planning on going for a walk." A walk right over to Ryan's cabin.

My rational, logical self kept reminding me that keeping my distance was the best thing I could do. The smart choice. I didn't want to lose his friendship.

But you could have so much more than just friendship! I'd never dated anyone seriously before. The idea of Ryan being my boyfriend, for real, was thrilling in a way I hadn't ever experienced. I wanted to be with him. It was time to take a chance.

After tonight's show we would have an entire week off. My brothers were going to rent a car and drive over to Billings because Parker's favorite band (entirely female, naturally) was playing. I had suggested flying home, but nobody else wanted to. I supposed I would tag along but didn't have any definite plans yet.

Maybe Ryan and I could spend some time together. Just the two of us. With no overprotective siblings nearby.

I decided to text Ryan to see if he was in his cabin. Often in the mornings and afternoons, he had radio and magazine interviews. I couldn't find my phone anywhere. I had just located it on the back of the toilet (?) when the front door opened and shut.

I heard Fitz's voice. I wondered if he had a secret rendezvous planned that I was about to mess up.

But Piper wasn't with him. He was on his phone. "We've got a few weeks left on the tour, and then we can get it ready to put on the market. If you're right about how fast it will sell, we need to be home in order to move our stuff out."

Unable to believe what I was hearing, I walked slowly to the living room. Fitz's eyebrows shot up his forehead. He was shocked to see me.

"I'll call you back later. Thanks." He hung up.

"What was that?" I half expected him to say it was none of my business.

"I told you about the house. I've been talking to a couple of real estate agents." He wouldn't look at me. He went into the kitchen, got out a glass, and filled it with water from the sink.

"You said we might have to sell. We're making so much money now, and I got us caught up." I'd been going through all kinds of things to make sure we were okay financially. I'd even been forced to give up my favorite guitar for it.

Fitz drank the entire glass, and I wondered if he was trying to avoid talking about it. But I was not going to let him get out of this conversation, and he seemed to know it. "We're gambling on the chance that we'll get more tours and more sales after this. We may not, Maze. This may be all there is. Especially with the way Ryan's fans are reacting to the news that the two of you are 'dating.'" He used his fingers to make air quotes. "We may be the most hated band in America by the time we're done."

He was saying this was my fault. I had agreed to something I never would have agreed to normally just to keep our mom in Century Pacific. And now he was saying it was my fault?

I was too mad to even speak.

"We have to act like this is all there is. If we sell the house, save all the money, and use just the interest, that will be enough to pay for Mom's care for as long as she needs it."

I noticed he didn't say the rest of her life, even though deep down, we all knew that was the case.

"Especially given how upset Ryan seems to be with you lately, I've been really, really worried. We have enough money from the tour to live off for a while, but we both have to realize that this could all go away tomorrow and act accordingly. We may not need the money from the tour once we sell the house, but your relationship will affect our ability to get future gigs. If Ryan's hurt or bitter, he could ruin our reputation with every venue, every promoter, with a single tweet. We'd never work again."

While he was not being explicit, his tone implied what he wanted to say. That he had warned me to stay away from Ryan. To not let it become real. Because as I knew too well, every real relationship eventually ended. And then we'd be fired because Ryan wouldn't want his ex-girlfriend on tour with him. He'd fired the previous opening act for less. I hadn't listened to Fitz, and now all our futures were threatened because of it.

"I'm sorry, Maze. I know how you feel. It's how we all feel. None of us wants to sell the house. But we don't have a choice. It's what has to be done."

My brother walked by me and patted me on the shoulder as he left me alone with my thoughts and regrets. I sank down onto the couch, letting my phone slip out of my hand. I couldn't text Ryan now. I couldn't do anything to risk my professional relationship with him. This job was too important.

It mattered more than anything else.

Including my heart.

CHAPTER NINETEEN

Later that afternoon, my brothers and I ran through our sound check, and I hid in our dressing room until it was time to perform. Then we did our show, ignoring some random boos and name-calling, and I tried my hardest to give everything I had to the music and the audience.

After we were finished, I should have left. Gone back to our cabin and avoided Ryan the same way he'd been avoiding me.

Instead, I stood off in the wings and watched his show. Like I was some kind of glutton for punishment. Reminding myself of all the things I couldn't have, no matter how badly I wanted them.

I knew every lyric, costume, and scenery change by heart. So when they altered it by bringing out a piano for Ryan, I couldn't stop my hopeful reaction. Would he want us to duet again? My heart leaped with excitement.

"I know fans hate when musicians do this, but I've been working on a new song, and if you don't mind, I'd like to sing it for you now." The arena erupted into cheers, which didn't surprise me. Ryan could have said he was going offstage to poop, and his fans would have been just as thrilled.

He started the song, and I immediately recognized the melody as the one he'd played for me at the after-party. The one he hadn't finished the lyrics for yet.

She's the one who's not easy to impress
She's the one who's just as beautiful in jeans or
    in a dress
She's the one, but she'll never confess
And in my dreams she's there beside me
Her head upon my chest

It's how she dances when she thinks no one sees
It's the way her touch knocks me down to my
    knees
Her laugh, her eyes, her heart, she drives me crazy
She's my girl
She's my Maisy

My heart beat so loud I was sure everyone around me could hear it. I leaned against a speaker for support since my legs wobbled so badly. No man had ever sung to me before, let alone written an entire song about me. It was both the most wonderful and the most terrifying thing I'd ever experienced. Terrifying because of how it made me feel.

And because of what it might make me do.

She's the one with long hair to her hips
She's the one comeback queen that never slips
And I'm the one moonstruck by her lips
Loving everything about her from her stare to
    fingertips

It's how she dances when she thinks no one sees
It's the way her touch knocks me down to my
    knees

Her laugh, her eyes, her heart, she drives me crazy
She's my girl
She's my Maisy

Oh she doesn't even know
The magic she holds inside her soul
And when I hear her voice I come undone
She's the one, she's the one

It's how she dances when she thinks no one sees
It's the way her touch knocks me down to my
     knees
Her laugh, her eyes, her heart, she drives me crazy
She's my girl, Maisy.

"It's a good thing we like that dude," Cole commented, his arms crossed. I hadn't even realized my brothers were standing behind me.

"Yeah, otherwise bad things would be happening right now," Parker agreed.

Bad things were happening. Because I had ceased to care beyond this moment. Without thinking, I walked out onto the stage. Ryan had already finished his song and seemed surprised when the cheers of the crowd suddenly grew even louder. He turned and saw me.

He stood and stepped away from the piano. He looked adorably unsure, as if he didn't know what would happen next.

When I reached him, he said, "I told you I was terrible with lyrics."

I couldn't help myself.

I kissed him.

The shock of our lips finally touching was like being pushed into a pool of ice water. I was shaking, drowning in him. Every part of my body was heavy and slow, my breath stolen. We didn't touch in any other way; only our mouths connected.

A few moments later, we both pulled back, like we'd just surfaced from that icy pool, both breathing heavily. Ryan seemed momentarily stunned.

Until he wasn't.

He gathered me in his arms, making a sound at the back of his throat that was deep and heart-flutteringly masculine. I had only a second to appreciate his strength and heat until one of his hands moved to hold my face. He stared into my eyes before his lips descended. This time it was fire. His mouth devastated mine, like a wildfire blazing, destroying, eating up everything in its path. He consumed me. I could only cling to him, unable to move or breathe as he burned.

Ryan inflamed every molecule in my body as he kissed me over and over again. My limbs seemed to melt away, leaving behind nothing but ash. I felt so deliciously light that I could have floated away.

The intense, crackling heat continued, turning my brain liquid and preventing any thought but this. *I want more of this.*

I wanted everything he could give me and more.

I'd imagined my attraction to him would diminish once we kissed. That I had built it up so much in my mind that reality couldn't possibly compare.

Reality was a billion times better.

My mouth opened to his, and he somehow made the fire burn hotter. The flame twisted and twined inside me, taking all that I had to offer. He wanted everything I could give him, too, and more.

His hands were everywhere—on my neck, around my waist, on my back, pushing me closer. Wanting to scorch and brand me his.

To make sure I wouldn't forget.

It was, without question, the most amazing kiss of my entire life. As if every other kiss before this one had been a rehearsal, and now I was finally playing for a sold-out stadium. Totally, completely unforgettable. I knew that even if I lived to be 107 years old, I would never forget for one second what this felt like.

It was better than when I played music, and I didn't know that there was anything better than that.

I would never be the same again.

The fire had a song all its own, a frantic rhythm that thudded through my veins, and I could feel the same music inside Ryan. Beating, pulsating, and dancing in the same way. We kissed with a perfect harmony, like our duet onstage together. Flowing and soul-piercing and beyond anything else I'd ever known.

At the moment I felt like I couldn't possibly take any more, that I would combust into a thousand glittery pieces, Ryan gentled the kiss. He made the fire he had stoked retreat, slowly dousing the flames until he softly, achingly, moved his mouth away from mine.

We were trying to catch our breaths, as the flames had consumed all the oxygen, leaving us without any to breathe.

I groaned in frustration, fingers curling into the fabric of his shirt, not wanting him to stop. He still held me tightly.

"Hi," he said, his voice tinged with desire that beckoned me to come closer.

"Hi," I responded. My lungs were too constricted to allow me to say much beyond that.

"We, uh, have company."

I turned my head in the direction he indicated. The entire arena had fallen silent. I had forgotten they were there. Where we were.

There had been only Ryan.

Then the audience exploded into applause and screams, louder than any I'd ever heard.

"Wait for me. In my dressing room."

In that moment, Ryan could have asked me for anything and I would have said yes. I nodded.

He reluctantly released me, and I pulled my own hands free, stepping back.

"Ryan?"

"Yeah?"

I couldn't wipe the grin off my face. "*That* was the best thing that has ever happened to my mouth."

He winked at me. "Told you."

Then he went over to the microphone. "Maisy Harrison, everybody!"

I gave a half-hearted wave and hurried offstage as quickly as I could. My brothers were no longer waiting in the wings, for which I was grateful.

Fox stood outside Ryan's dressing room. He nodded. "Maisy."

"Hey, Fox."

"That was some kiss."

"What? How do you know that?" It had just happened, and Fox was backstage. How could he possibly know about it already?

"I get alerts on Ryan. Just to keep an eye out for crazies. My phone about exploded a minute ago." He turned the screen toward me. There was a video of Ryan and me kissing. And it was almost as hot watching it as it had been experiencing it.

It bothered me that, thanks to technology, everybody would see our first kiss. But, to be fair, I was the one who had chosen to go out onstage and kiss a world-famous pop star with tens of thousands of witnesses.

"He is my boyfriend" was my weak response. I got the feeling, though, that Fox didn't miss a thing and knew exactly what was going on.

I went into the dressing room, ignoring his smirk. Fitz was going to kill me. He'd just gotten through lecturing me about how I'd put things in jeopardy, and now I'd kissed Ryan De Luna, and the entire internet knew.

Forget Fitz. The Luna-tics would be worse. If they were throwing eggs before, what would they throw at me now? Anvils?

As the endorphins and riled-up hormones began to wear off, I had a good forty-five minutes to completely freak out. What had I just done with Ryan?

Kissed him in front of the whole world?

I walked around the room, trying to distract myself. I found a large jar that was halfway full of red gummy bears. It seemed weird, considering Ryan didn't really eat sugar. I picked it up just as the dressing-room door opened.

Ryan.

I held the gummy-bear jar against my stomach, as if that would keep him at bay. Something in my eyes must have told him to keep his distance because he sat down on a couch, rubbing a towel over his sweaty hair.

"Why do you have a jar of red gummy bears?"

"It's part of my rider. I ask for a single red gummy bear at every performance, and then I add it to the jar."

I blinked. "Why?"

"Sometimes artists put extravagant things in riders because they're divas. Sometimes it's for comfort. And sometimes it's to make sure the venue is reading the fine print. Because if they're not, given a highly physical show like mine, it could cause safety issues. No red gummy bear, then we have a problem because we know they weren't paying attention." He leaned forward, resting his elbows on his knees. "But do you really want to talk about riders or gummy bears right now?"

"Honestly, I don't really want to talk at all right now." I wanted to escape and not face the choice I had made.

"I don't want to talk, either." He flashed me a wolfish grin that made even my toenails blush. "But we probably should, right?"

"I still can't believe I did that."

"There's video if you need proof." He held up his phone.

"I've seen it." And relived it about a thousand times, thanks.

"Are you worried about what people are saying online?"

"No. I'll start caring about internet trolls' opinions when I can start paying bills with them."

"Did you not like the kiss?"

"Not like . . ." Had he not been there? "You mean besides the fact that I saw through space and time?"

Another predatory grin. "Then I'm not sure why you're cowering over there instead of coming over here to enjoy round two."

I wasn't cowering! Okay, I might have been cowering a tad.

Ryan stood and began walking toward me slowly, like I was a wounded animal that would bite him if frightened. "Did you like the song?"

Like it? I'd been ready to have its babies. "No."

He hesitated, his face falling. "No?"

"I mean, no, I didn't just like it. It's . . ." I trailed off, not knowing how to convey to him what it had made me feel. "I spend all my free time trying to funnel my emotions into words, and I can't even think of anything nice enough to tell you how much I loved it."

"That's one of the best compliments I've ever received for my work."

"All those Grammy Awards don't count?"

"Not nearly as much." Now he was close. He reached out and gently pried my fingers off the jar, then put it down on the table.

"I haven't figured anything out," I blurted before he could do anything else. "Earlier? That wasn't a decision. It was . . . more of a reaction."

He had a slight frown that quickly disappeared. "I can wait."

"It's not just that. My brothers are all convinced that something will happen between us, we'll break up, and you'll fire us. We really need this job. And a good-enough reputation to get future jobs."

His hands settled on my hips. "Is that what's got you worried? I promise I won't fire you. No matter what. Even if I catch you cheating on me with Vince."

I smiled at the image of me kissing our bus driver.

"I also promise not to hurt your chances of getting any other gig. I'll put all that in writing if you want." He urged me closer, and I didn't resist. In part because he'd just erased one of the things I was most worried about. He'd lifted a huge burden off my shoulders, and I almost felt as light as I had earlier when we'd kissed.

He rested his forehead against mine. Our chests rose and contracted in unison, our breath mingling together. I closed my eyes, loving the feeling of standing so close to him.

"In an hour I'm going to California for the US Music Awards. Be my date for the show. Come with me."

To California? Together? We'd only just kissed for the first time. His offer made me take a step back. I wasn't worried about getting fired, but I was worried about my ability to resist his masculine wiles if we were alone. I wasn't ready for that. "What? I can't, you know, go away with you."

"Fox, Vince, and one of the other drivers are coming, too. It's an eighteen-hour drive, and they have to switch off."

I walked around him, rubbing my arms. His touch still managed to make me all shivery. It was better that he wasn't suggesting we go off alone together. But that would be a long road trip. I sat on the couch he'd recently vacated. "Flying must be terrible for you."

He sat next to me. "I've tried everything. Hypnosis, sedatives, therapy, special training courses designed to help you get over your fear of flying. I just can't."

I nodded. It wasn't like I had anything else planned, but this felt like a really big step. Was I ready to take that kind of risk?

"I'll make you a bet. If I win, you come with me. If you win, you stay here and be miserable and miss me every second." He leaned back and settled into the corner of the couch.

"What kind of bet?"

Ryan considered this. "I bet I can guess your birthday."

Well, he had a one-in-365 chance of getting it right. My birthday was actually in two weeks, something that had slipped my mind in the chaos that had become my life. He'd never guess it. I would win, and he would leave me behind.

Was that disappointment I felt?

"Do we have a deal?" He held out his hand, offering to shake on it.

"Deal." Tingles shot through my arm as he enveloped my hand.

Before we'd even stopped shaking, he said, "May thirtieth."

My mouth dropped open. "How did you do that?"

"Your brothers told me."

"That's cheating," I said, pushing against his shoulder while he laughed. "That doesn't count."

"I hedge my bets. It wasn't cheating. Besides, you didn't set that as a parameter at the beginning. The win is good."

It wasn't something I wanted to argue about. I was glad he'd won. And that he'd found a way for me to say yes that seemed less big and scary. "Then I guess I'm coming to California with you."

He tugged on my hand and jerked me forward, surprising me. I sprawled across his chest, and his lazy grin let me know that was exactly what he'd wanted.

"What's that saying? To the victor go the spoils?"

His hand went around the back of my neck as his gaze focused on my lips. Breathing became virtually impossible. His thumb caressed the bottom of my earlobe, and it took every ounce of willpower I had not to purr like a cat. I needed him to kiss me now to end this torment.

But he didn't move. Didn't lean his head forward to connect us. He stayed put, like he was enjoying just watching me. My frustration and tension began to mount.

"If that's your way of saying you're going to kiss me, I'm okay with it." I really was.

That first kiss had to be a fluke. Some kind of once-in-a-lifetime, stars-aligned, cosmically ordained situation. We could have only one first kiss, and nothing else could live up to all that anticipation, all that wanting and waiting.

Right?

"I like that we think so much alike. That we're so similar." His voice had that hazy, growly thing going on, and my stomach plummeted into my toes.

It wasn't true. There were so many ways in which we were complete opposites. "Not quite. Did you forget you're El Caliente and I'm the Ice Queen?"

"Sweetheart, do you know what happens when fire meets ice?"

"Water?"

He shook his head. "Steam."

He was right. Complete, total, and utter steam.

Our first kiss had been no fluke.

CHAPTER TWENTY

I packed quickly and explained to my brothers what was happening. Ryan had graciously extended the invitation to them as well, but they were either grossed out by the idea of watching us together or didn't want to intrude.

Fitz glowered disapprovingly in the kitchen. I told him about Ryan's promise, but it didn't seem to ease his mind. Cole made a perfunctory effort to talk me out of it, but I ignored him. I was an adult and could make my own decisions.

It seemed like a waste of money to use the entire bus for just Ryan and me, but I understood his flying phobia. Not to mention that since I'd spent so much time there already, it was starting to feel a little like home to me.

And whether that feeling was because of the bus or Ryan, I wasn't sure.

Once we got onboard, considering how late it was already, we decided to go to sleep. I went into the bathroom to change and brush my teeth.

When I came out, I was surprised to find Ryan climbing into Fitz's bunk above mine. "You have a huge, comfortable bed in the back," I said.

"I know. I'd rather be here."

That caused a series of funny twinges in my heart. I got into the bunk and lay on my right side. It was weird to think of Ryan being so close.

Then he put his left hand over the side. I reached up and interlaced my fingers with his.

"Good night, Maisy."

"See you in the morning, Ryan."

I fell asleep that way, holding on to his hand.

I wondered what Ryan and I would do with all that time together. Fox didn't really interact with us unless we stopped somewhere to get gas or grab something to eat. He pretty much stayed in his bunk.

Ryan and I played video games (where he got to experience repeated failure for the first time in his life), watched movies, and talked. A lot. About everything. Even though I kept telling myself we were from different worlds, we had more in common than we didn't.

My favorite activity (besides kissing) was playing music. We wrote. We played all kinds of songs together. I'd never realized it was possible to connect with someone on so many levels.

When we finally arrived in Los Angeles, Vince took us directly to Ryan's home. Ryan lived in an expensive, upscale gated community in Calabasas. As the bus driver unloaded our luggage, I realized it hadn't occurred to me that I didn't have anywhere to stay for the week we were here. For some reason I thought we'd stay on the bus, but that wasn't a possibility, given that Vince was currently driving away.

I could have gone home, but there were four guys I didn't know very well staying there. Fitz's friend had invited some buddies to crash, which my brothers were fine with, but I didn't feel comfortable staying there.

Angie would probably let me sleep on her couch. I tried texting her, but I didn't get a response. I grumbled, frustrated.

"What's wrong?" Ryan asked as we walked up the driveway to his ridiculous mansion.

"I just realized I didn't make any arrangements for while we're in LA. There're strange guys at my house, and Angie's not answering her phone."

"Stay here."

I desperately wanted to. My mouth even opened and started to say the word *yes*.

Which probably meant it was a bad idea. I didn't want him to get the wrong idea about what was going to happen between us. "I should go to a hotel." I'd have to rent a car as well. Spending that kind of money wouldn't make Fitz happy.

As if he understood my concern, he said, "Fox will be here, and so will my aunt Bibi. We will be well chaperoned, I promise. I have a lot of extra room in this house. You can choose whatever bedroom you want."

"Okay." The word came out involuntarily. I was only thinking of my brother. For Fitz's financial peace of mind, I would stay at Ryan's. To distract myself from the lie, I asked, "Your aunt Bibi?"

"My mother's sister. She's Diego's mom. She took me in after my mom died and raised us together. Until my dad decided I should be a pop star. Now she handles my fan club and most of my social media."

The front door opened, and a forty-something Hispanic woman with Diego's features stepped out. She folded Ryan into a hug before he could even say hello. "Welcome home!" she exclaimed.

After she finished with her nephew, she turned her attention on me. "You must be Maisy."

At first I was flattered, thinking Ryan must have talked about me, but if she was in charge of his social media, of course she would recognize me.

"Nice to meet you." I held out my hand to her.

"We don't shake hands in this house. We hug." She pushed my arm aside and pulled me in tight. Her perfume reminded me of my mom's, as did her embrace. It had been a long time since I'd had a motherly-type person hug me, and it was better than I remembered.

It made me want to cry.

"Much as I'd love to catch up, tonight is my book club. There is an enchilada casserole in the fridge. Give me a call if you need anything else." Bibi kissed Ryan on the cheek and then headed out through the front door.

Leaving Ryan and me alone.

"I thought we were going to have chaperones."

"In a sense. Bibi lives in the guesthouse, and Fox and the security team stay in the pool house. The bedrooms are upstairs. Come on."

I finally got a good look at his place. The first thing that struck me was how much light there was. Everything felt bright and airy. The ceilings were high, the windows enormous. The walls were gleaming white with a dark-wood trim.

His home managed to be comfortable and cozy while still being big enough to host a Super Bowl. Not a Super Bowl viewing party, the actual game itself.

"So nobody sleeps in this house except you?" I clarified. Would he understand that I wasn't ready to do anything beyond making out? Or that I was desperately afraid being alone together in his home might tempt me to change my mind? "This is not what I was led to believe about the sleeping situation."

"I promise I can control myself," Ryan said, dropping a brief kiss on my lips. "But just barely."

Trying not to blush, I followed him into a frilly, feminine bedroom. I'd never considered myself to be a girlie girl, but there was something about the canopied bed, mauve pillows, and sparkly chandelier that spoke to my inner princess.

"I thought you might like this one."

"You were right." I dropped my bags.

"I'll let you get settled. When you're ready, come downstairs and I'll feed you." He backed out of the room, grinning at me. "My bedroom is the third door down the hallway, on the right. Just in case. I want to make sure you know where to find me. If you want me."

I chucked one of the pillows at him and listened as his laughter trailed down the hallway.

I kicked off my shoes and let my toes luxuriate in the expensive rug that covered the hardwood floors. I decided to take a very long shower and get changed.

When I went downstairs to the kitchen, I saw that Ryan had done the same. He was so beautiful that sometimes he stopped me dead in my tracks.

"What are you staring at?" he teased as he pulled the casserole out of the oven.

"I was just admiring what a good job I did on your hair," I responded, sitting down at the kitchen table. "Or maybe I'm just in shock at the sight of you actually cooking."

"I can cook. As long as there're very detailed instructions and somebody else has done all the preparing and putting it together first."

"Which means you can reheat things. Not cook."

"What about you? Do you cook?" He took out a metal spatula and cut some square pieces for us. He put them on plates.

"I'm lacking that particular gene. The only thing I'm good at is brownies."

He brought me one of the plates and a fork. "Why brownies?"

"My mom has a secret recipe that's been handed down for generations. She promised to pass it along to me, but she had her accident before she could. So I've been trying to re-create them for years. Nothing's ever quite right."

"I'd like to meet your mom."

I had a bite of food almost to my wide-open mouth when his words made me freeze. "Why?"

Ryan shrugged. "She's someone important to you, and I've already met everyone else who's important to you. Just like you've officially met everyone important to me."

That caused a hysterical panic that I hadn't felt since . . . after I'd kissed him onstage. He seemed to bring out that feeling in me a lot.

Probably because his request indicated a level of seriousness and commitment that shouldn't have existed in our fake relationship.

Was it still fake, though? We were kissing. Being affectionate. Spending all our free time together. I was eating dinner with him in his house after traveling with him halfway across the country to get here. And I'd be sleeping here tonight.

"I have to meet with my agent and my dad tomorrow, and then there're a few rehearsals for the USMAs starting the day after that. Maybe closer to the end of the week, before we head back and meet everybody in North Dakota?"

"Okay." Much as I'd agreed to stay there without thinking, now I did the same thing about him meeting my mom.

Admittedly, some part of me wanted them to meet, even if she would immediately forget.

"Do you want to come to the rehearsals, too?"

That I definitely wanted to do. "Absolutely." Not for any business purpose. I should be doing my best to network and make some new connections in the industry. Instead, and despite the fact that I'd already seen him a bunch of times, I wanted to watch Ryan perform.

I wanted to be where he was.

My phone rang before I could finish my potential freak-out. I didn't want to interrupt our first dinner together, but if it was one of my brothers, they would call until I picked up. I glanced at the screen. "It's Angie. Excuse me a second."

I walked into the family room and answered. "Hey! Guess who's in LA?"

"You and Ryan De Luna. Your *boyfriend*."

"How did you know that?"

"I read ENZ every day, thank you very much." She sounded insulted that I'd questioned her knowledge of the movements of pop stars. "Ryan's supposed to perform at the USMAs this week. I figured he would come. I just didn't know you'd be here, too. This is excellent."

Ignoring her implication, I said, "I'm going to visit my mom tomorrow. Do you want to get dinner after that? And maybe hang out with me at the USMAs rehearsals? If you can get the time off?"

"I can probably take one sick day this week, but that's it. Your timing is perfect, though. Hector's parents asked to keep the baby for the next few days, so I'm free to hang out and do whatever. I would love to have dinner and go to some rehearsals! And make sure your man's good enough for you."

There was no point in rolling my eyes since she couldn't see me. "Sounds good. I'll text you later with the details."

"I'm assuming your lover boy is nearby, but when we're alone, you will tell me about that song and that kiss because I completely died when I saw it."

"Talk to you later!" I said, not knowing if Ryan could hear her or not. She tended to be loud on the phone.

"What did Angie have to say?" Ryan asked as I sat back down.

Nothing I could repeat to him. "We planned to have dinner tomorrow night." I have no idea what possessed me to add on, "Do you want to come?"

"Yeah. That sounds fun."

"Bring Fox. I want him and Angie to get married."

"Do they know that?"

"They do, but they're being stubborn." I told him about Hector and how he and Fox had served together. And all the cute little glances I'd observed between them the night Ryan and I met, and how Fox didn't deny that he had feelings for her.

We finished eating, and Ryan asked if I wanted more. I told him I was stuffed, and after I thanked him for the meal, I got up to clear the plates.

"What are you doing?" he asked. "You're my guest."

"You 'cooked' and served; I wash up. That's how it works."

Which consisted of rinsing off our plates and forks and sticking them in the dishwasher while Ryan packed up the rest of the casserole.

We were being so domestic, and it felt . . . strangely natural. Not like we were playing house. Like it was the real thing. As if we'd done this a million times before and would do it a million more.

"I'm kind of beat," Ryan said. "Feel like watching a movie and then turning in?"

"Sure. If I get to pick." Our bus choices had been mainly his favorites since it was his bus and his movies. He really liked movies about music stars and explosions, and old black-and-whites.

I dried my hands and followed him into the living room. He logged me in to the streaming service attached to his TV, and I chose one of my favorites, *Say Anything*. "Have you seen this before?" I asked.

"Nope."

"That should be listed in the Geneva Convention as a crime against humanity," I told him. "One of the greatest movies ever. My mom used to watch it religiously. Sometimes when I visit her, we just sit and watch it together. It's like the 1980s answer to *Romeo and Juliet*." *Say Anything* didn't come out until after my mom had graduated from high school, so at every viewing it was like she was seeing it for the first time.

He leaned against the couch, and without overthinking things, I cuddled into his side. His arm went around my shoulders.

Ryan, however, did not seem impressed with the movie, not even during the pivotal boom-box scene, where Lloyd Dobler stood outside Diane Court's house, willing her to remember how important "In Your Eyes" was. He wouldn't let her forget what it had meant to both of them. He was expressing his devotion through that song.

"Why didn't he try getting her flowers?" Ryan whispered, and I hushed him. He was silent for only a few moments before he added, "Take away what I assume is the happy ending, and this is just a restraining order waiting to happen."

I paused the movie, irritated. "You're saying that only because you have actual stalkers. This is romantic. He's serenading her. Like they used to do back in olden times. Telling her he loves her. That he's willing to make a fool of himself to win her back. Are you planning on watching the movie, or are you just going to annoy me?"

In an attempt to calm me down, he gently kissed my forehead and said, "I can do both. Because wouldn't his arms get tired? That thing looks heavy."

I elbowed him in the side and instructed him to be quiet. He chuckled. He did manage to keep his comments to himself and let me enjoy the rest of the movie.

When it was over, I told him I was tired. He walked me upstairs and stopped outside my room. "Are you upset with me?"

"Not upset. Aggravated." I'd get over it. My brothers aggravated me on a daily basis. I was kind of a pro at dealing with it. "I love *Say Anything*. I was hoping you would, too."

"We don't have to like all the same things. If anything, our differences will make things exciting. I do think it's funny that a hard-core rocker chick like you would be such a fan of a romance."

"I like romance," I said, feeling a bit insulted. "My music doesn't define everything about me. I like all kinds of romantic stuff. Movies. Books."

"Boyfriends?"

I realized I could really like a romantic boyfriend. "Depends on what he thinks is romantic."

He slipped his arms around my waist, and I sank into the feel of him. The tiny sparks he generated set off small flames inside my veins. "I can think of something romantic both you and I really enjoy doing, if you're interested."

I was interested.

After kissing me for a very long time and more passionately than he probably should have, I finally told him good night and fell asleep quickly. I had always been a ridiculously light sleeper. When my mom was in full-on lecture mode of the "Do you know what I've done/given up for you" variety, she always brought it up. "Do you know how many times I had to get up in the middle of the night with you because you heard some small noise?"

It was how I knew when any of my brothers snuck out of the house. They still owed me so many favors for keeping my mouth shut all those years.

So when my bedroom door quietly opened, I was instantly awake. Not afraid, because I knew Ryan would never let anything happen to me. But alert.

"Maisy?"

"I'm up." I glanced over at the small digital clock next to the bed. Three thirty in the morning.

I felt my mattress sink as he sat on it, next to my knees. I went to reach for the lamp on my nightstand, but he put his hand on my forearm.

"Leave the light off."

At the sound of his deep, husky instruction, my blood thickened, and my pulse hammered inside me. He didn't release my arm and instead locked his fingers with mine.

"There's something I want to say, and I think it'll be easier without the light on."

My heartbeat had become so loud that I was surprised it wasn't shaking the bed. I didn't know what I expected him to say, but I could tell from the tone of his voice that it was important.

"I know what I said. That I wouldn't pressure you or try to influence you. I wanted you to make a decision on your own. But, Maisy, I can't stay quiet. I want this to be real."

"What?" What did he want to be real? Us?

"I don't want to pretend to date you. I want to be with you. Because I think . . . I think I'm in love with you."

CHAPTER TWENTY-ONE

Every molecule inside me froze and then sped up, threatening to burst.

"I've never been in love before. All I know is that what I feel for you is different from anything else I've ever felt, so . . ." He let out a self-conscious laugh. "For someone who sings about it constantly, you would think I'd know."

He loved me? Ryan De Luna *loved* me?

I'd never been in love before, either. Did I love him?

I had spent so much time trying to avoid having any feelings for him that I'd totally suppressed them. I didn't know how I felt. I wanted to be with him. I liked him. The physical connection was out-of-this-world insane.

But despite me trying to close myself off to him and what he made me feel, this was more than casual. If I wasn't actually in love with him yet, I was definitely falling for him. It was like when I was younger and tried to stay away from music by picking a different career path. I kept telling myself that I couldn't trust or rely on Ryan. That he would hurt me. That what we had was pretend.

No matter what I did, no matter how much I'd told myself I wanted anything else, it always came back to him.

Regardless of how much that frightened me.

I felt his grip tighten. "I kind of went out on a major limb here." His tone was light, but I heard his vulnerability.

He deserved to know the truth. "I'm afraid to let this be real. You stayed away from me after the bee accident, and it devastated me. That was before we kissed. Before you said you . . ." I sucked in a deep breath. "Before you said you loved me. How much worse would it be if you walked away now? If you cheated on me with some pleech?"

"I stayed away after you got stung because I realized then that I had fallen in love with you, and you didn't respond. I thought you didn't feel the same. Now I know you didn't hear me." He was right. I most definitely would have remembered him saying that. "I'm not going anywhere. I don't want anyone but you. I don't see that changing."

"I'm scared." Not just scared.

Terrified.

Loving Ryan made me feel actual terror.

At that, he pulled me into a sitting position and wrapped his arms around me tightly. "You don't have to be afraid."

"I know it's not fair to you." My words were muffled into his shoulder. "This thing with my dad . . . it's like getting on an airplane for you."

"Are you saying I give you anxiety attacks?" He teased, but it was kind of true.

"I'm not sure I trust myself and how I'll react when I'm with you." Or what kind of lines I might be willing to cross.

His head pressed against the top of mine. "Then trust me. Give me the chance to prove I'm a good guy."

"I already know you're a good guy." That wasn't the problem.

"Let's take a chance. Clichéd or not, I think we'd make beautiful music together."

That made me laugh.

"I want you to be my girlfriend. I don't know if I'm supposed to ask you to go steady or give you a pin or something, but I want us to be exclusive."

My heart fluttered giddily at that. "Maybe start watching movies that happened after 1959 so you can have more updated references."

His arms tightened, and I could feel his smile against my skin. "I want to be . . . that guy from that stupid movie you just made me watch."

He was talking about Lloyd Dobler. "You're already so much better than Lloyd Dobler."

Ryan was asking for my trust. For me to let myself feel things for him. To break Rule #1. To give him my heart and hope that he wouldn't destroy it. To say he was different from every other musician I'd ever met. That what we had was special.

He wanted me to leap without looking.

I'd already taken so many leaps of faith where he was concerned, what was one more?

"If we're going to do this, be real, exclusive, boyfriend and girlfriend, then I need something from you." I had the feeling he might not like it.

"Anything. Name it and it's yours."

"I need to take things really, really slowly. Like, don't-come-in-my-room-at-three-thirty-in-the-morning slow. Glacier slow." Regardless of how attracted I was to him, I wasn't ready to take that next physical step. "I am planning on waiting until I'm married."

Ryan nodded, letting out a sigh. "I can't say I've ever had a relationship where that wasn't involved. Plenty of nonrelationships where it was involved, too."

"Okay, okay," I muttered. I got it. I didn't need to be reminded of his former reputation.

"You've been up-front all along about your boundaries, and I love you and respect you and will take things as slowly as you want me to. I think it'll be hard, but, Maisy? You're totally worth the wait."

It was, quite possibly, one of the most romantic things any man had ever said to me. He was right. I did like romantic boyfriends. My heart thudded fast and hard as I realized I could definitely love a man who said things like that.

And that I possibly loved him already.

He let go of me then, and we both sat there motionless in the dark. "So, is that a yes? We'll be real?"

"You already know the answer." It had been a yes before he'd even asked. Even before he'd come into my room.

"I know. Just like I know you love me, too, even if you can't say it yet." My heart caught at the truth of his words. He leaned forward and pressed a soft, gentle kiss against my forehead. One that stirred up the embers inside me, all poised and ready to ignite once he moved his mouth a little farther south.

He stood up.

"That's it?" The words burst out of me before I could stop them. "You tell me you love me, and all you're going to do is kiss me on the forehead?"

"Glacier slow, sweetheart."

He shut my door behind him, and I got the distinct feeling that despite the fact that it was a necessity and my idea, I was not going to care for glacier slow.

The next morning I went downstairs and found Bibi in the kitchen, singing to herself as she cooked. "Good morning! Ryan's already left for the day, but he said to make yourself at home." Honestly, I was both relieved and disappointed. Mostly relieved. I wasn't sure I was ready to face him in the cold light of day after our discussion last night and my tantrum over not getting more than a forehead kiss.

"He left you a note." She pointed to it at the end of the kitchen island.

Ryan could have texted me. Somehow it was more romantic that he'd taken the time to put paper to pen.

I'll be gone all day, but I should be back in time tonight for dinner. You can use any of my cars today if you want to go shopping or see your mom. Or Bibi can call you a driver if you'd prefer. I hope it's okay, but I went ahead and made reservations tonight at seven at La Isla Cubana, one of my faves.

I love you.

Ryan

Would I feel the same supercharged thrill every time he said or wrote that he loved me?

Cars? Plural?

"Can I make you some breakfast?" Bibi asked.

"Oh no. You don't have to do that for me. I've been feeding myself for a long time. Do you have any cereal?"

She pointed to the pantry and then to the cabinet where the bowls were. I grabbed a bowl and a spoon from the drawer just beneath it.

"Ryan told me about your parents."

"He talked to you about me?" I located the shelf with the cereal and sighed. Of course Ryan had only gross flavors like "Pencil Shavings" and "Inedible Tiny Rocks." I went with "Pencil Shavings." I found a container labeled Sugar and figured an undercover agent had somehow sneaked behind enemy lines. I hoped dumping a gallon or two of it on top of my cereal would at least make it edible.

"I'm probably not supposed to say anything." Bibi shot me a conspiratorial smile. "But he talks about you quite a bit. Has for a long time. Between you and me, I think he might even be in love with you."

That let me know she hadn't read his note. Where he'd point-blank said it. I put the cereal and sugar on the counter, feeling the blush that started in my cheeks and blossomed out everywhere.

I grabbed some vanilla almond milk (no animal milk of any kind around) and sat at the island to eat. I didn't respond to her educated and correct guess. Because what could I say?

"If he is, I hope you'll be careful with him. He has a delicate heart. He's always been artistic and sensitive. He is strong and confident, but underneath he's still that little boy who lost his mother and was abandoned by his father."

That made my own heart twist in sadness because I understood it all too well. "Is that why he uses De Luna instead of his dad's last name?" It was something my brothers and I had discussed for ourselves, but it had always been important to our mother that we use our father's name. Out of respect to her, we left it alone.

Ryan's aunt broke some eggs into whatever batter she was making. "Diego's father left before he was born. I gave him my last name because I thought his father didn't deserve that honor since he wouldn't be around to help raise him. With Ryan, his dad made the choice. He was Ryan Shaughnessy up until his fourteenth birthday. His father thought they would sell more records as Sofia De Luna's son."

"That's . . ." I tapped my spoon against my cereal bowl, not sure what to say. "Mercenary of him."

Bibi nodded. "Now, I think Ryan prefers it for the same reason Diego and I do."

I chewed my shavings and tried to swallow them down. The sugar was not helping. Maybe I should go shopping. I could buy a dress to wear tonight and food with absolutely no nutritional value that tasted less like wood.

As I sat there, I wanted to ask Bibi questions. About what Ryan was like as a little boy. How Diego could act so cold to me despite his mother being such a lovely, open person. What made her think Ryan loved me? Even though she was being so sweet to me, her implication earlier had been clear, her allegiance spelled out. She was worried about Ryan and didn't want me to hurt him.

I couldn't tell her that the opposite was far more likely.

Instead, I asked her what it was like to run his fan club, and that filled up the time until I decided I couldn't take any more soggy shavings. I rinsed out my bowl and told her I would be heading out to see my mother.

"The car keys are in the mudroom, near the garage. Choose whichever one you want."

After I retrieved my purse and my phone, I picked a sparkly silver car. Mainly because it was the only automatic and I didn't know how to drive a stick. I took a picture and sent it to Parker. He was going to die. He loved expensive cars.

I stopped by my favorite vintage store and found an adorable dress to wear to dinner. It was sleeveless with a tucked-in waist and slightly flared skirt. It was a dark-blue-and-white floral print. It hit that sweet spot where it wasn't too fancy but not too causal, either. Because if we were going to one of Ryan's favorite restaurants, my guess was that it wouldn't be a flip-flop-and-tank-top kind of joint.

I decided to go to the grocery store after I saw my mom (so the multiple cartons of ice cream wouldn't melt), and I drove over to Century Pacific. I texted Angie when I got to the parking lot, and she was waiting in the lobby, ready to pounce.

"Did you die? I would have died. I did die, and his song wasn't even about me! Did you just completely melt?" She said this while hugging me hello.

"Yes, I died. And obviously I melted. You saw the kiss." Everybody saw the kiss.

"And?"

And . . . I wasn't ready to tell her everything yet. I kind of wanted to tell my mom first, then I could share it with other people. It was something I'd always done growing up. I told her everything. She had been my best friend. I missed getting her advice.

When I was a senior, Kori Bryant had started spreading rumors about what I let guys do to me under the bleachers after her loser boyfriend smiled at me. I wanted my mom to make it better, to tell me how to deal with it. My poor brothers were at a loss because they couldn't punch Kori in the face and make it all go away.

So Mom first, Angie second. "There's not really much to say. He wrote an amazing song about me, which gave me all the feels, and I had to kiss him. I didn't have a choice."

Angie nodded. "The same thing happened to me the night Hector and I met."

"He sang to you?"

"No," she said with a laugh. "He was so scrumptious I just had to kiss him."

That was the second or third time I'd heard her talk about Hector without getting choked up. I didn't point it out to her, though. "I'm going to say hi to my mom and let you get back to work. Ryan made reservations for seven at La Isla Cubana, FYI."

"I will see you there. I can't believe I'm about to have dinner with Ryan De Luna!"

I wondered what she would say if I told her how many times I'd already kissed Ryan De Luna.

Thinking about him, the fact that we were now exclusive and he loved me (and that I probably loved him) made me happy. I hummed the tune to "Maisy" and let one of the orderlies introduce me to my mom again.

We chatted for a little while, and this time she asked me more questions about myself than normal. Like where I lived and whether or not my parents were still married.

"They were never married," I told her. "My dad was hardly ever around. He took off permanently a few years ago."

"I'm sorry. That sucks. My dad died when I was little, so it's just me and my mom, too."

My grandmother died when my mom was in her early twenties. It must have been nice for her to be living in a world where that hadn't happened.

"Are you a musician?"

My mom's question interrupted my train of thought. "Uh, yes. I am."

"I heard you humming. The song sounded pretty."

"My boyfriend wrote it for me. We just became official last night. He told me he loves me."

Her eyes got big. "Did you say it back?"

"Not yet."

"Oh. Well, that's exciting."

"It is. He's a musician, too, and we're actually touring together right now." Realizing she'd have no idea who Ryan was, I added, "He's newer but pretty popular. You've probably never heard of him. Ryan De Luna."

"That name sounds familiar." I tried not to laugh at my mother's attempt to appear cool, like she was up on all the new artists. Although "new" meant something completely different to her than it did to me. "And you're touring with him? Wow. You're young and have already accomplished so much. Your mom must be really proud of you."

My chest tightened, my throat thickened, and tears sprang to my eyes. "I hope so. Because I am really grateful to be her daughter."

A nurse interrupted me, a concerned look on her face. "There's someone here to see Cynthia. Maisy, I thought you should talk to them first."

I told my mom goodbye, and my pulse pounded as I walked to the front desk. Had Ryan come early?

It wasn't Ryan. It was an older blonde woman I didn't recognize.

"I'm Cynthia's daughter. Can I help you?"

"Of course you are. You look just like her. You probably don't remember me. I'm Elaine Jorgenson. I was your mom's best friend when we were younger. We lost touch about ten years ago, and I only just heard about what happened. I was hoping I could visit with her."

I asked Elaine if she could sit with me, and I told her about my mother's condition. That seeing Elaine would be a shock, given that my mom thought she was still a teenager. "She doesn't even have any mirrors in her room."

Elaine fiddled with her purse straps. "I certainly don't look the way I did when I was sixteen. I didn't know. Last year I moved about half an hour away from here, and when I got in touch with some old high school friends, they told me about the accident. They didn't say we couldn't visit."

"It's probably better for her that you don't. I'm sorry."

"Oh no, don't be sorry. I should have called first. I just felt awful when I heard. She was always such a good friend to me. I remember how our freshman year in college she'd make me her special brownies every time I got my heart broken."

"Brownies?" I repeated, hopeful anticipation rising inside me. "Do you know what recipe she used?"

"The recipe? You mean the one on the back of every box of Betty Crocker brownie mix?"

Wait. Was she saying what I thought she was saying? "My family's secret recipe is Betty Crocker? What about the frosting? Is that Betty Crocker, too?"

Elaine let out a little laugh. "It is! Your mom was not very happy with her mother when she found out. She'd thought it was something complicated and mysterious, and it turned out to be something you could buy from the store. They were still delicious, but she was disappointed."

I totally understood how my mom had felt. I'd spent years trying to perfect something that hadn't existed to feel closer to her. It crushed me to think I could have picked up a box at any time and made her brownies. It was disappointing to think of all the time I'd wasted wanting to connect with this family tradition that turned out to be something so simple.

We walked out to the parking lot together. Elaine and I exchanged information, and I promised to keep in touch and let her know how my mom was doing, especially if there were any changes. I almost told her to follow me on social media, but I didn't want her to see what the Luna-chicks and Luna-tics were saying about me.

I got into Ryan's car as she drove off. Unable to help myself, I went on YouTube to watch the video of Ryan singing my song and then us kissing. I scrolled down to look at the comments. Most of them were about how pathetic I was to throw myself at him; how I wasn't good enough for him; that I must have seduced, manipulated, or tricked him; or how I should die so he wouldn't be forced to spend time with me.

Although I knew I shouldn't care, and usually didn't, self-doubt flooded my mind. Maybe it was because Ryan had just told me he loved me, which made me feel more vulnerable. Despite what I'd told him earlier about internet trolls, their comments did bother me. They hurt my feelings. Their comments made me insecure.

He made me feel like I was a complicated, mysterious, special kind of brownie.

But what if I was just a regular old mix?

CHAPTER TWENTY-TWO

Instead of letting myself sit there and wallow, I drove to the grocery store and loaded up on enough junk food to feed my entire family. After I went to Ryan's house and put my groceries away, I went out for a run and let all the stress and anxiety get eaten up by the pounding of my feet against the pavement. Then I took a long, steamy, relaxing shower and got ready for dinner. I heard Ryan come home, and he called out to me. I told him I was getting ready. I didn't want to see him yet. I took the time to blow-dry my hair and put on makeup. Like it was some kind of armor against the world and what they thought of me.

Or maybe I was just afraid he'd see through me. See what his fans saw.

At six thirty I went downstairs and found Ryan sitting at a grand piano, playing a tune I didn't recognize. My heart constricted when I saw him. He was so gorgeous. He'd styled his hair and put on a dark-blue button-down shirt with rolled-up sleeves and black slacks. We almost looked like we'd coordinated our outfits. He must have heard my heels against the hardwood floor because he turned when I entered the room.

"Wow. I don't want to objectify you, but in my mind I just totally objectified you. You're beautiful."

How did he manage to make me blush and laugh at the same time? "I would say the same, but you already have the whole world telling you how handsome you are." He didn't need me to make his head any bigger.

"But your opinion is the only one that matters." He crossed the room to hug me and then kissed me gently. I reached up to brush my lipstick from his mouth.

"In that case, you're gorgeous, and you know it."

He rewarded me with a bone-melting smile and said we should be going. He called Fox and told him we were ready.

"Does he know?" I asked as a black SUV rolled up the driveway.

"He has no idea. He just thinks he's coming to watch out for me."

On the drive to the restaurant, Ryan told me about his day. From his tone it sounded like his meeting with his father had not gone well after Ryan told him he'd already handed over the financial aspects of his career to a business manager.

"You should fire your father." Ryan needed someone looking out for his best interests. Someone who would put him and his career first.

"He's my dad."

"I know. But look at what he's put you through. The sacrifices he forced you to make because of his bad decisions. You can't make the music you want. You can't do the kinds of shows you want. You're stuck. You need someone who will fight for you." Although I didn't say his father was not that person, I hoped my implication came through loud and clear. *Bah.* Screw implications. "You deserve better."

Ryan nodded and squeezed my hand. He stayed quiet, but it wasn't uncomfortable. Like he was considering what I'd said, and I gave him the space to think about it.

We arrived at the restaurant, and Fox told us to stay in the car while he scouted the place. A minute later he returned to let us know we were okay to go inside. I watched as the hostess eyed my boyfriend and tugged on her shirt to give herself more cleavage.

I also watched as my boyfriend totally ignored her advances. Which gave me the strength to not trip her as she showed us to our table.

Ryan helped pull out my chair, which I thought was so sweet.

Then I reconsidered my not-tripping decision when the hostess bent down in front of him and said, "My name is Anna. I would be happy to help you with any of your needs. Your server is Jordan and should be over shortly."

Ryan didn't even seem to notice her flirting, and I tried not to gloat when she left, disappointed. Instead, he beckoned Fox over with his hand. "Have a seat."

"A seat?" It was like Fox had just realized that we were at a table with four settings. So much for those keen detection skills.

"We insist," I told him, clamping my lips together to keep from ruining the surprise.

But he stood behind Ryan's chair, hesitating.

Then Angie came in wearing a baby-pink sheath that made her look stunning. As Fox's expression made perfectly clear.

Ryan stood when she got to the table. His mother and aunt had certainly raised him well. My mom would have loved his manners.

Angie said hi to us and seated herself before either man could move. With a dazed look on his face, Fox took the seat next to her. I reached over to grab Ryan's hand, excited as Angie and Fox said hello to each other, both surprised.

Our waiter, Jordan, came over to get our drink order and see if we wanted any appetizers. Ryan ordered the *empanadas de tasajo* for the table. Jordan left, and Ryan told us to order whatever we wished; tonight was on him.

"Oh, I couldn't possibly let you—they have lobster tail?" Angie said, going from demure to giddy acceptance in less than five seconds.

I asked Ryan for his recommendations, and he told me what he liked best. They were mainly vegetarian or low-carb/low-fat options. I decided to pick something he hadn't listed.

And to ignore all the fiery tingles he caused by leaving his hand on my knee.

The server returned with our drinks, took the rest of our order, and promised to be back with the appetizers shortly.

Ryan had a greenish drink that smelled disgusting. "What is that?"

"A bunch of stuff. Mostly spinach and acai berry."

"Gross. I'm not kissing you after you drink that."

"Yeah, you will." He was right. I would. "I'll have you know that acai berry is a superfood."

"Is its superpower that you can't drink it without getting sick?"

He laughed and kissed the tip of my nose.

"So, Ryan, are you excited for the US Music Awards this week?" Angie asked, and I immediately felt guilty that we weren't being very attentive to the couple across the table.

"Excited might be a strong word. I love performing, but it's work."

I put the linen napkin on my lap. "Angie, you're still coming with me to the rehearsals tomorrow, right?"

"Yes! I'm so excited. It will be a lot of fun." She turned her attention back to Ryan. "What award are you up for?"

I wanted to laugh. Like Angie didn't know exactly what Ryan was nominated for, who his competition was, and the odds of each one winning.

"I'm going to win for Best Male Artist—Rock/Pop." Then he leaned toward me. "See how rock and pop go together?"

"That's some confidence," I shot back. "That veered into arrogance territory."

"It's not arrogance. It's knowledge. So many of these awards shows are rigged. The winners know beforehand so they'll be sure to show up. You can even read the fine print on their websites. They say they can give awards to whomever they want. Especially ones like these that the fans vote for. Have you ever noticed how they never show you the voting totals?"

Angie's mouth hung open. "My inner fourteen-year-old is now furious that she spent so many hours repeatedly voting for Justin Timberlake to win best video."

Ryan grinned. "It's more about the fashion and performances. Nobody really talks about who won but about what they wore and what they did when they were onstage. The networks are looking for viewership and social media engagement. Sometimes they'll make the fans happy; sometimes they'll push them to be unhappy because of the uproar they'll cause online when they feel like their favorite artist has been slighted somehow."

"I'll be sure to tune in for the performances and fashion, then. Speaking of, what are you wearing to the awards show, Maisy?"

Something else I'd totally overlooked. Ryan really did distract me. "I have nothing to wear."

"I bet showing up wearing nothing will get the show a lot of attention," she teased.

"I know I wouldn't mind it." Ryan winked at me. He took out his phone briefly and then slid it back into his pocket. "Done."

"Done?"

"I just tweeted that my gorgeous girlfriend needs a dress for the USMAs. At least twenty designers will call my agent by ten o'clock tonight, and you'll get to pick and choose which one has the privilege of providing you a dress."

It was hard to imagine a life like his. Ryan seemed so normal and down-to-earth when we were together that I often forgot about how wealthy and famous he was. Moments like this really drove it home, reminding me how different we were.

Just like the Luna-tics had pointed out.

Angie stood, and then so did Ryan and Fox. "I'm going to visit the ladies' room. Maisy, come with me?" She had to tug on my arm to get me to join her.

"You got that panicky look on your face," Angie said once we were out of earshot of the guys. "The one where you're about to say or do something stupid."

"Thanks for saving me from myself."

"Any time. That's what friends are for."

The pristine bathroom had this elegant old-world feel to it. We used the facilities, washed our hands, and touched up our makeup.

"You probably should have told me this was a setup," Angie said, looking at me in the mirror.

"I was worried you wouldn't come."

"I would have come. Did Fox know?"

"Nope."

"That's probably a good thing. He gets really nervous on dates. Hector told me this story once about Fox's first date after they finished basic training."

As I listened to her recounting Fox's disastrous date that involved inadvertently breaking an expensive statue and setting the tablecloth on fire, I realized that for the first time in a long time, Angie seemed really happy. Even if nothing happened with Fox, at least she was willing to take a step in that direction. She would have come even if I'd told her it was a setup. That Angie might be willing to love again.

I knew she'd never forget Hector but was glad she was open to the possibility of finding someone new to share her life with.

"Why are you looking at me like that?"

"You just seem happy," I told her. "I've been noticing you've been able to talk about Hector and say his name without getting emotional."

"I have?" She seemed to ponder this. "I guess you're right. I have. I still miss him all the time, but every day does get a bit easier. Turns out that time-healing-all-wounds thing might have some merit, after all."

Angie put her powder compact in her purse. "Okay, now I want to know what's going on with you and Ryan. Nothing about you two seems like a fake relationship. What changed your mind about being together?"

"I saw another side of him, I guess. He's a really good—"

"Kisser?" Angie supplied, making me laugh.

"Yes, but he's also a good guy." Maybe too good.

"It's like you're living an actual fairy tale."

I couldn't help but let out a little laugh. I knew this was no fairy tale. "Don't get ahead of yourself. I don't think there will be a happily ever after in our future. He's in the major leagues, and I'm not even on the farm team."

"I don't know what that means. But if you're trying to say he's out of your league, not true. You are fabulous."

This was why we were friends.

"Even if it doesn't end well," she continued, "at least the middle part will have been completely awesome."

Time to tell her all of it. "We made it official last night."

"You did? How did you make it *official?*" She waggled her eyebrows at me.

"Not like that. We agreed to be exclusive, and he . . . he said he loved me." Telling Angie made it feel more real.

"What?" Then she screamed. Actually screamed with excitement while jumping up and down. Like she was at one of Ryan's concerts.

A few seconds later, Fox came running into the women's bathroom, his hand on his weapon in his belt. "What happened?"

"We're fine," I told him. "Angie's just happy for me."

Fox took another quick look around and left, muttering something about giving him a heart attack, which struck both of us as hilarious, and we busted out laughing.

"Did you see that?" I asked when our laughter finally faded.

"Did I see what? Fox run in here like a crazy person?"

"Fox left Ryan and came running in to save you. He's being paid to protect Ryan, and he didn't think twice about leaving him behind." I knew Fox had feelings for Angie, but I wanted her to know it, too. "Isn't that interesting?"

She looked thoughtful. "It is interesting."

We left the restroom and rejoined Ryan and Fox. This time Fox took a cue from his boss and helped Angie with her chair.

I whispered in Ryan's ear. "We should go. Have the server pack up our food, and let's leave Fox and Angie alone."

"Are you trying to have me all to yourself, Miss Harrison?"

"Absolutely." I pressed a soft kiss against his jaw, right under his ear.

He immediately stood. "We have to get going. Something's come up. But please stay and enjoy—my treat. Before you say anything, Fox, we're headed straight home."

Home. It wasn't my home, but when Ryan said the word, it felt like it was.

The server was at another table nearby, and after he finished, Ryan gave him his credit card with the instructions to take extra good care of Fox and Angie. Then he asked him to pack our food. We waited at the bar for it to arrive.

"Why did you tell Fox we were headed to your house?"

"Because it's the only place he would let us go without him." He had his arm around my waist. His nose nuzzled my neck, and I used the bar to help me stay vertical. "It's cute how much of a matchmaker you've turned out to be."

"Just for Angie. She deserves all the happiness in the world."

"So do you. I plan on making sure you get it."

What else could I do but kiss him again?

Jordan interrupted us by bringing out a big bag, and we thanked him. Ryan's driver waited out front, and a single paparazzo stood on the sidewalk, taking pictures of us. I wondered how he knew where we were. Who would have called him? The hostess?

I didn't have long to think about it before we were in the car and on our way. Ryan told the driver after he dropped us off he should grab one of the bodyguards and go back to give Fox keys to a car to use to drive Angie home.

Sometimes the logistics of his life were a little exhausting.

Ryan tugged me over and wrapped me in his arms. I settled my head against his shoulder and sighed when I felt him drop a kiss on the top of my head. "It seemed like something was bothering you earlier, but we spent the ride over talking about my dad. Did something happen?"

My experience growing up with men had taught me they were generally oblivious. I liked that Ryan recognized when I wasn't quite acting like myself. I told him about Elaine and the recipe.

"That's good. Now you have the recipe you've spent so much time searching for."

He was missing the point. "But it's not what I thought it would be."

"It doesn't matter what you thought it would be. You have it, and you can make your mom's brownies for the rest of your life. That's what matters."

"I actually bought the mix and frosting at the store today. I was thinking about making them when we get ho—when we get back to your house."

If he noticed my slip, he didn't comment on it.

Embarrassed, I rambled, "The whole thing made me sad, and then I did something I probably shouldn't have. I went online and looked at comments on YouTube. They were not nice. At all. Your fans do not think we should be together, and it made me feel, I don't know, insecure. They don't think I'm good enough for you."

He reached over and lifted my chin so I could look at him. "Remember earlier when I told you the only person whose opinion matters to me is yours? When it comes to us, the only voices you should be listening to are yours and mine. It doesn't matter what a million teen girls think of our relationship. It matters only what we think. I love you. I also like that you think of my place as home."

So much for him not noticing.

Then he kissed me, softly, briefly, lovingly.

Being with Ryan made me feel better. Being held by him, loved by him, made all those other awful words, insults, and doubts slip away.

"So, Mr. De Luna, what exactly are your plans when you get me home?"

"I can't say. I've been told it's not polite to kiss and tell." His fingers ran across my collarbone, up my neck, and over my jaw. I couldn't help but shudder.

"Then maybe we could do some kissing and not telling."

He grinned. "Okay, you talked me into it."

CHAPTER TWENTY-THREE

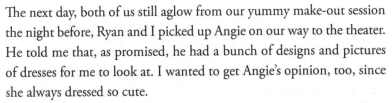

The next day, both of us still aglow from our yummy make-out session the night before, Ryan and I picked up Angie on our way to the theater. He told me that, as promised, he had a bunch of designs and pictures of dresses for me to look at. I wanted to get Angie's opinion, too, since she always dressed so cute.

We huddled together, scrolling through the photos. So many of the dresses were short, black, and covered in metal studs. Probably to appeal more to my rocker vibe. But I didn't want to show up to the awards show looking like I'd just escaped from a biker gang.

"I like this one" was something Ryan said repeatedly. Like the one that had a neckline down to the navel (navelline?). Or the one with the leg slit that went up to the same spot. Or the multiple dresses sporting see-through bodices. Now he was saying it about a strapless pink minidress that looked like it belonged at a prom on a much shorter girl.

"I'm not wearing something strapless. I'm not dealing with tugging that thing up all night or trying to sit in something that short."

"I don't see the problem. I think it would be flattering. I'm thinking only of you."

Yes, I was sure he was thinking only of me. I rolled my eyes. "Flattering? Yeah. Okay. Thinking only of me? By the way, you're not as slick as you think you are."

"I am the very definition of slick," Ryan said, his eyes twinkling. "Subtle. Totally mysterious."

"You are unmysterious. Obvious."

He wouldn't give in. "I am an enigma."

"Not even a little." He was such a guy.

"Maisy, what about this one? So pretty!" Angie showed me Ryan's phone. She'd continued going through the dresses while Ryan and I bantered. It was a full-length chiffon gown with a bodice that resembled a halter top. It had beautiful crystal-and-silver beading not only on the bodice itself but also on the crew neckline, which almost looked like a giant, sparkling necklace. There were two delicate jeweled straps that crisscrossed in the back. It was the perfect mix of "I rock out" and "I'm a girl."

Best of all? It was the same pale green as my eyes. I loved it. "This one. Tell them this one."

Only a minute after he pressed SEND, there was a reply. "The designer, a woman named Erika Chang, is going to come by later tonight and do a fitting."

We pulled up to the theater's private entrance and ran past the waiting paparazzi to get inside. A man who introduced himself as Pablo gave Angie and me passes to wear. He said there would be a barbecue in the back of the theater at lunchtime, along with a craft-services table set up backstage. Then he told Ryan to follow him. Ryan kissed me too quickly, promised to see me soon, and was off.

"What now?" I asked Angie. I didn't want to come across like some pathetic groupie. Even if Christa Harbinger had just walked by and I almost passed out from the thrill of seeing one of my idols in person.

"I'm worried that if we wander around backstage, we might piss off the wrong diva and get kicked out. I vote we sit out front and watch."

We were not the only ones to do so. A lot of the people appeared to be journalists or bloggers, ready to share their experiences at the rehearsals and what the stars would be doing two nights from now.

A boy band was currently onstage, discussing the logistics of their set while their dancers stretched and gabbed. As they started their sound check, I turned to Angie.

"You never did tell me what happened with you and Fox last night."

She kept her eyes trained on the stage, her mouth twisting. "We ended up staying at the restaurant until it closed, and they had to kick us out. Then he drove me home, and we stayed in the driveway all night, talking. I never realized how much we have in common. Or how much I enjoy hanging out with him."

"Seriously? That's amazing!"

She let herself smile. "He asked to see me again tonight. I said yes."

"I'm so happy for you."

"I guess some part of me feels bad. Like I'm betraying Hector, even though I know I'm not. Fox actually gets that. It makes it easier that he loved Hector, too."

"I get to pick out my bridesmaid dress. You're not sticking me in some neon-orange monstrosity."

"Stop," she said, nudging me with her arm. But she was still smiling.

The boy band finished, and five more acts ran through rehearsal. Some I knew better than others, but it was fun to get a behind-the-scenes look at the process.

I sat up straighter when Ryan finally came onstage. Even though I'd spent so much time with him, he still exuded that charisma and magnetism that made him impossible to ignore and resist. Like if the music thing hadn't worked out for him and he'd become a long-distance truck driver, he'd have a different woman waiting for him at every truck stop.

Then Skyler Smith glided onstage. She was a tiny, curvaceous, platinum blonde and absolutely stunning. She looked like the kind of woman who got dressed every morning with the assistance of animated woodland creatures.

Skyler gave Ryan two air kisses. Which I was totally fine with.

Fine-ish with.

Then she wrapped her arm through his and stayed put, resting her head against his upper arm.

That was my bicep she was leaning on.

Jealousy just about crushed my windpipe.

"I always like when people carry their dogs around in their purses," Angie said. "Makes it much easier to spot their crazy."

I'd been so focused on how that . . . that . . . wannabe man-stealer was touching my boyfriend that I hadn't even noticed her yappy Chihuahua in her oversize bag.

"Maisy? Are you okay?"

"Why is she hanging on my boyfriend?"

"I'm sure they're just friends. It's not something you need to care about."

I did care. A hundred and crazy percent. Because if Skyler Smith didn't control her whoremones and get away from my man, I was going to have to knock out America's Sweetheart.

"They dated," I reminded her.

"For like two seconds. It probably wasn't even real. Like a publicity stunt or something."

Did she mean like how Ryan and I started out? That did not help.

Ryan ran through "Be With You," and it made me think of the music video, which helped relieve some of my anger.

That Skyler perched on a box in the corner of the stage did not.

"Let's grab some lunch. It's about time."

That was probably a good idea. I didn't particularly want to see Skyler's rehearsal anyway.

It took us a little while to find our way to the back, given that most of the crew members were unhelpful (since we weren't famous), and we didn't dare speak to any of the music stars around us. I had to hear Skyler singing in that nasally, breathy baby voice that set my teeth on edge.

Finally, we found the back exit of the theater. The barbecue was set up in a courtyard, surrounded by thick, high bushes. I wondered what they normally used this area for. Angie and I stargazed a little bit, pointing out some of our favorites while trying not to be obvious. So much talent gathered in one spot!

Then, probably after making some people uncomfortable, we decided to check out what kind of food they offered. There was almost a line of demarcation between two tables—food for regular people like chips, soda, and hamburgers; and food for famous folk, including quinoa, lettuce, and kale.

"If vegetarians love animals so much, why do they eat all their food?" I asked Angie, filling my plate.

A voice behind me said, "Maybe you should try it. Veganism, I mean. It looks like you need it."

I turned to see Skyler Smith glaring at me, flanked by two very tall, very thin women. She was attempting to insult me. Why?

"I'm not interested in being vegan or vegetarian. Thanks anyway." She sucked at insults. I was happy with the way I looked. The whole thing was random and weird. I was about to say as much to my best friend, but Skyler kept talking.

"Why? Do you have something against vegetarians? Ryan is a vegetarian."

Since she'd brought Ryan into this, she must have known we were together. But why would she care? Although he ate a lot of vegetables and other weird stuff, Ryan was not a vegetarian. I'd seen him eat plenty of meat.

"I don't have anything against vegetarians or vegans. Cows are vegans, and I love them."

Skyler gasped, and I remembered that she was super into animal rights. "The only thing cheaper than your sarcasm is your perfume. Until human beings start seeing animals as our friends and not as a food source, there's no hope for us as a species."

"Seriously? Just how many cow friends do you have?" I was starting to enjoy myself, but Angie looked horrified.

"Meat is murder."

"Then I'm about to commit a homicide. I'd like one burger, please." The man stationed at the barbecue slid a patty onto my plate. "I have something for you, Skyler. It's called go away, and it's located somewhere not here."

She crossed her arms. "Ryan will never end up with some nobody like you. He needs a woman like me on his arm. Someone with millions of followers who will get him all the publicity and fame he needs for his career. Your little band has no fans."

"Untrue. We have a fan." Joe. It was weird that she seemed to know things about me.

"The only fan you have is on the ceiling."

I wondered if she hurt herself coming up with that one. "We're outside. That might have been a solid burn if we'd been indoors."

Her face turned slightly red. At first I couldn't tell if it was anger or embarrassment. I quickly discovered it was anger. "I am going to dedicate my time to ruining you. I will say whatever lie, spread whatever rumor, do whatever I have to do to destroy you and your career. When Ryan sees how much you're dragging him down, he'll beg me to take him back."

All of Ryan's fans already hated me. I couldn't see where Skyler adding to it would do much more damage. "Do you have a life goal to be a James Bond villain? You're just going to spell out your whole evil plan for me? What do you think's going to happen when I tell Ryan what you're planning to do? Because I will tell him. I even have a witness." I pointed at Angie.

It was like that thought hadn't crossed her teeny mind. "Whatever. You're not even worth my time. I'm leaving because I can't stomach another second of being around that dead flesh on your plate."

To add to her whimsical unkindness, she called me some names a woman should never use against another woman.

"I understand why you have to rush off. I'm sure you need to get back to luring children into your gingerbread house." Now I was annoyed, mostly by the inappropriate name-calling. Why did America love her so much? She was horrible.

"I would have smacked her, but I didn't want to get skank on my hands," I muttered to Angie.

"It's been a long time since I've witnessed that much girl-on-girl crime. I can't believe how awful she is. I always thought she was so nice."

We walked in the opposite direction from Skyler and her crew and found a table.

Angie smiled as she sat. "Now I wish Ryan had been here. To personally witness how possessive you are over your man."

I finished chewing a bite of my extremely delicious hamburger. "He doesn't belong to me. It's not like he's the box set of *Buffy the Vampire Slayer*. She is awful. Don't you remember what she did to Katsia Evanovich?"

Angie pursed her lips together and shook her head.

"Katsia and Skyler had some kind of falling-out, and when Katsia released her debut album, Skyler released her own secret album the same day. To kill Katsia's numbers." Katsia's album had failed, and she hadn't put out another song since.

Even though I'd blown off her threats, remembering what she did to Katsia made me reconsider. What if she did the same thing to me? Singled out my band and me and did everything she could to wreck our careers? She had a lot of influence. Not only with fans but also with important people in the music industry. It would kill my brothers if she ruined our chance before we even really had one.

It would kill me.

"Are you going to tell Ryan?"

"At the first opportunity."

Maybe he would be able to undo some of the damage that Hurricane Skyler was about to inflict on me.

I didn't tell Ryan right away. The next couple of days were a blur. When he wasn't working, Ryan took me on multiple dates. Out to eat, to a private beach, even to the movies. (He'd had to rent out the whole theater so our date wouldn't be interrupted by someone trying to steal a lock of his hair.)

I even got the chance to introduce him to my mother. Who flirted shamelessly with Ryan. It was humiliating, but he was amazing about the whole thing. I wished she understood, and would remember, how important he was to me.

Erika Chang, the designer, came and took my measurements. She reminded me a lot of myself. Just starting out, determined to make a name in the fashion industry. I was excited to wear the dress and to tell everyone that she had designed it. She promised to get me some shoes and a purse, too. She had everything delivered by messenger.

Then it was the night of the US Music Awards. Ryan offered to hire someone to do my hair and makeup, but given that I'd done actual training in that sort of thing, I felt like I had a good handle on it. I did my eye makeup heavier than normal, wanting to emphasize the color. As for the rest of my makeup, considering all the bright lights that would be there, I made it more stage appropriate. I had originally planned on leaving my hair down, but given that the dress was basically backless, I put it up in a braided chignon. Which is much easier to do on someone else than it was on myself.

When I reached the top of the stairs, Ryan was waiting for me at the bottom. Smiling up at me like some hero out of a movie. My heart stopped entirely and then started slowly with a low, hard thudding. He wore a slate-gray, perfectly tailored designer suit and gave a whole new meaning to the word *delicious*. His five-o'clock shadow kept him from looking too preppy, lending him a slightly wild edge. Made him a little bit rock and roll. He was just so perfect-looking. Like he'd been artificially created and brought to life by some mad spinster scientist. He turned my knees hollow. I grabbed the bannister for support.

"Wow. Look at you. I'm unable to form a single coherent thought," he said, his eyes devouring me.

"You just did."

"That's the only one. Everything else in my brain is just . . . wow."

I knew the feeling.

We had a limo for the event, and, given his current expression, I warned Ryan not to mess up my makeup on the car ride over.

"Not even a little?" he asked.

"It's my first red carpet, and I'm already nervous enough. I don't want to have to worry about that, too."

So he settled for kissing me on my neck and shoulders, which I did not object to.

We waited in a line of limos, giving me time to get more and more nervous.

"You'll be fine. They'll love you," Ryan said in between kisses that were not nearly as soothing as his words.

Then it was our turn.

"Follow my lead." Ryan got out first, and I could tell the moment the crowd figured out it was him. The screams were deafening. He held out his hand to me, and I took it.

Photographers' flashes surrounded us, making it hard to see. Ryan pulled me up the red carpet, waving and smiling as we went. I clung to his arm, feeling like I'd entered some undiscovered country.

Reporters from television shows called out his name, and Ryan stopped for the one from *ET*. Janelle something.

"Ryan! So good to see you out here tonight. Who are you wearing?"

"I don't want to talk about that. Have you met Maisy Harrison? Of the band Yesterday?"

Only the slightest flicker on Janelle's face let me know she wasn't pleased to be pushed in a new direction. "I haven't. Maisy? Gorgeous dress. Who are you wearing?"

"Erika Chang. She's an up-and-coming designer."

"Maisy and her band are opening for me on my Moonstruck tour."

Recognition lit up her eyes. "This is the same woman you've been rumored to be dating?"

He put his arm around my waist. "Yes."

Janelle asked, "Ryan, what can you tell us about your next album?"

But his response was "Thanks for chatting with us," and we moved on.

The same thing happened with every other reporter. Ryan refused to talk about himself, about the tour, his upcoming album, or his soon-to-be released single. He wanted them to talk only to me and ask me questions.

Which completely threw me. I wasn't ready for that. I thought I'd just be on his arm, smiling, nobody caring who I was. Instead, Ryan made me the focus, and I hadn't been trained to give interviews the same way he had.

Like when they asked me to tell them about my hobbies. My answer was "Other than music and Ryan? Feeling inadequate, eating chocolate, and napping."

I faced question after question until I felt dizzy. We finally reached the end of the line, where there was one reporter determined to flag us down. She had a microphone that said MTV.

"Maisy! Over here!"

I don't know if the word had spread, but she cleverly called out my name instead of Ryan's, ensuring that he pulled me right over to her.

She made small talk, asked me how the tour was going. How long Ryan and I had been dating.

"Ryan, when did you know that Maisy was the one for you?"

If he wouldn't answer questions about himself, he had no problems answering them about me. "The first night I laid eyes on her, I knew she was special. I've never met anyone who challenges me or understands me the way she does. It didn't surprise me when Maisy became the most important person in my life. Or when I realized how much I love her."

He looked down at me with total love and adoration in his eyes. My heart fluttered and flapped all over the place, like it wanted to break free of my chest and hug him.

"What about you, Maisy?"

"The first time I laid eyes on him, I did not know he was the one."

That made Ryan laugh and kiss me on the forehead.

The reporter was relentless. "So when did you know?"

I thought about all the things Ryan had done for me. Kept my mom in Century Pacific. Took me and my brothers out on tour, paying us a ton of money to live out our dreams. How he made me laugh. How comfortable I felt with him. How he'd given me someone to talk to about music in a way that I never had before. How he carried me out of the club my dad played in. Rushed me to the hospital after the bee sting and stayed by my side. How he confessed his love to me, and even tonight, when it should have been his chance to shine, his chance to drum up publicity, he instead focused the spotlight on me.

The realization that I'd been in love with him for a long time hit me harder than an egg to the head.

"I don't know if there was just one moment. It's been more like a bunch of little moments all combined together that made me love him."

Ryan's reaction seemed to happen in slow motion. I watched the different emotions cross his face—surprise, confusion, doubt, and then total and complete joy. "You love me?"

"You already know the answer."

Before I finished the last word, his mouth was on mine, demanding, grasping, desperate. As if he'd been waiting impatiently for this very moment, and now that it had arrived, he couldn't contain himself. Fiery stars exploded in front of my eyes, forcing me to squeeze them shut, to sink in and savor the feel of his kiss.

He pulled me close against him, his entire body a strong, hot line of fire that should have burned me but instead only made me feel deliciously hazy and pliant.

His warm, strong fingers pressed into my bare back, and I sighed with pleasure, which he matched with a rough sigh of his own. I shook from the intensity of his kiss, from the blaze he seemed to so easily control inside me.

At some point my nerve endings rearranged themselves to be connected to my lips so that every movement, every change in pressure, caused them to spark into ever-increasing flames. And each flame stole a breath, and another, and another. I'd never felt more safe or more sure than I did completely breathless in his arms, against his lips.

I pushed against him slightly, not wanting this moment to ever end, but finally remembered myself. "Ryan? As you once said, we have company."

His breathing was labored, his eyes unfocused. It took him a second to regain control of himself. I brushed away a lock of his hair that had fallen over his forehead, and he grabbed my wrist and pressed a hot kiss against it, causing my tremors to start up all over again.

Which made me almost forget about that whole-being-surrounded-by-thousands-of-people thing.

"That wasn't a glacier, Maisy Harrison. That was a bonfire. In front of everyone."

There was a certain symmetry to it, I supposed. I'd kissed him for the first time in front of the whole world. It somehow seemed appropriate that I would tell him I loved him for the first time in the same way.

"Sorry, what was the question?" Ryan asked the reporter, eliciting laughter from everybody nearby. He thanked them, and we went into the theater. Once we were briefly out of sight of the cameras, Ryan spun me up against a wall and pinned me in place.

"You love me."

"I do."

"I want to hear you say the words."

"I love you, Ryan De Luna."

Then he proceeded to show me, without words, just how much he loved me in return.

CHAPTER TWENTY-FOUR

During Skyler's performance at the awards ceremony, I told him about her threats. He laughed for about five minutes, which I think the cameras caught and would probably spin another way. Like we were making fun of Skyler or something. When he finally calmed down, he told me I had nothing to worry about.

"There is zero chance of Skyler Smith and me ever getting together. We were never even together in the first place. We went out on one 'date' because we were with the same label and our agents arranged it. Not to mention I'm not exactly her type."

Not her type? Was she blind as well as stupid? "What do you mean?"

"Those friends? Her 'crew'? Not just friends. More than friends. If Skyler said she wanted me, it's only to be her beard."

Oh. "Did she tell you that?"

"No."

Then he was just assuming. He didn't actually know. "If it's true, why would she hide it?"

"A lot of famous people do. They don't want to get pigeonholed. Like I told you, perception is everything. But know that I'm enjoying your jealousy."

"I'm not jealous." I was jealous. A Jealous McJealouson. "I just don't want your ex-girlfriend to ruin my life."

"You don't have to worry about her. What do you think about sneaking out of here early? My performance is done. I have my pseudo award. Want to go?"

I looked up, as if actually considering my answer. I desperately wanted to leave, to be alone with him and not surrounded by cameras or fans.

"Come on, Maisy. Say yes, please."

In a low voice I told him, "Yes, please."

He let out a groan. "Unfair. You can say things like that when I have to behave." Then he kissed me hard but all too briefly. "You're going to be the death of me."

"Won't it be a fun way to go?"

"I don't know. Let's find out."

The tide of the internet turned in my favor after the awards show. Skyler had so many Twitter feuds with so many different celebrities that nobody paid her much attention. The consensus seemed to be that she came off as desperate and pathetic while I, by maintaining my silence, seemed classy.

The comments on the YouTube video of Ryan singing to me had also changed in their tone.

Lunachick4Life 1 hour ago
Look at the way he watches her. He's obviously in love with her.
REPLY 👍 👎

Sofia Ferreira 1 hour ago
That's real love
REPLY 5 👍 👎
View all 2 replies ⌄

Anni 1 hour ago
If Ryan loves her, I'm going to love her, too.
REPLY   3 👍 👎
View all 1 replies ⌄

enji aoren 1 hour ago
He wrote a freaking song for her. I wish someone would write a song for me and perform it the way he did for her.
REPLY   👍 👎

AwesomeMari77 1 hour ago
I'd maim somebody to be Ryan's girlfriend
REPLY   6 👍 👎
View all 4 replies ⌄

Girl Power 1997 1 hour ago
She seems nice and down to earth. Like one of us.
REPLY   2 👍 👎
View all 1 reply ⌄

Bijoy Chondo 1 hour ago
I wish somebody would kiss me like that.
REPLY   👍 👎

real name 2018 1 hour ago
I wish somebody would just kiss me.
REPLY   7 👍 👎
View all 4 replies ⌄

Estrella Crystal 1 hour ago
Does she know she's the luckiest girl in the whole world?
REPLY   👍 👎

I did know I was the luckiest girl in the whole world. With the awards show over, Ryan and I traveled back to meet the rest of the crew and continue the tour. On the way, I helped him with his revenge prank on Cole, which involved a ton of Ping-Pong balls being stuffed into his bunk and held in place by industrial-strength plastic wrap.

Cole was not happy, but it was really hilarious. I then asked both sides for a cease-fire because I knew how quickly this could escalate.

As we traveled to new cities and new stadiums and arenas, something funny started to happen. People knew the words to our songs. Our downloads increased dramatically, as did our video views. We even got rid of one of the covers from our set list and replaced it with another original song.

Bloggers and magazines started calling us for interviews. In every single one, Parker and Cole were relentlessly charming and hilarious, which everyone seemed to respond to. At the venues, people were waiting to meet us, wanting our autographs. Girls even screamed and jumped up and down for my brothers, which I still did not get.

On top of everything else, Ryan's "Be With You" video dropped and earned the highest number of views in a single day ever.

One fan. Skyler Smith could kiss my butt.

After sound check at the venue in Chicago, Ryan and I were hanging out in his dressing room, cuddling on the couch. They had insisted he do a meet and greet. I listened as he told me all the reasons why he didn't like doing them. Then in the middle of his monologue, he interrupted himself.

"Do you ever think about the future?"

"Um, all the time. I worry about my mom, mostly."

He held up my hand, studying it. "I mean a future for you and me."

My pulse exploded, skittering frantically underneath my skin. Because, no, I hadn't. I'd been living day to day, taking things as they came. I didn't think about tomorrow when it came to Ryan.

"Have you?" I asked.

"It wasn't something I ever considered before, but recently I've been thinking about things like getting married."

I think I blacked out for a second because he couldn't possibly have just said what I thought he said.

Could he?

"What?" I whispered.

"I think I'd like to have kids. A big family, like yours."

It was like my entire body had turned into one giant heartbeat, drumming so hard I couldn't hear or think. In my life rules, the unspoken Rule #3 was "Never marry a musician." How could I marry and have a family with someone who would always be gone? Who would always have to deal with an unending horde of women who would constantly offer themselves to him?

"Any thoughts?"

I was glad we were both facing the same direction and he couldn't see my panicked expression. I gulped. "When I think about the future, it's mostly about making the band work out. I don't have to be famous. I just want to make enough money so we can earn a living from it without having to do crappy second jobs. And still take care of our mother. I've honestly never thought about marriage. Ever."

"Really? Never?"

"I've thought about it in the abstract sense. But it terrifies me. The same way that becoming intimate physically terrifies me. I've never wanted to care that much about someone. Never wanted to give a man that kind of power over me that he could destroy me the way my dad destroyed my mom. I joke a lot about my overprotective brothers driving guys off, but the truth is that I'm the one who drives them off."

The silence between us felt physical. Like it was shaping itself into a wedge and setting between us.

"So not only am I the first man you've let yourself care about but also the first one you haven't tried to scare away."

I nodded.

He turned me on my side so I could look up and into his eyes. "Maisy, you do realize that whatever power or control you think I have over you, you have that same kind of control and power over me. I could never hurt you because I would only be hurting myself. I'm not your father, and you're not your mother."

There was a knock at the door, telling Ryan it was time for the meet and greet.

He stood up and kissed the back of my hand. "Maybe think about our discussion. About whether or not you see possibilities for us."

Maybe think about it? It was all I was going to think about from now on. And panic about.

Ryan De Luna saw a future with me in it.

I probably should have gone back to my own dressing room and done vocal warm-ups. Instead, I found myself on the outer fringe at the meet and greet. I knew his heart wasn't in the event, but his fans would never have been able to figure it out. He made everyone feel special. He comforted the crying girls and got them to laugh. Whenever a gorgeous woman flirted and acted all seductive, his eyes automatically flickered back to me, ignoring her. Like I was the only woman he could see.

A little bald girl in a wheelchair came through. The flirting women got seconds with him, but he spent a good five minutes talking to this girl, signing everything she wanted signed and taking picture after picture with her. Ryan even called Fox over and upgraded their seats, giving them VIP passes.

When they were done, the girl's sobbing mother threw her arms around Ryan's neck, thanking him for giving her sick daughter such an amazing gift. My own eyes welled up with tears. Ryan calmed down the mother and sent them on their way.

Watching him with that girl, with all the kids who came to meet him, made me realize he would be such a good father. I knew he'd be a good husband because he was already the most amazing boyfriend in the entire world. He was right. I wasn't my mom, and he wasn't my dad. It wasn't fair to make Ryan pay for crimes he'd never committed.

Marriage had always seemed like an overwhelming, frightening concept. A fire-breathing, scaly dragon I couldn't face alone. But with my own devoted knight at my side, it didn't seem nearly as scary or unconquerable as it had even minutes before.

After the show, I got on the bus and was shocked when everybody yelled out, "Surprise! Happy birthday!"

Ryan bringing up marriage earlier had consumed my every thought. I'd forgotten it was my birthday.

Balloons covered the ceiling, and streamers hung haphazardly along the walls. I wondered if my brothers had been in charge of those. All my siblings were there, along with Ryan's band, Piper, and the dancers.

Ryan grabbed me and picked me up off my feet. "Happy birthday."

"Thank you. I can't believe you threw me a surprise party. I've never had one of those before."

"Well, in honor of it being your twenty-second birthday, you get two of everything. Like . . ." He gestured to where two big pies decorated with birthday candles sat on the kitchen counter.

"Are those pumpkin pies?"

"I know, birthday pie is not really a thing. But that's your favorite, right?"

It was. How did he remember stuff like that?

Because he loves you.

I couldn't stop the tear that fell onto my cheek. "My mom used to make me pumpkin pie. All the time."

"Sweetheart," Ryan said, rubbing away the tear with his thumb, "I didn't want to make you sad."

I leaned my head against his chest. "You didn't. You made me really, really happy. Thank you."

"Don't thank me yet. We haven't even gotten to the presents."

My brothers came over to hug me and wish me a happy birthday. They told me to sit at the table, and everyone sang to me as they brought both pies over. I'd never heard such a beautiful rendition of the birthday song before. Totally on key, with perfect harmonies.

When it was time to blow out the candles, I made the same wish I did every year. For my mom to get better.

Everyone cheered and applauded and started loading up the table with presents. Fitz gave me his first so he could help Piper cut up the pie and serve it. The card said it was from both of them. They had bought me a pair of emerald earrings, the stone for my birth month. Parker threw his present at me: two expensive-looking pairs of sunglasses. Cole gave me a set of guitar picks that he claimed had once belonged to Christa Harbinger.

I was touched not only by their thoughtfulness but also by the fact that they had obviously dug into the money we'd been saving to buy me presents. I thanked them, hugging them as best I could, given the crush of people surrounding us.

The other presents were also two-themed, and everything was meant for me to use while on tour. A pair of small throw pillows, a set of comfy slippers, and some wool-lined socks. Nothing big and bulky that would be difficult for me to lug around.

"Ryan's turn!" Parker announced when I'd opened all the other gifts and thanked everybody.

To be honest, I was a little bit afraid of what Ryan might do. If he might have a wedding ring in his pocket. My heart expanded into my throat, choking the air from me. He wouldn't do that, would he?

"What do you think I got you?" he asked as if he could read my mind and knew just how much I was freaking out.

"Jewelry?" I could barely squeak out the word.

"Not jewelry."

Powerful relief surged through me, allowing me to relax.

"Because what would Maisy Harrison love more than jewelry?" he asked.

"Being right," Cole yelled out, just avoiding my swatting hand.

"Could you be any more annoying?" I asked my brother. "By the way, that was rhetorical, not a challenge."

"Come see," Ryan said, gesturing me over. He stood in front of the closed bunk-alley door. "Open it."

Just beyond the doorway stood two guitars: a custom acoustic Martin guitar just like he had, and a blue-edged Fender Stratocaster. These were not guitars that cost hundreds of dollars. They cost thousands. Maybe tens of thousands.

"I wanted to replace your broken Dreadnought. I bought you two in case you lose one or some random crazy person breaks it," Ryan said. He went over and picked up the Fender. "This one I had signed." He turned it over, and Bonnie Raitt's signature was on the back.

He handed it to me.

"Ryan, I couldn't possibly accept." But I said it even as my fingers curled around the neck of the guitar. It was so beautiful. And the perfect weight. I plucked at the strings, excited to sit down and tune it.

"Seems like you just did. Are you going to tell me I spent too much money?"

"No." I turned over the guitar and ran my fingers over where one of my idols had signed it. "You can afford it. And it would be really selfish of me to deny you the pleasure of giving me a gift."

He threw his head back and laughed, and it filled me with such an overwhelming wave of love that I wrapped my arms around him, squeezing tight. "Thank you, Ryan. This is literally the best gift anyone's ever given me."

"Hey!" Parker protested somewhere behind me, but I didn't care.

I looked up at the most incredible boyfriend in the entire universe. "Thank you. I love you, Ryan."

"Because I bought you guitars?" he teased.

"No. I love you for who you are. I see you, the man. Not the money, not the pop star. And that's who I love."

He kissed me then. The gentle warmth of his mouth blurred my mind with hazy pleasure. Each kiss was longer, slower, and more intoxicating than the last.

"Gross! Give her the tonsillectomy later, dude. There's a party going on!"

We broke apart, but the promise and want in his eyes nearly made me reconsider. We went back into the lounge, and Fitz handed me a piece of pie. I asked Ryan to hold my guitar for a second.

The pie was delicious. "This is now the second-best thing that's ever happened to my mouth."

Ryan laughed at our private joke. When I finished, he gave me back the Fender and retrieved the Martin. I wouldn't let anyone else touch my guitars, and I sat there holding them, not knowing which one to love and play with first. I wondered if this was how mothers of twins felt.

"What kind of jewelry did you think I was going to give you?" Ryan asked, sitting next to me.

I felt my eyes get big. "Nothing." Not only wasn't that an answer to his question, but also it was basically untrue since I'd already announced that I thought he would get me jewelry. I saw Fitz and Piper's present on the table. "Earrings."

"You didn't think I'd give you a ring, did you?"

"Of course not. That's silly." My voice sounded pathetically unbelievable even to my own ears.

Ryan smiled at me like he didn't believe a word I was saying. He kissed me on the cheek. "When I know you're ready." He got up to join the group of guys playing a video game.

When he knew I was ready, what? He'd give me one? He'd said only half a sentence.

But did I want him to finish it?

People started drifting back to their own buses, and Ryan's band-mates turned in for the night. It was just me, my family, and Ryan.

It turned into a "Let's embarrass Maisy" party. My brothers told Ryan story after story about me, and no amount of threatening to reveal their secrets stopped them.

"She was a total band geek," Parker said, laughing.

"Please tell me you wore a polyester uniform. And that you marched in a parade."

I stayed quiet for a moment. "I'll have you know we were in a parade at Disneyland."

For some reason they all found this totally hysterical.

"And band camp? Did you go to band camp?" he asked when he could breathe again.

"I'm not dignifying that with a response."

More laughter.

"Did you know what a huge crush she used to have on you?" Fitz asked, making me gasp. I threw one of my new pillows at him, and he easily caught it.

Parker didn't look away from the TV screen as he replied, "I forgot about that. When she was a teenager. Didn't she have his poster on her wall?"

"Really?" Ryan sounded far too pleased. "I thought you hated my music."

"I do. Some of it. Not all of it. I'm particularly partial to 'Maisy.'"

"That's because you're an egomaniac," Cole informed me.

"That's enough of that," I told them. "You have sufficiently humiliated me, and it's late."

Catching my drift, Fitz and Cole wished me happy birthday again and said good night.

"What's it like getting to make out with your teenage crush?" Ryan teased as he pulled me close.

"Shut up."

"Not a chance. I'll be bringing this up a lot. Also, do you still have your band uniform? I think I'd like to see you in it."

"It's not attractive," I told him.

"I'll be the judge of that." He kissed me with feathery, teasing kisses and pulled away before I could press for real ones. "Is there anything else you want for your birthday?"

"At the moment I can think of one or two things."

His eyes darkened at my tone and expression. "Just so you know, you can unwrap me anytime you'd like."

At that, Parker called out, "Gag. I am sitting right here!"

"I know where you are," I told him. "Take the hint and go."

He finally did, leaving me somewhat alone with Ryan.

"Where's Fox?" I realized I hadn't seen him at the party.

"He gave me his two-week notice this afternoon. He wants to move back home to LA. My guess is to spend some more time with your best friend. I told him to go now and gave him the money for the two weeks and a generous severance package."

Even though Ryan didn't say it, I knew he'd done for it me. Because of how much I wanted Fox and Angie to be together. Even if it inconvenienced him or the other guards on the tour.

"You are seriously the best. Do you know that?" He was. Ryan De Luna was more than I could have ever hoped for.

"I've been told."

"And the most humble."

As his arms tightened around me, holding me close, I decided that life couldn't possibly get any better than this.

CHAPTER TWENTY-FIVE

For the next few weeks I traveled from city to city with my family and the man I loved. I knew Ryan had his faults. Like how he was temperamental, refused to eat food with flavor, and was sometimes prone to yelling. But there were so many good, amazing things about him that the bad stuff didn't seem to matter. All those years I'd spent avoiding musicians—his musical side was easily among the things I liked best about him.

And he totally tolerated my quirks. He didn't care if I wanted to lock myself in a hotel room all day to write. I'd seen how many relationships my brothers had lost over things like that. Their girlfriends always felt less than. But Ryan got it.

Sadly, though, the tour came to an end. We did our last concert in New York City, and after the performance Ryan promised that early the next morning, he would take me to his SoHo apartment and afterward show me all the touristy sights like the Statue of Liberty and Broadway. Then tomorrow evening the buses would be heading back to California. My brothers and I would put our house on the market when we got home while Ryan ramped up the publicity for his upcoming album and presumably planned his next tour.

He told me he already had a good idea who the opening act should be and advised me to clear the band's schedule.

The next morning he brought me to his apartment. Which he should have called a penthouse, given how ridiculously big it was. On the top floor of a building that housed everyone from movie stars to athletes to foreign royals, it had the biggest windows I'd ever seen and the most amazing view. Exposed brick along the one interior wall, some industrial piping across the high ceiling, and a kitchen so bright and beautiful it looked as if it had never even been used. There weren't any inside walls, just a large open space broken up by furniture.

"How many homes do you have?"

"Seven," he replied.

"That may be part of why you went broke," I told him.

Ryan smiled and shook his head. He wasn't broke any longer. This tour had netted him a fortune. Not only in ticket sales but also in merch, downloads, and preorders for his next album. Thanks to his new business manager handling his finances, he no longer had to worry about the bottom falling out from underneath him again.

"This place is so huge. Do you live here alone? Or do you have a housekeeper or something?"

"I have a service that comes in to clean once a week. But today it's just the two of us."

"Just the two of us?" We hadn't been completely alone together since the music awards.

He slid his arms around me. "Yep. Any suggestions on what we should do?" He began nuzzling my ear, which made my eyes roll into the back of my head. While Ryan had remained respectful of my boundaries, he reminded me of an explorer traveling up and down a river, looking for a place to ford it. If I let the waters recede just a little, he'd happily cross over.

But I didn't let him. Because despite how much I liked kissing and touching him, there always came this moment when we were together when I froze up, like I'd slammed into a massive iceberg. When we had reached a point where we had to stop because things could get out of control. Yes, I loved him, but I didn't feel like I had to prove it. I loved myself and the decisions I'd made about how far I would take things physically.

Not to mention that, given my father's fertility, I was pretty sure despite whatever precaution might be used, I'd wind up pregnant. Much as I adored my own single mother, I was in no hurry to be one.

"I think," I said, wrapping my arms around his neck, "that you should take me sightseeing like you promised."

"Not nearly as fun." He sighed. He held on to my waist and put a bit of space between us.

"I know. I have thought about what it would be like. How it might feel." I already had some indication from what we had done. I wanted him to know he wasn't totally alone in this.

At that, he let out a soft groan, lowering his forehead against mine. "You can't say things like that. I'm not made out of stone."

The muscles in his arms begged to differ as I trailed my fingers along his biceps. "I'm not trying to make things harder for you. I want to be honest."

His lips pressed against my forehead. "Sometimes, for my sanity, it's okay to keep your honesty to yourself."

"Noted. But I'm grateful to you for how respectful you've been."

"It has been a massive sacrifice, because every time I get close to you like this, my brain turns off completely, and I can think of only one thing."

His words sent a series of delicious chills through me. "How *Say Anything* is the best movie you've ever seen?"

That got me one of his wickedly charming smiles. "No. I think about touching you. Holding you. And a lot less clothing being involved."

The chills turned into streams of fire. I gulped, hard. "You could maybe keep some of your honesty to yourself, too."

269

That made him laugh. "I'm going to go take a very cold shower." He gave me a quick kiss. There was a spiral metal staircase on the south side of the apartment, and he followed it upstairs. "You're more than welcome to join me."

"I'm good." I was trying desperately not to think about him undressing.

I walked around, giving myself a little tour. It was probably supposed to be a bachelor pad, but the apartment didn't give off that vibe. It felt like a family should live here and fill this vast space with love and memories.

The weird thing was, I could see this being my home. I could envision myself in this corner of the apartment, next to the piano, writing a new hit song. Holding a baby while a toddler played at my feet. Ryan chasing our oldest in circles around the kitchen island. I could hear the laughter and feel the love and the happiness.

Maybe I was being overly sentimental because the tour was ending, or maybe it was because ever since he'd first brought up the idea of marriage and babies, I'd spent an inordinate amount of time thinking about it. Imagining it.

Now I wanted what I was imagining. Despite how scary and life-ruining it had always seemed before, spending all that time with Ryan had changed how I felt. I wanted a commitment and kids and everything. Some people might have thought I was too young, but I'd had to grow up practically overnight after my mom's accident. I'd been an adult for a long time.

Despite my rules, I wanted all of it with Ryan. Which overwhelmed me and then made me all emotional.

Ryan found me in the middle of the living room, crying.

"Sweetheart, what happened?" He sat down on the couch next to me and pulled me onto his lap. "Did you go online again?"

His still-wet hair dripped against my skin. "I've thought about it."

"Thought about what? Going online?"

"No. Our future."

A second earlier his hands had been stroking my hair and rubbing my back, and then he went totally still.

"And?"

"I can see you in mine. I can see marriage and babies."

"And it makes you cry?"

"It doesn't make me cry like that," I told him. "The idea of it happening makes me happy. For someday. Not tomorrow or anything."

He let out an exaggerated sigh. "That means I'll have to cancel the private jet to Vegas."

"Ha ha. Like you'd get on a plane."

"For you I might consider it." His hands went back to soothing me.

"You really love me that much?"

"I do. And, hey, maybe you should practice saying 'I do.' Not for any particular reason. Just in case."

"Ryan?" I turned my face up. "I do."

Then I kissed him. I kissed him with all the hope, all the longing, all the dreams and promises of someday bursting inside me. Every cell inside me exploded with light, heat, and happiness.

He kissed me so softly and tenderly that I sighed against his lips. "Promise me something," I said.

"Anything."

"Promise me I can trust you."

He pulled back, his eyes serious, his expression truthful. "I promise you can trust me."

The next few words nearly caught in my throat. "Promise me you'll never hurt me."

Ryan blinked, nothing wavering on his face. "I promise I'll never hurt you."

He went back to our kiss, and his words caused a swell of love that I'd never experienced before. I could trust him. He wouldn't hurt me. Everything he'd said was true, and I knew it. My last clear thought was that I wished I could thank whatever pleech, groupie, or girlfriend had taught him to kiss this way. He used easy, delicious glides that had me clinging to him, trying to get closer.

He moved in a steadily increasing rhythm, a constant drumbeat, that robbed me of my breath and ability to think. Our lips were like two pieces of a puzzle fitting perfectly. We pressed them together, moving in warm, sensual strokes.

As always, Ryan kept the kiss in that controlled range where we both really enjoyed it, but I could sense the wall he stayed behind. The line he wouldn't go past because I'd told him not to. His restraint felt like a physical barrier erected between us. Behind that wall there was a passion I wanted. I didn't know if it was because of our earlier conversation, or his promises, or because I now knew I would marry Ryan De Luna, but I found myself wanting to experience it. With him.

I pushed into him. Wrapped my arms around his neck. I broke the kiss off long enough to say, "I want more."

"More what?"

"More," I repeated in a breathy voice that sounded nothing like my own.

I saw his Adam's apple bob and a slight nod, and then he captured my lips with a desperate, hungry urgency.

This was what I'd wanted. More of this.

Restraint gone, walls demolished, lines erased.

His lips feverishly explored mine as if he wanted to memorize every square inch of them completely. I let out a little groan of pleasure, and I felt his hands tighten around my ribs in response.

Then he used those same hands to separate us. To pull back. To hold me in place so I couldn't keep kissing him.

"Maisy." I heard the warning in his roughened whisper, but I also heard the longing in it. "We should stop."

"Don't you want this? Don't you want to kiss me?"

He closed his eyes as if my questions physically hurt him somehow. "I want you more than I've ever wanted anything."

His words embedded a hot spike in the pit of my stomach, sending flares of heat everywhere.

Ryan opened his eyes slowly. "But I'm trying to be respectful."

Swallowing hard, I told him, "It's not your respect I want right now."

As if that was all he needed to hear, Ryan crushed me against him, his fierce, hot lips seeking and devouring. His hands were in my hair, stroking my face, rubbing my neck. His touch turned my heart volcanic, pumping lava through my veins, making my skin flush in response.

Ryan's strong body molded against mine as he laid me on the couch, never breaking the contact between our mouths. When he had me flat against the cushions, he leaned back to look at me.

"So beautiful," he murmured, running his fingertips against my skin, leaving pools of molten fire behind. It was the kind of heat that brought tiny beads of sweat to my hairline and along my lower spine.

He closed in, totally intent on only me, his scorching kisses demanding more and more, just as I had wanted. Every fiber of my flesh was alight with fire, as if somebody had tossed me onto one of those funeral pyres. I burned. Ryan burned.

He kissed me like I'd made all his wishes come true. He kissed me like he was desperately afraid of losing me. He kissed me like I was cold water and the only person who could douse the flames.

Instead, I made it burn brighter and harder.

I ran my fingers along his flexed biceps and over his broad, muscular shoulders, loving all the pent-up strength just beneath the surface. Then I brushed them against his smooth jaw, missing his shadowy stubble that usually turned my delicate skin bright red after he'd finished kissing me. I let the strands of his damp, silky hair caress my fingertips.

As I explored the feel of him, Ryan did the same. Only he used his mouth. I felt his hot breath skim across my neck, my shoulder, leaving a fluttering, tingling sensation that increased a thousandfold when his mouth finally made contact with my skin. I gasped as his lips glided across my throat. My pulse sizzled beneath his touch, sensations spiraling out.

"I love you, Maisy." His rough, husky voice sounded thick in his throat and caused heat to pool into my abdomen.

"I love you, Ryan." His feverish hands turned my body into one frantic ache, my back arching against him.

It was going too far. Everything was about to spiral out of control. He had been right earlier. We should have stopped. Or we should stop now. There was no iceberg moment, though. It was more like somebody had nudged a tiny snowball in my direction.

With a strength I didn't know I possessed, I pulled my mouth away from his and pressed against his shoulders. "Ryan, wait. You were right. We need to stop."

His eyes were unfocused, his breath ragged. "I don't want to."

I didn't, either, but I kept that piece of information to myself. I felt a tad guilty; I hadn't meant to lead him on. It was just . . . I understood where he was coming from when he said being close made his brain turn off. It did that for me, too.

"I know. But we need to."

A few moments passed, and he pressed one last scalding kiss against my jaw before he sat up and moved to the opposite end of the couch. I tried to sit up, too, even though my bones currently had the same consistency as broth. Like every muscle in my body had failed to report to work today and refused to move or respond to my internal commands.

"Are you sure I can't talk you into that Vegas flight?" His smile was rueful, and even though he was teasing, I seriously considered it.

"Maybe." I didn't joke. Ryan's expression changed, and he reached out to me with one hand.

"Maisy, are you saying that you would—"

I became aware of a buzzing sound that I thought was coming from somewhere inside me until I realized it wasn't.

"What's that?" I asked.

"My intercom," he said dismissively. "Some Luna-tic site posted my apartment number, and it's usually some teenagers hoping I'll come down and see them. Ignore it. This is more important."

I couldn't ignore the sound because it kept happening. "Ryan. You should answer that."

With a growl and a choice word, Ryan got to his feet and stalked to his front door. He pushed a button on an intercom and said, "What?"

"Mr. De Luna, I'm sorry to bother you, but there's a young woman here named Cecilia Williams, who is demanding she be let up to see you."

"I don't know anyone named Cecilia Williams." Ryan leaned his forehead against the wall as my muscles started to show signs of life.

There was a pause, and the doorman on the other end answered, "She says you'd know her as CeCe."

I saw Ryan straighten up, his back tighten. He turned to look at me with trepidation in his eyes. "Can you tell her I'll text her?"

Now I had the strength to stand up. What was going on?

"She says it's an emergency and she has to see you."

I crossed my arms as goose bumps broke out. What kind of emergency? Had something happened to Ryan's dad? To his aunt Bibi? Ryan stared at me as he pushed the button. "Let her come up."

"Who's CeCe?"

Ryan walked over and grasped my hand tightly. "Someone I used to date a long time ago. An actress. It's been over for years."

"What does she want?"

"I don't know."

Another guy might have tried to speak to her alone first to find out what she would say. Or ask his current girlfriend to leave the room.

Ryan didn't. We stood hand in hand, ready to face whatever this was together.

There was a knock on his front door, and I went with him to answer it.

The first thing I noticed was how tall, beautiful, and willowy this CeCe was.

The second thing I noticed was the toddler in her arms.

A little boy who looked exactly like Ryan.

CHAPTER TWENTY-SIX

"I'm sorry to just stop by. But I saw your tweet earlier today about showing off your apartment here in New York and figured this was as good a time as any. I didn't know you had company." CeCe's gaze flickered to me for a second, her eyes full of pity. "May I come in?"

Ryan moved out of the way and let her inside. CeCe put the little boy down. He stayed close to her, wrapping his arms around her leg.

"What are you doing here?" Ryan asked.

"There's no good way to say 'Surprise, you're a daddy,' so surprise. You're a daddy. This is Thomas. He's a little over two years old."

My whole body tensed as fingers of dread wrapped around my spine. My heart raced erratically. Ryan? A father?

I'd known the truth of it the second I saw Thomas. One night when we were in California at his house, his aunt had spent the evening showing me photo albums of Ryan as a baby and small boy.

Thomas was the spitting image of Ryan at the same age.

Some of his features were different. He had a small cleft in his chin, where Ryan didn't. Thomas's coloring didn't match Ryan's, either, but he must have taken after CeCe.

As if somebody had punched me hard in the gut, I realized Ryan was a dad. He had fathered a child he hadn't even known about. An empty hollowness started in my chest and slowly spread until I felt completely numb. I wasn't angry or sad.

There was just nothing.

Ryan's face had gone pale. "I'm sorry for asking, but how do you know he's mine? We were always so careful."

"Nothing's a hundred percent effective. And you were the only person I was dating at the time. I mean, if you don't believe me, you can get a paternity test. But I'm not lying to you."

"Of course he's yours." I spoke up without meaning to, especially since this was none of my business. "He looks just like you."

"Why . . ." Ryan seemed at a total loss for words. "Why tell me now? Why didn't you tell me as soon as you knew you were pregnant?"

CeCe patted the top of Thomas's head. "I wasn't sure what I wanted to do. If I was going to keep him. And then I saw an ultrasound and fell head over heels in love. You weren't exactly father material back then, and I thought Thomas would be better off without you. But everything I see and read about you now makes me think you've changed. That you'd be capable of being a good dad. I grew up without a father, and I don't want that for my son. Our son."

I'd played a part in this. My fake-then-real relationship with Ryan was meant to convince the record label about his growth and maturity. To show that he had changed from that silly party boy into a more serious, adult artist.

I heard CeCe say, "I want you to know this isn't about money but about a relationship."

My knees felt weak, and I collapsed into a nearby chair, feeling the blood draining from my head.

Ryan was a father.

That cute little boy clinging to his mother's leg was physical proof of everything I'd feared about falling in love with Ryan. I saw myself in Thomas, with a musician father who would be in and out of his life, never really there. I couldn't take it. I couldn't live through this again.

My soul began to break, and it fractured from the pressure more and more until it shattered completely, scattering shards everywhere.

I couldn't be here. I couldn't be a part of this. I grabbed my purse off the counter and headed to the door.

"Maisy, wait!"

Ryan caught up with me in the hall, grabbing my arm and spinning me around. "Where are you going? I need you here."

"I can't do this. You had a baby with someone else. When I finally got to the point where I was ready to be the one to have—" I had to stop as my throat swelled, a knot of tears lodging inside it. "They were supposed to be our babies. Not your babies with someone else."

"Let's straighten everything out first. Let me get a paternity test and make sure he's mine, and then we'll figure out where we go from there. Together."

Together? How could he say that to me, as if we still had a future? As if I could just get over the fact that he'd impregnated some random fan? Like that shouldn't matter to me? I hit his shoulders out of frustration. "There is no more together. No more us. I told you and told you how I felt about this. You're exactly like my father!"

Ryan looked stricken, as if I'd slapped him across the face. He knew that for me, it was the worst possible insult I could have given. "Maisy, that's not true. You know me."

Breaking free of his grasp, determined not to cry, I held up my head. "Stay with your baby mama, and work out whatever you have to work out. I'm done. I'm done with us. I'm done with you. Don't call or text me ever again."

Not wanting to wait for the elevator, I ran for the stairs. Ryan called after me at least three times that I heard, but there was no way he could follow me, given that CeCe and Thomas were waiting for him in his apartment.

Nausea roiled in my stomach as the doorman got me a taxi. The second he closed the door behind me, I dissolved into tears. My shoulders curled in, and I brought my knees up, wrapping my arms around them. My chest ached as I cried and cried so hard that I nearly hyperventilated. How could Ryan do this? Have a baby with some woman he'd never even mentioned?

In a single moment, my entire life had been totally destroyed. Just as I'd always feared it would.

The only other time I'd felt this kind of hopeless despair was the night I found out about my mom's accident.

My phone rang. It rang and rang and rang. All the calls were from Ryan. I turned the phone off.

The cab driver brought me to my hotel, and I tipped him extra for leaving my tears and snot all over the back seat. My brain pounded, making it difficult to think or see. I don't know how I got to the right floor. I found Fitz's room, not wanting to be alone.

He called over Parker and Cole, and in between sobs I told them I needed to go back to California. I didn't give them any details. I couldn't talk about it yet. My brothers made a bunch of threats about going over to Ryan's apartment, but I begged them not to. I just wanted to go home. And not on Ryan's tour bus.

Fitz got online immediately and bought us four plane tickets. My brothers helped me pack up and took me and all our stuff to the airport.

Three hours later we were onboard a California-bound flight. I would go home, and things would be better. I'd get back to normal and live my life the way I had before I ever met Ryan.

Exhaustion claimed me, but as I drifted off to sleep, I knew there would be no going back. We were going to sell our house. I didn't have a job or a place to live.

And Ryan had ripped out a huge chunk of my heart. I didn't know how I'd go on living without it.

We sold the house to a pregnant couple. It gave me some measure of happiness to know that a family would live here and love it the same way we had.

Since that money would take care of Mom's facility, Fitz split up all the money we had earned on tour with Ryan. It wasn't a small amount, either. It enabled us to go off on our own. Get our own places. I bought a brand-new phone and had the salesman give me a new number. I found a reasonably priced studio apartment in Venice Beach. The area felt comfortable, familiar.

I would move on with my life.

Angie asked over and over again what had happened with Ryan and me, but I still wasn't ready to talk about it.

"Just tell me this. Do I need to have Fox take him out for you?"

I laughed and cried at the same time, but I said I didn't want to talk about him anymore. From time to time, I'd catch her with this look in her eyes, where I knew she wanted to tell me something about him, but she respected my wishes.

Today she and I were shopping to find her a new dress to wear. She was going to meet Fox's parents and wanted to look perfect. We'd been to three regular women's stores already, and now we were at a bridal shop. When I'd asked why, Angie told me they had informal dresses for sale, as well.

"It's a big step. The parent thing," she told me as she thumbed through any number of cocktail dresses that would have looked amazing on her. One of them had a blue-and-white pattern, which made me think of the dress I'd worn the night we'd surprised Angie and Fox into going on their first official date. As if where I'd be stopping for lunch wouldn't be enough of a reminder.

It had been happening more and more. Instead of remembering why I was mad at Ryan, how he'd promised not to hurt me and then immediately did, I kept thinking about all the fun we'd had together. How much I still loved him.

This is Angie's day, I reminded myself. I would not wallow, and I would be a good friend and do what I had been asked to do.

One of the clerks came over and offered us a tray with champagne on it. "I thought they did that only for brides."

"When in Rome, right?" Angie accepted a flute, but I waved it off. The last thing my morose self needed was to be drunk.

"Meeting Fox's parents is a big step. But they'll love you. And Hector Jr. If they don't, then they can just . . . I don't know. Suck it."

Angie laughed as she pulled out a red sparkly dress. She knocked back the rest of her drink before setting the glass on a shelf. "I'm going to try on this one."

A song came over the trendy boutique's speakers. At first I thought I was hallucinating, but no, it was "One More Night." The words twisted painfully against my heart, like they were enclosing it in barbed wire. I closed my eyes and leaned against the wall, remembering when Ryan and I sang it together. How I'd felt an intimate, soul-deep connection with him.

Before I could start crying, Angie came out and twirled around in her dress. "What do you think?"

"You look gorgeous," I told her, my voice tight. "But ask yourself, what kind of dress is this? Is this The Dress? The one you'd wear to the Governor's Ball? The one you'd want to get proposed to in? Go to the Academy Awards in?"

Not hearing my none-too-subtle slip of the tongue, Angie sized herself up in the mirror. "It's probably not formal enough for that stuff, but I do love it."

"Then you should wear it out of the store. Be fancy for lunch."

"You know what? I will," she said, smoothing down the material over her legs.

After she paid for the dress and got the tags removed, we went back to her car. Angie had become very good at carrying on one-sided conversations with me.

"You should probably let me drive," I said, interrupting her. I'd finally figured out the best way to finish up this afternoon. "I know you didn't have that much champagne, but better safe than sorry, right?"

"Absolutely." She tossed me her keys, and I caught them. I had to adjust her seat and mirrors when I got in, since she was so much shorter. As she put on her seat belt, she glanced at me. "Maybe it was just the champagne talking. Won't I be really overdressed for lunch?"

Not at all. "It'll be fine. Who cares what other people think?"

"Where are we eating?"

"It's not far," I told her. That was all the information she'd be getting out of me for the rest of the day.

She was in the middle of telling me a story about something adorable Hector Jr. had done with a bowl of spaghetti when I pulled up in front of the restaurant.

"La Isla Cubana?" Angie asked, her face full of worry and concern. She had no idea what was about to happen, and instead of wondering, she thought of me first.

I got out of the car, forcing her to follow. "All your answers are inside."

She hesitated on the sidewalk, but I pulled open the door and gave her a gentle nudge. Just beyond the hostess station, I could see they had cleared all the tables except for one. Fox knelt in the middle of the floor, surrounded by a sea of flowers, holding out a ring box to Angie.

Since her back was to me, I couldn't see Angie's expression, but I saw her hands fly up to her mouth in what I hoped was excitement. I let the door fall shut, letting them have their moment. I would be really and truly happy for them both. I would not stand out here and wonder if Ryan had been involved with this. If he was somewhere close by even now.

I wouldn't think about how I'd been ready to marry Ryan.

Even though it made my heart break all over again.

When I got home, I tried, again, to write a song about Ryan and the breakup, thinking it might help me process my pain. It didn't. It just brought back the agonizing grief. I decided it was better not to think about him.

As if that were possible when every song on the radio was his, and I saw his face practically every time I turned on the television.

He hadn't told the media about our breakup, and I didn't want to share that information, either. If they knew, it would have turned into a feeding frenzy. They wouldn't have left me alone.

My still-intact privacy was one of the few things I was currently grateful for.

I should have known it wouldn't last.

CHAPTER TWENTY-SEVEN

Not even twenty-four hours later, my life blew up.

"Maisy! Over here!"

"Maisy! What do you think about Ryan and Skyler? Did he cheat on you?"

"How long have you been broken up?"

"Did you know he was with Skyler Smith the entire time you were together?"

Startled, I threw my hands up in front of my face, not only because I couldn't see past the flashing lights but also because I didn't want them to have a picture of me reacting to their words. How had the paparazzi found me at my new apartment? Why were they saying those things? Skyler Smith? What were they talking about?

I made it to my car, keeping my head down. Ryan and I had been apart for over a month. It was possible he'd started dating again. I quickly called Angie after I locked my door.

When she picked up, I said, "I know I told you I don't want to talk about him, but why are the paparazzi taking my picture? What's going on with Skyler?"

There was silence for so long on her end I thought the call had dropped. "Um, the tabloids say they're dating."

My heart scrunched up inside my chest, and it felt like someone had dipped my lungs in lead. They fell into my stomach, making it impossible to breathe. "I'll call you later."

I turned off my phone and started up my newly purchased used car. For some reason I'd thought being able to buy myself a car would make me happy.

It hadn't.

I carefully pulled out of the parking lot, avoiding the paparazzi, who were still yelling my name and taking pictures of me. Fitz had called a family/band meeting, which was why I'd actually bothered to leave my apartment.

When I arrived at his complex, with no reporters trailing after me, I turned on my phone and went to the ENZ website.

Pictures of Ryan and Skyler. The captions indicated that they were recent. Laughing over dinner. Walking her Chihuahua together. He looked happy. I let my fingers outline the shape of his face.

I read the article under the pictures. Several insiders talked about their love rekindling, with Ryan telling Skyler he'd never really gotten over her. They talked about how perfect they were as a couple, so alike in every aspect. The title of the story even asked, "Maisy Who?"

There was a crushing sensation pressing down on my chest, making it hard to catch my breath. I felt completely destroyed. Skyler had promised to ruin my life, and it looked like she'd finally figured out a way to do it. She'd said she'd get back together with him, and she had. As if I'd never existed. Never even mattered to Ryan. I leaned forward, folding in on myself. My arms and legs shook as if they wouldn't support me if I tried to stand.

But Ryan said she didn't like guys.

He was assuming, I reminded that inner voice. *Maybe he was wrong.*

These pictures seemed to indicate that he had been.

I got out of the car, feeling like a shell of myself. Nothing had been right in my life since I'd walked away from Ryan.

Fitz opened the door before I could knock and gave me a hug. I tried to smile at him but didn't quite manage it. He offered me something to drink, but I declined.

Cole and Parker arrived together about a minute later. Fitz asked everyone to sit down. "I have some good news and some great news."

"Isn't it traditional to start with the bad news?" Parker asked, nodding his head toward me.

My other two brothers turned toward me. "Maisy?" Fitz asked gently. "Is there something you want to tell us?"

"Nope," I managed. "All good."

"Lie," Cole said. "If you don't want to talk about what's bothering you right now, that's fine. But I think it's time you told us what actually happened between you and Ryan. It's been bothering me for weeks. I feel like I should have beaten somebody up for hurting my sister and didn't."

Large tears fell on my cheeks. I shook my head. "I can't."

Fitz came over and knelt on the floor in front of me, taking my hands in his. "Maisy, we're the people you can trust. You know we're always here for you. Let us help you carry this burden."

I needed to tell someone. Through tears and sobs, I told them in a cracking voice everything that had happened when CeCe showed up at Ryan's apartment.

When I finally finished, I expected . . . something. Threats of bodily harm, promises to make Ryan pay, a dramatic leaping to their feet and swearing to enact vengeance. Instead, I saw them exchange uneasy glances with one another.

"What?" I demanded.

"I'm sorry, Maze, but to be honest I don't get why you're so upset," Parker finally said.

I blinked, too shocked to respond.

"It's not like he knew about the kid and kept it from you," Cole added. "Then you'd have a right to be upset."

"Yeah. He didn't make this happen. It sounds like he was just as surprised as you were."

Fitz had moved onto the couch and put his arm around me while I'd recounted my story. "Maisy." He said my name gently, like he was worried I might break. "Have you considered the possibility that Ryan needed you when he found out?"

The heartache inside me quickly shifted to anger. What was happening? "How are you guys not on my side? Don't you see he's just like our father?"

Cole folded his arms. "Ryan is nothing like our dad. And him having one kid he knew nothing about doesn't make him like Louis. At all. Why would you even say that? I thought you loved Ryan."

"I did," I sputtered.

I do.

Then, annoyingly enough, my brothers started talking about me like I wasn't in the room.

"She needs to get over this anger at Dad and move on with her life. It's going to destroy any future relationship she ever tries to have."

"I can't believe she just took off. It must have killed him."

"You can't really blame her for that. Maisy has a tendency to over-react to things. She jumps to conclusions without having all the facts. Hopefully he already knows that about her."

"I don't even believe in love, and I thought they were really in love."

"She's going to regret this for the rest of her life."

"Stop!" I yelled, my fists balled up in my lap. I wouldn't be able to take much more of this. I felt completely overwhelmed by their observations. It was all too much to process. "Enough. I don't need your judgments. I came here for Fitz's news. Can we please get back to that?"

Parker looked like he was going to argue with me, but Fitz stood up, holding out one hand toward Parker. As if he was trying to placate him instead of me. "Okay. The first thing I should tell you is that Piper and I decided last week to become exclusive."

That was what he wanted to tell us? Like it wasn't bad enough that I already had three knives sticking out of my back? He wanted to make sure he twisted his in nice and tight?

"And Piper wants to become our manager. She's ready for a change in her career, and she's been doing this for long enough that she's got the right kind of connections."

"I thought Piper didn't crap where she eats," Cole said.

"She does now."

Ugh. That was completely gross. "What if you break up?"

"We're adults and professionals. We'll be fine."

Raging anger blinded my vision for a second. So it would be fine for Fitz, but it hadn't been fine for me. They'd all given me such a hard time about dating Ryan, fearful for their careers. I guess now it didn't matter. I really couldn't call Fitz out on his hypocrisy, given how badly Ryan and I had ended and that we were no longer together. Another sharp, stabbing pain throbbed in my belly.

"The great news," Fitz went on, "is that Piper has already booked us another tour. We'll be flying over to Europe to tour with Many Maus."

"We're going on tour with Minnie Mouse?" Parker asked.

"No, the German rock band. Many Maus. Bunch of Top 100 European hits. It won't be as nice as . . ." Fitz's voice trailed off as he looked at me. "But if we want, they'll send us the contracts tomorrow, and we can all sign. So I thought we should take a vote."

While I wanted to vote no on Piper as our manager purely out of spite, I reluctantly and angrily raised my hand as a yes for her and the tour.

"Is that it?" I asked, standing up. I wasn't sure how much more brotherly love I could take.

Fitz nodded. "Yeah, that's everything. But, Maisy, I really think we should talk."

I went to his front door and put my hand on the doorknob. "You know, after all we've been through together, the one thing I could always count on was my brothers having my back. No matter what."

Cole got to his feet as well. "We still have your back. Just not the way you wanted. You messed up. Who else is going to tell you that kind of truth?"

Furious, I slammed Fitz's front door behind me before Cole could say anything else. He was lucky I didn't punch him first. How could they pretend that they were on my side and trying to help me after the horrible things they'd accused me of? Weren't they supposed to love me no matter what? The utter and total betrayal of my brothers not standing by me was more than I could bear. Tears blurred my vision as I stomped out to my car. I was careful not to take my anger out on the road. My brothers' idiocy was not worth getting in an accident over.

Problem was, I didn't know where to go next. I didn't want to go home. Where I would sit and seethe.

I wanted my mom. I needed her.

So I drove to Century Pacific, and I wiped away my tears of frustration and anger as I followed behind the orderly. This really wouldn't do me any good. She couldn't actually help me. Not the way I needed her to.

I couldn't even hug her.

Taking in a big breath, I reminded myself to be thankful for what I had. At least she was still here, in some form.

I introduced myself again, and she immediately started chatting about the prom. "You seem sad," she commented in the middle of her monologue.

"I am. My boyfriend and I broke up."

"This close to prom? Why?"

I so badly wanted her to comfort me and tell me everything would be okay! "Because he got another girl pregnant."

She gasped. "Is she going to drop out of school?"

"No, she's done with school." It was probably a lot more shocking to think this had happened to a couple of teenagers than to adults.

"He cheated on you, then?"

"No." I blinked. "Technically he didn't cheat on me. It happened before we ever met." Saying it out loud made me realize that my brothers, stupid and awful as they were, had been sort of right. Ryan hadn't set out to hurt me or betray me. Which just aggravated me more. I tried to justify my anger. "The thing is, my father always does this. He has a bunch of different kids with a bunch of different women. It ruined my life. My mom's life. I can't go through that."

My mom nodded, looking thoughtful. "Do you think you'd feel the same way if your dad wasn't the way he is?"

"I don't know. Maybe." Maybe I would have felt angry or betrayed, but if I didn't have such a dysfunctional parent, would I have gotten over it? "That's hard to imagine, though."

"It doesn't really seem fair to punish your boyfriend for your hang-ups."

"I'm punishing him for not using birth control correctly. It isn't about my hang-ups."

"Okay." My mother raised one eyebrow at me, the way she used to do when I was little and she didn't believe me. It made my heart squeeze. "Whatever you say. I think you should forgive him."

"What?"

"I go to church with my mom every week. I don't know if I believe everything they're saying, but I do think forgiveness is important."

My mouth literally dropped open. My mother had never once taken us to church. She'd grown up religious? How did I not know this?

Was this why she put up with my father for so long?

"So I just forgive him?" The way she had when she adopted Cole? "Just get over it?"

"Well, yeah. You'd be a lot happier. Like when my best friend and I got into this massive fight junior year over Frank Cadieux. He was my boyfriend, and she kissed him! We didn't speak for months. I was mad for a long time, but then I missed my friend, and it was all just . . . stupid. A waste. So I forgave Elaine."

I let out a sigh. It wasn't quite the same thing. "And then everything was fine?"

"Not so much. Elaine was still mad at me. The thing is, though, when you forgive someone, it allows you to let go of your anger. When I stopped being angry, I found a way to fix our friendship."

I realized she was right. That this could be the answer to my situation. Maybe it wasn't what I had come here for, and even though she didn't know who I was, she'd still managed to help me.

Not wanting to keep talking about Ryan, forgiveness, and the doubts that had started to creep into my mind, I said, "Hey, I don't know if you remember, but I told you about how my family has a secret brownie recipe."

"Mine, too!"

"Right. Anyway, I found out the secret. It was made from a mix."

She let out a low whistle. "That must have been a letdown. I would have been furious."

"It was a letdown. But I've been making them, anyway."

"Are they good?"

I twisted my lips and cleared my throat, making the tears go away. Then I reached over and put my hand on her arm. "They're good. But it isn't the same."

CHAPTER TWENTY-EIGHT

Over the next couple of weeks as I got ready to go on tour again, I had nothing but time to think, to keep running my brothers' words through my mind over and over. I had my groceries and the occasional takeout meal delivered so I could avoid the paparazzi still camped out in the complex's parking lot. I also ordered some books online about forgiveness.

I found some measure of relief after I confessed to Angie the truth of everything that had happened. She told me she'd be there for me but didn't have much else to say about it.

It left me even more time to sit and think, and to read advice from a number of different experts. Eventually it dawned on me that my idiot siblings had been right.

Ryan didn't need my forgiveness.

I needed his.

With some time and distance, I was able to think more clearly about that situation with CeCe. Ryan had been shocked. He hadn't known, hadn't kept me in the dark. He hadn't betrayed me or cheated on me. Something life-altering had been dropped in his lap, right after I'd told him I wanted to be his wife. Where I would promise to love, honor, and support him. Instead of doing any of that, I took off.

Ryan wasn't like my father.

I was.

Leaving when it suited me, not standing and fighting for my relationship when I should have. Walking away when things got too hard. That wasn't how relationships were supposed to work.

My Harrison temper had made me do something so dumb.

No, I mentally corrected myself, not willing to keep passing the blame. It wasn't my DNA that was to blame. My father hadn't forced me to be a terrible girlfriend. That was a choice I'd made.

A choice I needed to beg Ryan to forgive me for.

Like my mom had said, it was all a waste. Of time, energy, love.

Forgiveness, obviously, had never been my strong suit, and now I was the one who needed it from the man I loved. If he couldn't forgive me, it was what I deserved for reacting so badly. For saying things to him that were so blatantly untrue. Ryan had never been, and never would be, like my father. Ryan had been attentive, loving, and devoted to me the whole time we were together, despite what the tabloids were saying. And he was that way even before things were official between us.

I also realized I needed to learn to forgive before I could ask for it from other people. Not Ryan. He didn't need my forgiveness.

My father did.

Or, more accurately, *I* needed to forgive. Parker had been right. I'd never be in a functional relationship if I couldn't get past my anger at my father. Because the only person my anger was hurting was me. My father was who he was. I didn't have to let him be a part of my life, but I wanted to stop giving him power over me.

I had to find a way to let go.

I knew it wouldn't be easy, but I used my new forgiveness guides to help me. To make me into a better person.

Admitting my own faults, that I was the one to blame when it came to Ryan, made it so that I could write music again. Like I'd unlocked some door that had been sealed shut because I wasn't being true or authentic. Creation couldn't come from lies.

It came from truth.

And pain.

I also started looking up information on Ryan so I could see what he was up to. I saw more pictures with Skyler that made my stomach twist and turn. After a few calming breaths, I told myself that if he'd moved on with her, well, I deserved that, too. I wanted him to be happy. If it was with someone like her, I'd have to learn to accept it.

My books were making me very Zen.

Then I found a press release where his label announced an upcoming single, a duet between him and Skyler.

That gave me a sliver of hope, something I hadn't felt in a long time.

If they wanted him to do a duet, maybe all this "Skyler and Ryan are dating" stuff was just publicity.

Maybe, if I could earn his forgiveness, we could find our way back to each other.

I found a recent clip from an entertainment show. An interview. I both wanted to watch it and didn't want to.

I gave in and pressed PLAY. It hurt my heart to see the animated expression on his beautiful face, to hear his voice. To hear the laughter in it, like he'd totally moved on and wasn't sitting in a small, dark apartment feeling sorry for himself.

The interviewer asked him about the Moonstruck tour, and I actually forgot to breathe. Would Ryan talk about me?

He told a couple of stories about his bandmates, one about Anton always sleeping, but nothing about Yesterday. Nothing about me.

Until the interviewer asked, "What about you and Maisy Harrison? The lead singer of your opening act? Are you two still together?"

As my heart cartwheeled like an Olympic gymnast in my chest, all the emotion left Ryan's face. He looked like he'd been carved out of granite. "Next question," he instructed.

Freezing grief—all-encompassing, numbing, and painful—swallowed me up.

I'd lost him.

And it was all my fault.

Then they talked about Ryan's next album, and he spoke excitedly about how different the sound would be. More adult. More rock. More real instruments.

It was everything he'd wanted. The reason we'd had a fake relationship in the first place. Despite my own pain at losing him, I was happy for him.

I wanted to tell him.

Why couldn't I tell him? There was nothing to stop me from texting him. We were leaving for our tour the next day. I didn't know how texting would work once I was in Europe. This might be my last chance.

Before I could talk myself out of it, I grabbed my phone and entered his number.

> This is Maisy. I have a new phone/number. I saw your interview and I wanted to tell you that I'm so happy you're getting to make the album you wanted to make.

I pushed SEND, my fingers shaking. I waited. And waited.

No response. Maybe I needed to stay away from small talk and tell him how I felt.

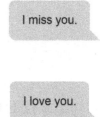

I miss you.

Still nothing.

I love you.

What was he thinking? Had I really screwed things up so badly that he wouldn't even respond to my text?

I completely messed up. I overreacted and I am so sorry. Can you ever forgive me? I would do anything to make it up to you.

Finally, two hours later, I put my phone away. There wouldn't be any response.

Ryan had just let me know, loud and clear, that we were 100 percent over.

CHAPTER TWENTY-NINE

Angie had offered to drive me to the airport, and I agreed. She talked about her wedding plans with Fox, and I promised to fly back for the event. I kept my gaze pointed out the window, only half listening. I hadn't slept at all last night, devastated by Ryan's lack of response.

It had hit me all over again how much I missed him. How much I had missed him ever since New York. Missing him became so all-encompassing that it was like a black hole had opened up inside me, sucking up everything else so that I could no longer do anything but think about him.

"Ryan troubles?" Angie correctly guessed. She knew all about my epiphany.

"I texted him last night, and he didn't answer. I guess it really is over." My voice caught on the last word, and I focused on breathing in and out.

We came to a red light, and Angie held out her hand. "Let me see."

I gave it to her, and she quickly read through my short messages. "I can't believe Ryan didn't say anything back. I mean, if you could see him . . ." Her eyes went wide, as if she'd just admitted to something she shouldn't have. "What I meant to say was if he could see you, see how much you've grown and that you're willing to own up to your mistakes, I think it would change everything."

"Yeah, I'm super self-actualized now." And super alone.

"I didn't mention it before, but Ryan's throwing a party tonight to celebrate his new single."

With Skyler Smith, I reminded myself.

"If you want, I could find out what's going on."

"No!" I told her, taking my phone back. The light turned green, and Angie reluctantly moved with traffic. "He was pretty obvious here. I have to take the hint."

"If that's what you want."

What I wanted was Ryan back in my life, but I was trying to accept that as a non-option. "The worst part is the guilt. I really wish I could at least apologize, if nothing else."

"The best thing you can do with guilt is learn from it. And move on."

"I'm trying," I told her. "But I feel like this horrible, selfish brat." No wonder Ryan got over it so quickly.

"You are an emotional, fiery artist and a wonderful daughter and sister and friend who made a mistake. You are allowed to make those. You're human, after all."

I knew she meant well, but it didn't really help.

About twenty minutes later, we arrived at the airport. I hugged her goodbye and promised to text or email or whatever I could do when I was overseas. I grabbed my brand-new passport as I jostled my way through the crowd. This would be my second time on a plane, my first going out of the country.

Thinking about flying made me remember the first time I'd been on a plane. After I'd walked out on Ryan. A thousand sharp icicles pierced my heart, and I nearly doubled over from the pain of it all.

I found my brothers waiting for me next to the computerized ticketing station of our airline. They all looked at me warily, most likely not sure what I would say or do. I hadn't talked to them since the vote at Fitz's apartment, when they'd tried to help me see the reality of my situation.

Better to admit to the truth up-front than let this thing drag out. I set my Martin guitar case down. "You guys were right. I messed up and was a total idiot with Ryan."

All three of them grinned in unison.

"You should apologize to him," Parker said. "Someplace private where none of us will be forced to watch."

"Yes. I don't want to see Maisy groveling," Fitz agreed, putting his arm around me.

Parker nodded. "There is something fundamentally weird about that image."

"You guys are crazy," Cole interrupted their exchange. "I'd pay good money to see Maisy publicly admit she was actually wrong about something."

I punched him in his arm, and he pretended to be wounded before winking at me.

"Come on," Parker said. "Let's get this new tour started. Tickets are this way."

"So are you going to apologize to him?" Fitz asked me, keeping me close to his side as we followed our brothers.

"I already did. I texted him. He didn't answer. So I guess that's it, then. Chalk it up to a learning experience and move on. Right?"

Fitz looked thoughtful. "That surprises me. That doesn't seem like something Ryan would do."

I shrugged one shoulder to indicate he already had done it. "At least I'll always have you guys."

"You'll always have us," he agreed, but his voice sounded distant. Like he was thinking about something more important than this conversation. I saw Piper walking across the terminal, hips swaying as she smiled and waved at us. Fitz smiled lovingly, dropped his luggage, and ran across the airport. When he reached her, he picked her up and swung her around in a circle. Piper threw her head back and laughed before settling in to kiss him hello.

I did have my brothers and the band. For now.

But how long would that last?

CHAPTER THIRTY

"Why can't I get this chord change? What's wrong with me?" I asked.

"Hang on," Cole replied, jumping up. "I gotta get my list."

I laughed as he ran out of the room. We'd been on tour with Many Maus for about two weeks and were currently staying in an adorable bed-and-breakfast in the heart of Amsterdam. It was a beautiful city, with old buildings lining waterways and cobblestone sidewalks. Sunlight beamed in through the open wooden shutters, lighting up the entire third floor.

Parker walked past my room while reading his phone. "Did you guys see this review? The actual music critic liked us, but the commenters are vicious."

"Don't let the trolls win," I called after him. It was something else I'd figured out recently. I'd been so reluctant at every step of my relationship with Ryan because of my parents and my fears of what I felt for him both physically and emotionally. But those internet voices? The ones who disparaged me and said we'd never work, the same ones I'd claimed I didn't care about and didn't listen to? I did care, and I did listen. I let total strangers make me doubt myself and doubt Ryan.

Never again.

"Hey, Cole?" I heard Fitz call from another room. "Remember we have that thing right now. You coming?"

Thing? My brothers hadn't mentioned any plans.

"Yeah," Cole replied. "Give me a second and I'll meet you downstairs."

Before I could ask where they were going, Fitz and Parker left. Cole stuck his head in my room and said, "The only thing wrong with you is that you gave up on love too quickly."

Easy for him to say. He wasn't the one who'd texted Ryan and never heard back from him again.

"And, uh, stay here. Don't go anywhere."

Before I could ask Cole why he'd said that, he was already gone. Weirdo.

I tried to make the quick change again on my Fender but finally gave up and set it down on the bed. I wondered where Ryan was now. He had been at a fund-raiser in LA last night. I'd continued doing my best Luna-tic impersonation and spent most of my free time stalking him online. Still wondering why he didn't respond to my texts.

Maybe he was dating CeCe again, and he would be a happy little family with Thomas. That image made me feel queasy.

But I also knew I could have loved Thomas. Just like my mom took Cole in, I would have adored Thomas because he was Ryan's son.

I wished I could tell him that.

Given that I had the place to myself, I decided to take a nap. I lay down on my bed and closed my eyes.

I heard music coming from outside. That wasn't all that strange; there were often performance artists on the sidewalks, busking.

The strange thing was that I recognized the tune.

And the voice.

My pulse hammered as I ran over to the open window and looked outside.

Ryan was there. Singing the same song to me that my mother had when I was a little girl.

He was Lloyd Dobler-ing me.

There is a flower within my heart
Maisy, Maisy
Planted one day by a glancing dart
Planted by Maisy Ell

Whether she loves me or loves me not
Sometimes it's hard to tell
Yet I am longing to share the lot
Of beautiful Maisy Ell

Maisy, Maisy, give me your answer do
I'm half-crazy all for the love of you
It won't be a stylish marriage
I can't afford a carriage
But you'll look sweet upon the seat
Of a bicycle built for two.

He sang the song while leaning against an actual tandem bicycle that was locked up to the fence.

The man I loved was serenading me. I wanted to fall at his feet and beg for his forgiveness. I wasn't worthy of his song.

I couldn't believe he was here. Singing to me. The crowd of people who had gathered around him applauded when he finished, and some of them even tried to give him some cash. I wanted to laugh as he politely refused.

"What are you doing?" I yelled down at him. My heart was in my throat, making me feel like I was going to choke. This had to be good, right? Had he finally found a way to forgive me?

"Can I come up?"

That was probably a smart move, considering how many people had stopped to take his picture or film him.

Not to mention I wanted him to come upstairs more than I wanted my next breath or my next heartbeat. "Yes! Take the stairs up to the top floor!"

My hair was in a bun, my face scrubbed clean. I so wished I was wearing something besides yoga pants and a tank top.

He knocked on the door and on my heart at the same time. I opened both to him and whatever he had to say.

"Hi." Just hearing his voice again was enough to make me swoon.

"Hi. Come in." I let him into our small sitting room. Like my brothers, he had to duck from the roof eaves on this level. I sat down on the tiny love seat, and Ryan sat across from me in a 1960s-style orange armchair, setting his guitar on the floor.

I greedily drank in the sight of him. He looked a little thinner, tired. Stubble lined his face; his hair was tousled. But he was still the most beautiful man I'd ever laid eyes on.

Then it occurred to me how truly impossible it was for him to be here at this moment. "You were in Los Angeles last night."

"I was."

"Then how are you here now?"

He rubbed his jaw. "After the fund-raiser, I got on a red-eye to come here and see you."

It was a fifteen-hour flight. A pang of love and disbelief hit me hard, and I put a hand on my chest. "You got on a plane for me?"

"I did. Some noise-canceling headphones, a sleeping mask, and heavy sedatives were involved."

He was too good. Too amazing. I didn't deserve any of this. I started to cry. "I'm so sorry. So, so sorry."

In seconds he was on his feet, pulling me up from the love seat. He held me tight, and his embrace felt every bit as good, as right, as I remembered. He rubbed my back, laying his head on top of mine, soothing me.

"I was such an idiot," I said in between sobs. "I completely over-reacted and ruined everything. I'll never forgive myself."

"You have to forgive yourself because I already did. A long time ago."

I pulled back. His face looked blurry through my tears. "Then why didn't you answer my texts?"

"I didn't find out about those until Angie told me at my release party. After you left in New York, I sort of threw my phone against the sidewalk and left it. When I went back to get it, it was gone. So I had to get a new phone, and my security team made me get a new number. Just in case. I never got your texts."

Blinking hard, I tried to process what he was saying. "But your release party was two weeks ago."

He ran one hand through his hair. "This was the first opening in my schedule, and I wanted to come say what I needed to say to you in person. It wasn't textable. I have to tell you about Thomas."

Nothing else in the world mattered as long as he was here, holding me. "I will love Thomas. He's a part of you."

"Not in the way you think. Thomas isn't my son. He's my brother."

Not his son? His brother? Immediately I got squicked out and wondered what was wrong with CeCe. "You mean your dad and CeCe? That's . . . totally disgusting."

"When she found out that my dad didn't have any money, she came up with a plan to say Thomas was mine so I would pay child support. I think she was hoping the resemblance was strong enough that I wouldn't question her. But I had a paternity test done."

The resemblance had been enough that I hadn't questioned her and put all the blame on Ryan.

For something he hadn't even been guilty of.

"I'm so sorry," I told him again. It felt like I couldn't say it enough. "I shouldn't have reacted the way I did. I should have stayed and worked things out with you, just like you asked me to. I promise I won't ever run from you like that again."

Ryan squeezed me tightly against him, making it impossible to breathe. I didn't care. "There's nothing to forgive. I love you."

"I love you. I never stopped."

He smelled the same. Felt the same. This was where I belonged. With him. He really was my home.

"I fired my dad."

I lifted my head. "You did?"

"I'm going to help take care of my baby brother, but I'm tired of bailing out my dad. It's not my responsibility to pay for his life so he can do nothing but make bad choices. He had a job before I became famous. He can get another one. I hired Dean Bruno to be my manager. He thinks the first single for my next album should be 'Maisy.'" Dean Bruno was one of the top managers in the music industry.

Who was already employed, last I'd heard. "But wasn't he working for . . ."

"Yes. I lured him away from Skyler Smith."

My heart was back in my throat again. "Wouldn't that upset your girlfriend?" Even though he'd just said he loved me, I needed to clarify where things stood.

His hand rested against the back of my neck, cradling my head. "Skyler and I didn't date. That was all publicity. You're the only one for me."

"You know that makes me love you more, right?" I asked, wanting to collapse into a puddle of relief.

He kissed my forehead, and it felt like all was right in the world again. "I got you a present." Ryan reached into his back pocket and pulled out a piece of paper. He handed it to me.

"What's this?" I asked.

"It's the deed to your house. I bought it from the people who bought it from you. I know how much it meant to you. I wanted your mom to have a place to come home to, in case she gets better."

"Are you serious with this right now?" Ryan De Luna was too good to be true.

"Don't cry, sweetheart."

"How can I not cry? You're amazing, and I suck."

"You're amazing, too. I wouldn't love a sucky person."

That made me laugh, and Ryan tenderly wiped away my tears.

"I sold my house in Gstaad to buy yours. That couple you sold to were quite the negotiators."

He sold one of his many houses for me? "Aw. That is so . . . stupid that you had a house in a place with a name like Gstaad."

Now it was Ryan's turn to laugh.

"But seriously? Thank you. This means everything to me."

"You're welcome. And I have another present for you." Had I imagined it, or had his voice just wobbled?

He let go of me and this time reached into his front pocket.

He pulled out a tiny box that could hold only one possible thing.

I covered my mouth with my hands. "I don't understand what's happening right now."

Ryan got down on one knee, opening the box. "Didn't you ever listen to the lyrics of 'Daisy' before? It's a proposal song. I'm proposing to you. Be my wife, Maisy. I love you, and I don't want to live without you. These last few months have been among the worst of my entire life. I don't want another day to go by without you in it."

My mouth just hung open. I was unable to take in the enormity of what was going on. I didn't know anything about diamonds, but it was huge, glittery, and gorgeous.

"This isn't a fake engagement, is it?"

He grinned. "Not fake. It was never fake for me, Maisy. With you it was always real."

Would I ever stop crying today?

"Also," Ryan added, "I can absolutely afford a carriage. A stylish marriage, if that's what you want."

"I can't believe you're proposing to me while I look like this."

"I think you look hot. You're the most beautiful woman I've ever known."

Okay, that was not true, considering the crowd he ran with, but I figured being in love might have skewed his perception. Which worked for me.

"That diamond is so big," I said as Ryan took it out and put it on my finger. "Maybe too big."

"Said no woman ever," he teased. "I actually considered some larger diamonds, but I didn't want it to weigh down your hand while you're playing. Because I want you to keep pursuing your dreams and your music. I don't want marriage to mean an end to either your or my goals. We'll figure out a way to make it all work. But I also want the whole world to know that you're mine. So I got something reasonable."

I held my hand aloft, letting the diamond sparkle in the sunlight. It was light. I wouldn't have any troubles playing. But reasonable? "It's not reasonable. As I once said, I'm not selfish enough to deny you the pleasure of giving it to me."

Voices came up to the window from the sidewalk. They were calling our names. We walked over to see my three brothers standing there, smiling up at me. Those jerks had known what Ryan had planned and been in on it.

I had never loved them more.

"Are you done?"

"Did she say yes?"

"Are you our new brother?"

Ryan turned to me, resting his hands on my hips. "I know Rule #1 is to never date a musician. But what about marrying one?"

I put my arms around his neck and grinned. "You already know the answer."

THE MUSIC OF #*MOONSTRUCK*

You can check out the music video for "One More Night" at:

https://www.youtube.com/watch?v=5XPquxeTF2s

You can check out the music video for "Maisy" at:

https://www.youtube.com/watch?v=qk_HWl0cy5Y

AUTHOR'S NOTE

Thank you for coming along on this journey with me! I hope you enjoyed Ryan and Maisy's story. If you'd like to find out when I've written something new, make sure you sign up for my newsletter at www.sariahwilson.com. I most definitely will not spam you. (I'm happy when I send out a newsletter once a month!)

And if you feel so inclined, I'd love for you to leave a review on Amazon, Goodreads, the bathroom wall at your local watering hole, on the back of your electric bill, or anyplace you want. I would be so grateful. Thanks!

ACKNOWLEDGMENTS

For everyone who is reading this—thank you. Thank you for your support, for your kind words, and for loving my characters as much as I do!

My biggest thank-you is to Megan Mulder, my favorite editor. I was so excited when we went out to dinner, I told you my idea for this story, and you immediately said you'd been hoping I'd do one about a musician. Thanks to the Montlake team for everything you do for me, including all that behind-the-scenes stuff I never know about (Sally, Elise, Kelsey, Kris, Jessica [I miss you!], and Le). Thank you to Charlotte Herscher, not only for pinch-hitting but also for helping #*Moonstruck* become about a thousand times better. Thank you to Elise, Sally, and Jill for their proofreading and editing skills. Thanks to Eileen Carey for my gorgeous cover!

A special thank-you to singer Jenny Phillips, who sat and talked with me about what it feels like to be famous and a musician.

Thank you to the musical group TREN (Taylor Miranda, Richard Williams, Eliza Smith, and Nate Young) for helping me make Maisy's and Ryan's songs real. Special thanks to Taylor for running point on this, and thank you for fixing the lyrics so they would go with your beautiful music!

For my children—I love and adore you. Kaleb, I miss you every day, but I'm so proud of the choice you made to serve others.

And Kevin, who takes the things I imagine and makes them into real images for my stories—I couldn't possibly love you more than I do.

ABOUT THE AUTHOR

Bestselling author Sariah Wilson has never jumped out of an airplane or climbed Mount Everest, and she is not a former CIA operative. She is, however, madly, passionately in love with her soul mate and is a fervent believer in happily ever afters—which is why she writes romances like the Royals of Monterra series. After growing up in Southern California as the oldest of nine (yes, nine) children, she graduated from Brigham Young University with a semi-useless degree in history. The author of *#Starstruck*, she currently lives with the aforementioned soul mate and their four children in Utah, along with three tiger barb fish, a cat named Tiger, and a recently departed hamster who is buried in the backyard (and has nothing at all to do with tigers). For more information, visit her at www.sariahwilson.com.